BLACK DRUMS TALKING: THE COMPLETE

TALES OF KINGI BWANA, VOLUME 3

BLACK DRUMS TALKING:
THE COMPLETE TALES OF

KINGI BWANA

VOLUME 3

GORDON
MacCREAGH

ALTUS PRESS • 2014

EDITED AND DESIGNED BY

Matthew Moring

PUBLISHING HISTORY

"Black Drums Talking" originally appeared in the March 1934 issue of *Adventure* magazine. Copyright 1934 by The Ridgway Company. Copyright renewed 1962 and assigned to Adventure Pulp LLC. All Rights Reserved.

"Wardens of the Big Game" originally appeared in the April 15, 1935 issue of *Adventure* magazine. Copyright 1935 by Popular Publications, Inc. Copyright renewed 1963 and assigned to Adventure Pulp LLC. All Rights Reserved.

"Raiders of the Abyssinia" originally appeared in the April 1936 issue of *All Aces* magazine. Copyright 1936 by Popular Publications, Inc. Copyright renewed 1963 and assigned to Steeger Properties, LLC. All Rights Reserved.

THANKS TO

Doug Ellis, Joel Frieman, Everard P. Digges LaTouche and Gerd Pircher.

TABLE OF CONTENTS

BLACK DRUMS TALKING

KINGI BWANA'S safari wound like a monstrous snake through low, rolling hills of parched brown grass and dusty mimosa scrub—like a black snake with a swift, olive-drab head. Over a low rise came King, tall, khaki-clad, tireless, his face tan as his ragged shirt, his quick gray eyes scouting ahead from under his shapeless double terai-hat. At his heels trotted, like a dog—or rather like a well trained monkey—his wizened little Hottentot whose name was longer than all his shrunken body. Kaff'enk wa n'dhlovo, abbreviated even by his own tribe, who loved staccato, monosyllabic stanzas of names, to Kaffa.

Behind them in an undulating line hurried the Shenzie porters under light loads. And last of all a resplendent figure of a black man all decked out in leopardskin *moocha* and monkeyhair garters at knee and elbow. His great, sword-bladed spear and his nodding black ostrich plume showed him to be an *elmoran* of the Masai, a single-handed slayer of lions—and of men.

From time to time the Masai would utter a gruff shout of—

"*Bado, m'panze, bado!*"

Which was quite unnecessary, since the porters were keeping up splendidly with King's fast lead.

Anybody could see that the safari was hurrying on the home trek; and anybody who knew Africa could see why.

Brilliant clouds, as white and as hard edged as if cut out of

paper, were piling up on the horizon. Within very few days the clouds would drift up to spread over the sky, and their clear cotton white would turn to gray, from gray to threatening purple-black. Then would come the rain. People who know Africa try to avoid being caught out on trek by the rainy season.

The sun, that had been doing its brazen damnedest, poised in the exact zenith throughout the whole day as tropical suns seem to have the power to do, began to drop. And having so decided, it fell as fast as a hot rivet, dull red in the dust haze.

King, squinting through narrow eyelids to right and left, pointed to one side with his rifle. The big Masai at the far end of the line barked orders. The black line of Shenzies swung over toward the thorn patch that King had indicated.

King and the Hottentot, without looking back, strode on and were quickly lost to view over the next low hill.

The Masai expertly marked out a rough circle with his steel-spiked spear butt where the labor of thorn bush clearing and piling up would be least. Under his growled directions a boma quickly began to grow. This was bad country.

The Shenzies chanted mournfully as they dragged the spiny, stunted mimosa trees to form a tangled wall. This was to be another dry camp. Water would be handed out by the gourd

measure, just sufficient to every man's need. But African safari porters grumble when they can not be appallingly wasteful of everything, even of the turbid, befouled water of the ending dry season's water-holes. So with all armies on march.

There was no water-hole. King was not trekking a standard route, zigzagging from one hole to the next in easy stages. He was making a bee-line across country, and he camped wherever the nights caught him.

Presently the sound of a far shot drifted in on the still air; and quickly after it another.

"*Hau!*" grunted the Masai. "There will be meat. Two bucks. In this country they will be *kongoni*. Let four men go, and swiftly."

When the four returned with King and the Hottentot—and sure enough with two *kongoni* antelopes—the swift darkness was falling like a blanket. Within the boma, cooking fires smoked and stank under the profuse grease drip. The porters gorged themselves with meat, recklessly wasteful. They forgot about the water shortage and were happy.

Stars blazed overhead, but from the horizon line came low rumbles of thunder. The rain gods growling in their bellies, working up their rage for the fury of the monsoon, said the natives. Deep, moaning rumbles sounded nearby, awesomely close, yet impossible to locate with exactness. The windless air was filled with guttural sound. Somewhere out in the dark reverberated a series of vibrating roars which coughed away to silence.

"Better get the doorway thorns dragged in, Barounggo," said King. "Game was scarce today. They'll be hungry."

"It is done, bwana," boomed the voice of the Masai.

KING LAY back with his hands folded under his head. The hard angles of his face were lighted in red outline by the glow from his pipe. Another far rumble throbbed across the night. King raised himself on his elbow to listen.

"What man among you can perhaps read that drum talk?" he asked.

The chattering of the porters ceased. They remained dumb—which is characteristic of African porters when speech is required. Fitfully the sound eddied and faded and surged in again.

"It will be a *ngoma*—a dance at some village," hazarded the Masai.

But the Hottentot, crouched like a blanketed gnome over the fire at King's feet, screwed up his face and clucked derisively.

"We passed no *shambas* by the way," he argued. "Nor, by the movements of the scattered game, was any village in that direction. Who then would dance in this empty country, unless it be the devils of the dust?"

King nodded toward him.

"Wisely spoken, apeling. It is no dance, but a talk. Can you of your experience read that talk?"

The Hottentot gathered his blanket closer around his shoulders.

"Nay, bwana. It is a talk that I do not know. But the skin within my belly is cold, by which sign I know that it is an evil talk."

The Masai's figure loomed immensely naked beyond the fire. His voice rumbled like a lion's.

"Evil walks always in the outer dark. But what is that to us? We are men; we are in boma; we have weapons. It is enough."

King knew that the Shenzie porters, huddled in the farther dimness, listened wide-eyed to every word; he knew, too, that panic came to porters more easily even than hunger. He nodded this time towards the Masai.

"Wisely spoken, warrior," he said. "In boma and armed. Let the outer evil walk where it will. It is no affair of ours."

Yet in Africa, where evil things are many, some things can force themselves most unexpectedly upon the affairs of people comfortably secure in a well constructed thorn boma.

With the suddenness of a rising sky rocket a scream cut into the normal noises of the night. Long drawn and wailing, it quavered and faded and rose again to a high shriek.

The Shenzie porters cowered.

"*Aie! Awowe!*" they moaned. "It is a bush devil that calls one to his death. Let the fires be fed and let no man venture forth."

But the little Hottentot, despite the coldness of his internal skin, was coolly alert.

"A fool," he said. "A fool who tells the lions where he is. Yet the trouble of a fool is none the less trouble." Already he was applying a match to the camp lantern.

King was on his feet, feeling in the chamber of his rifle to assure himself that the load which he knew to be there was intact.

"Quick, Barounggo! Six men with spears. Both lanterns, Kaffa. And you take charge of the boma. Let nothing enter. Haul clear the doorway there. Each man armed? Come along."

Outside the boma the fires from within made a tangled tracery of shadows through the thorn branches; but within a few feet these merged into the darkness. Soon the party was swallowed up in the outer dark of the African night where there lurked bush devils and other things.

Certainly other things. Yellow-green spots of light, always in pairs, looked at them with the unwinking intensity of night creatures. Given time an opportunity for observation, an experienced hunter might attempt the supremely difficult feat of judging distances in the dark and then, from the space between the eyes, guessing whether the owners might be jackal or hyena or lion.

But there was no time for any such calculation now. No chance for anything but to rush straight ahead, making as much display of the lanterns and as much noise as possible, hoping that the creatures that stared so steadily might not be too hungry.

THE SIX conscripted Shenzies crowded on King's very heels, stepping upon his boots till he cursed them fiercely over his shoulder. Behind them, as always, came their herder, the Masai—which was the only reason why all the six had not shrunk back into the boma the moment that their leader had passed beyond the doorway. But they made up for their reluctance by the volume and quality of their yells.

Before the onrushing hullabaloo the staring eyes blinked, then swung away and disappeared. More than likely this diversion drew the attention of prowling beasts away from the human thing that wailed its grief into the open night. The big cats hunt as much by sound and sight as by scent.

Again the shriek split the air, closer now. The rescuers, stumbling through the hot night, chilled at the note of terror. Even King, as the wild screech rose out of the blackness ahead, felt a tingle along his spine, in apprehension of he knew not what.

"That," panted the Masai, "is the voice of a man whom the devils have caught." And a little later, as the sound quavered again into the higher atmosphere, "The voice, too, of a white man."

Yet the word that was distinguishable now was a native word. "*N'gamma!*" it wailed. "*N'gamma!*"

And, *n'gamma,* whatever it might mean, seemed to be the focus of its fear.

"Hello!" yelled King. "Where away? Hold tight. We're coming."

But only, "*N'gamma!*" screamed back at them out of the dark.

And then a shape was apparent in the lanternlight. A shadow that ran on all fours like an ape, then rose and tottered forward on its hind legs and lurched and crawled again on hands and knees.

In another second they were up to it, surrounded it. Light from both lanterns in unsteady hands showed it clear.

"Lord!" gasped King. "A white man it is!"

He lifted the groveling creature, the weight hanging on his arms.

"Steady, old man," reassured King. "You're safe now. We'll see you through."

But the man only whimpered and averted his swollen eyes from the light, clawing away with an emaciated hand. And what a sight of a live human thing it was—rag-wrapped; thorn-gashed; knees and palms cut to raw shreds by gravel, sharp chips of which were still embedded in the pulp-like flesh. Every visible surface was a blood streaked mess of caked grime and sweat.

"Lord!" King stared at the man. "What new horror of Africa is this?"

Suddenly a spasm of renewed vitality came to the sagging figure. It jerked upright.

"*N'gamma!*" it shrieked again, and fought to break away from the hands that held it.

The Shenzies shrank away.

"*Awo!*" they muttered. "Surely have the devils of the bush laid hands upon this one."

But the effort was soon spent. Panting and whimpering, the

man hung in King's arms. King motioned with his head to the two sturdiest Shenzies.

"Make a chair with your joined hands," he snapped. "We must carry him back to camp. Quick."

IN THE boma, the Hottentot, wise in the unexpected ways of the bush, already had a can, one-third full of water, heating over a fire.

"Thirst is for tomorrow," he grunted. "But trouble is here tonight. See, bwana, the bandages are ready and I have taken the medicine box out of the pack."

King grunted a brief appreciation.

"It was well done. There will be a gift. Now lay out a blanket and help with the washing. Barounggo, if those Shenzies hold not the lanterns steady, beat their heads together."

The exhausted man struggled no more. He lay and moaned, now and then a tremor passed over his wasted body. As the encrusted blood and grime soaked away from the derelict's chest, a curious mark emerged and held King's eyes. A queer sort of crude design that had been smeared on with some yellowish ochre stuff: on each breast a circle with a dot in its center, and down over the abdomen a wavy line that divided at the navel and pointed away to each groin, like a crudely drawn inverted letter Y.

King raised his eyes, narrow and perplexed, to look into the round, simian orbs of the Hottentot. The little bush dweller screwed up his face and shook his head.

"I do not know this thing, bwana; yet it is in my belly that it is a mark of evil."

"And this word that he mutters?" asked King. "*N'gamma?* Is that known to you? Or anything like it?"

Again the Hottentot shook his head. King continued the washing and dressing of the innumerable wounds in frowning silence. When it was finally done the man was a mummy swathed in antiseptic bandage, torn trade cloth, and sticking plaster.

"If those Shenzies have left any meat, put a piece on to stew," ordered King. "Then sleep. I watch. Later I will wake you."

In the silent camp King stood on widespread legs and scowled into the night. Outside, throaty rumblings and snufflings circled the boma. Lambent lights in pairs stared at him out of the dark. Dull thunder grumbled. Fitfully the far drums talked their black secrets to one another.

"What mystery is this?" muttered King. "What hellish mystery of Africa?" And a little later, "Drum talk and a hunted man. Guess we'll know soon enough. They'll surely follow."

IN THE morning the man was still alive, which was surprising enough, considering what he had been through. The letdown after his terrific strain, of what must have been many days of privation, was upon him. He lay and moaned. At intervals a spasm contorted his face. Fear. Horror of something beyond human sanity.

King shrugged.

"Well, we can go no faster than we're going. Two days ought to see us at Archer's Post, and maybe there'll be a medico there. Barounggo, two men at a time in relays for a blanket hammock. Divide loads accordingly. *Bado-bado*—and trek."

That day was like the preceding one. Whirling dust devils and merciless sun and thorn scrub. Like many previous days, except that the safari edged over to the westward off the straight line to pick up a water-hole somewhere along the Ol-Doinya foothills. Behind them drums still muttered to one another. King frowned into the heat haze.

The next boma was like the last. King personally saw to it that it was a particularly strong one. The drums that had been talking all across the horizon seemed to be converging upon the camp. King whistled tunelessly through his teeth and directed, that half a dozen large piles of dried thorn and debris be gathered in a circle thirty or forty yards outside the little fortress.

The darkness closed down, and, unlike the previous night,

the drums seemed to have said all that they had to say and were silent. King smiled thinly. The Masai squatted over a fire that threw red highlights and ebony shadows upon his great muscles as with a small whetstone he stroked the long blade of his spear. Far away the thunder grumbled.

After a long silence King spoke.

"Have the Shenzies each man his shield and spear?"

"It is done, bwana. They will fight, for they are afraid."

At last it came. Jackals howled to one another—the demoniac low and high notes of gray-backed jackals.

"And that," said the Hottentot, "is foolish. For here are no gray-backed jackals."

"By which sign," added King, "we may know that those drum talkers have followed their man far; strangers, otherwise they would know. Douse fires within," he told Barounggo, "and send a man out to set light to those prepared piles of thorn."

But the Shenzies huddled together and chattered, clinging to one another like so many monkeys for protection. No man dared to venture out into the dark where there was a most mysterious kind of menace.

With superb disdain the Masai plucked his standing spear from the ground. Unhurriedly he stooped to pick up a brand and with a magnificent swagger stalked out and made the circuit of the stacked woodpiles. He knew that King with ready rifle covered his march. But so had the Shenzies known it. That was the difference between one man and another.

King grinned through tight lips as the bonfires blazed up. Within his own boma, shadowed by the interlaced thorn, was darkness. In the outskirts of the outer glare he could see figures flitting between the bushes.

Now a queer quirk of King's character, hard and efficient as he was in all his dealings with the difficult problem of the African in reasonless emotions, was that he hated to resort to the white man's ultimate argument of guns.

"They're just dumb fools," he maintained. "Barely descended

from the trees. A swift kick in the tail or just the right kind of hokum, according as circumstance and opportunity demand. It will always bring them around grinning."

But here was no opportunity for the persuasive psychology of a stiff boot well placed to the nether loincloth. King was no sentimentalist about his theories. He knew very well that people who came as did these furtive forms in the night came for war, and he knew the persuasive psychology of the first move in a war.

One unwary figure was too slow in dodging between bushes in its advance. King snapped up his rifle and fired. The man flung up his arms and pitched into the thorn bush.

These strangers who had come from some far place behaved as no East African tribe that King knew would have. They did not yell, and gather to adjust their minds to the suddenness of it, to shout encouragement to one another, to work up the necessary rage for attack. They did yell; but with their first shout they charged in to the attack.

"*Whau!*" grunted the Masai. "These be good people. Shenzies, let no fool throw a silly spear. Thrust through the thorn barrier."

It was by that simple defence that the attack was broken. The horde of dark forms surged up to the boma. But stiff acacia thorns are as effective a barrier against naked savages as ever was barbed wire against khaki clad soldiers. Around the boma dark shapes pranced, howling the typical demoniac accompaniment of African fighting.

Thrown spears flicked over the thorn wall. But they were without aim. Within the enclosure was darkness. The leaping shapes were clearly outlined against the outer circle of bonfires. From the inner darkness spears licked out at them. Blood spurted, shiny as dark oil. Yells of attacking fury were interspersed with yells of sudden pain. King deftly slung his rifle over his shoulder. His Luger pistol spat viciously. Leaping shapes writhed or lay still.

IT WAS a strong defence. But the attackers, as the Masai

had said, were good people. A group of them snatched off their loincloths, and, stark naked in the fire glow, wrapping their hands, they set to dragging away a section of the thorn barrier. Half a dozen interlaced thorn bushes began to tear away in a series of jerks under the strong tugs. One of the group started a grunting chant as with a will they heaved together. If that section were torn clear there would be a breach at which numbers would count. Inside, Shenzies clawed madly to hold the barrier in place.

King shouted at them. But in their unreasoning fear his voice only added to the dark pandemonium. With arms and legs he fell upon his own men from behind, and kicked and cuffed at them indiscriminately, till they shrank away, jabbering.

"Kaffa," he ordered then, "the shotgun here. Step well back. Let it spread all it can."

The twelve-bore roared out. The bunched group beyond the thorns fell away, shrieking.

The defence—the strong boma with an outer ring of light— had been prepared with an experience that these attacking strangers, good men though they were, found to be beyond all their expectations.

"Bwana." The Masai's eyes showed white; his nostrils were twitching wide. "Bwana, they waver. A charge now with shield and spear will catch them in their fear and will slaughter many."

"So speaks Kifaru the rhinocerous who has little sense," said King. "But another weapon is given to us."

Little blazes, offspring of the bonfires, were beginning to flare among the dry bunch grass. The lesser blazes began to meet in a flickering line. The attackers looked behind them. King watched with hawk eyes.

"Kaffa, give me that shotgun."

A few charges of No. 4, sprayed wherever there seemed to be anything like an organizing group, were a devastating argument. Isolated from one another, the attackers' hot courage waned. Dark forms began to leap back over the spreading line of flames. Shrill whistles of recall sounded. Black shapes raced past, bounding high like frightened bucks, to join the others before the fire should grow too wide.

King grinned mirthlessly.

"Take note, Barounggo, that wit must be added to courage. Had these men had any, they would have gathered on the windward side of our fires instead of senselessly in the direction from which they came. Take men quickly now outside the boma and stamp out fires that creep toward us from the other side."

The soft night wind blew with persistence. In a little while the boma was a dark island with little waves of fire flowing past it on either side. Beyond was a widening sheet of flame and sullen, red, low-hanging smoke.

King peered out at the scene with critical eyes.

"I guess that's that—" he grunted—"though if they are wise they can backtrack and close in as the embers cool. Barounggo, take those Shenzies by the ears and tell them that it was well fought. To each man there will be a blanket. And swift now. Get the wounded who lie outside into our boma for whatever protection it may offer the poor devils. We have won the first fight and a breathing space of time. Up loads then, and a hard all-night trek. It seems, that it is his fate to win free—this white man whom the drums have followed so far."

AT ARCHER'S POST life still remained in the man who had been the object of that relentless pursuit. His mind still wavered on a borderland of some horror that had driven it into the outer blankness.

The young medico at the post complimented King on his emergency first aid.

"He'll owe his life to your poisonous trade cloth bandages, if he pulls through. And he may—he must have had incredible stamina. I suppose you have no idea how long he was out, or where from?"

King shook his head.

"Must have been days. A long succession of ghastly days with the drums driving him on. Is he talking any?"

"Only that word, *n'gamma*, or whatever it is, and he mutters something about those painted symbols. 'Dedicated', he mumbles, and then he escaped."

King scowled into the far nothing.

"Dedicated, eh? Some hellish juju stuff he must have run into. Must have busted right into their secrets or they wouldn't have kept after him so hard." He strode a short turn up and down the room, thumbs hooked in his belt, head forward, frowning. A twisted smile tightened his mouth. "And I suppose I inherit a choice dose of voodoo vengeance for snatching him out of it. Well, that's Africa. Who around here knows anything about cults up north? That drum talk was new to all my people."

"Nobody knows much. North of Uasu Nyiro River is pretty well back of beyond. And I'm afraid—" the doctor shook his head soberly—"I'm very much afraid our patient will never tell us. Whatever it was has been a terrible strain on his reason. The fever is coming on him. I'm wondering whether we'd better put him in a car and rush him down to Nairobi where there'll be ice, or whether the jolting over the veldt trails will be worse for him than staying here. It's a devilish fix for a man as sick as he."

"There are many devilish things in this country," said King darkly. "If you take him down I guess I'll come along. If he ever talks I'd like to know for my own sake."

IN NAIROBI a military attaché, immaculately incongruous in the hotel where traders and white hunters congregated, waited upon King. No less a personage than the governor desired to have speech with him.

"O-ho, so he's a somebody!" was King's instant conclusion. "What does the governor want to know?"

But the attaché knew nothing, or at all events would say nothing. Whatever was on the governor's mind, his Excellency would communicate if he saw fit.

King grinned at the official formality and went along. The

governor dismissed the faultlessly dressed secretary and regarded with quizzical thoughtfulness the tall brown figure in
rough shirt and riding breeches. He knew King of old, and King
knew him. The attitude between the two men was one of
friendly disagreement on almost every subject.

"And what trouble have you picked up now, Kingi Bwana of
the wild places?" was the governor's characteristic opening.

King shook his head.

"Hanged if I know, Governor Bwana. It's a dark mystery to
me."

"Honest? You don't know anything more than you reported
to Archer's?"

King grinned at the implication.

"Not a thing—this time. Cross my heart. I picked the man
out of the night, and nothing that he has babbled since has
enlightened me."

"Hmh! Well, sit down. I'm going to ask you to take on one
of these jobs that you're always refusing."

King's expression became obstinate. He disliked official as-
signments. His whole soul revolted from their encumbering
red tape and the ponderous tedium of their reports.

"Now this is confidential, Kingi."

King nodded in silent agreement. The governor was serious.

"The man is dying. He will never enlighten us—his mind
won't recover in time. If you know nothing his case will remain
one of the dark mysteries of Africa—unless you can find out."

King made no sign of acquiescence. He waited to hear more.

"The man," said the governor slowly, "is a guide and safari
conductor of wide experience. An ex-soldier, in Africa since
the War. A first class man. He was one of a confidential mission
that we sent out to discover, if possible, evidence about the
constantly recurring complaints about Abyssinians raiding
slaves across our borders."

"Aa-ah!" King was immediately antagonistic. "The old imperial policy. Anything that happens along the border, blame the Abyssinians for it. Somebody stands up in Parliament and clamors for indemnity."

"Yes, yes." The governor nodded amiably. "I know you think that everything we do is just another move toward the acquisition of more territory. But I'm afraid, I'm very much afraid, my dear Ethiophile, that in this case our men must have found the evidence."

"Listen, Governor Bwana." King was positive. "I've got friends among the Abyssinians; they may be black men, but they've treated me white. Let me assure you that the new Abyssinian law imposes the death penalty for slave raiding. And figure it out for yourself: no Abyssinians could ever have chased this poor devil so many days through British territory; no East African tribe could have chased him through the country of other tribes. There's only one explanation. Your mission ran into some high juju stuff. Only a secret cult gang could pass tribal borders that way."

The governor was one of those officials who had won to his position through long service in Africa, not through the fortune of blue-blood. He understood Africa and African needs—though always from the imperial viewpoint—better than King would have thought possible. He frowned thoughtfully.

"Perhaps you are right. We may be much more deeply involved than for a few black slaves. If it's juju there's hysteria with it. Tribal uprisings have started from less. But we *must* have information, accurate and reliable information, before we can crush the thing in its inception."

"Aa-ah." King breathed understanding. "So you offer me the sweet job of sticking my nose into whatever deviltry of African imagination it was that overtook your mission and drove this other fellow shrieking crazy through the night—to say nothing about their being a heap of territory along your Abyssinian border, and very presently it's going to rain a whole lot over all of it."

"Kingi Bwana," said the governor seriously, "we've got to follow up this trail while it is hot. You know Africa. You know how quickly the most murderous happening can be buried in native secrecy and remain a dark mystery forever. We must trace this thing to its source; and if there has been murder or treachery there must be swift retribution."

Cynicism hardened King's wide mouth.

"Yeah, retribution. Military police. Machine guns. That's the history of Africa. I don't hold with shooting up the dumb feed African just because he's been an African fool."

"My dear Kingi—" the governor spoke with the conviction of all imperial policy behind him—"British lives must be protected in our farthest borders. British prestige must be upheld. That is our undeviating principle that affects every white man in the country."

"Yeah?" King's own principle was sacrilege to imperial tradition. "I'm strong for the principle of top dog. But in my home state of North Dakota a man's prestige is exactly as good as he can hold up with his own two hands, and if he rides into somebody else's range and gets into trouble that's his personal hard luck. Who all was the rest of this secret mission that's so important to British prestige?"

The governor looked into King's stubborn face with a wintry smile.

"Just one other man," he told him slowly. "Sir Henry Ponsonby. The man you found was his orderly."

"The devil you say!" King's whole expression changed. "Ponsonby was—*is* too good a man to fool away his time on any wild goose chase after a slave rumor. Governor Bwana, if it was Ponsonby who went up he's quite likely to be marooned in some juju den, holding his end up with a stiff grin and packing more white man's prestige in his own two hands than a whole platoon of military police. And you can't turn the constabulary loose on a case like that. This juju stuff needs to be handled with kid gloves, else there are killings and general hell to pay. You know that."

The governor's smile was almost undignified enough to be a grin.

"Kid gloves, do you say? I have been informed, my Kingi, that your method was a stiff cowhide boot. But since even that is preferable to what you so aptly describe as general hell to pay, I shall make you a concession that will upset the whole system of our colonial government. I shall instruct the comptroller of accounts to pass your expense sheets—scribbled as they will be upon scraps of wrapping paper and what not—and to honor them without question."

King was blasphemous.

"To hell with your system of colonial government! But listen, Governor Bwana—Ponsonby owes me pretty nearly three dollars on a shooting bet. If I should go slopping around in the rain to collect I'd need letters to all outposts to requisition supplies and relay porters to relieve my own when they'd stick in the mud and die. And I'd need a game law waiver—water-holes being flooded and game scattered—to shoot whatever I could get for safari meat whenever I needed it. I'd need a double fly tent and porter tents and half a ton of quinine and tarpaulin covers and slickers and—oh, hell, a twenty-man load of dude outfit."

The governor's smile was now undisguisedly a grin.

"I knew you would need all of that and an armed escort besides. In the circumstances I think your bet is worth collecting. I have already signed a blank requisition for you upon military police stores. When do you start?"

KINGI BWANA'S safari was once again at the place where the cry of gray-backed jackals had signaled the determined but ill-judged attempt to recapture a man whose reason had left him, but who still might know too much of things that white men must never know.

But this was a very different safari. Tents glistened wetly in the light of the sputtering fires. A huddle of narrow, steep-sided shelters fit only for a dog and aptly named pup tents; and a trim green one with a wide double fly under the eaves of which, raised from the ground on logs, were stacked boxes and bales. A tarpaulin covered another pile of lumpy shapes. There was no thorn boma. There were men enough to stand an all-night guard. Fifteen were *askaris* pure and simple, men who carried no pack loads save rifles of an outmoded military pattern which they could shoot off with a lot of noise and whose united front looked very formidable.

King would just as lief have dispensed with these noisy bravos who always caused envy and discontent among humble Shenzie beasts of burden. But since they were pressed upon him at the expense of his Majesty's imperial government, he shrugged and said to Barounggo, the safari driver—

"At least these be fifteen strong men; and when the strength of our porters fails in the clinging mud—"

The Masai placed a great hand over his mouth to cover a chuckle like the rumble of a lion and completed the thought:

"Out of our own good porters have we made not-so-bad fighting men, thou and I together, bwana. Surely then, when the more obstreperous of these not-so-good fighting men have eaten stick, can we make not-so-bad porters out of them?"

But it was a strong safari. King knew better than anyone in Africa what he was deliberately going into, and he was prepared for it. He knew that he was going into something that nobody knew. Africa at its darkest. Something that had swallowed up one white man because he came too close. Something that had driven another one crazy. And the latter had escaped from the immediate horror only because he had been a man of wide African experience, a first class man—a man perhaps as good as King himself.

There would be first the blank wall of honest ignorance: actual lack of knowledge on the part of the great dumb majority. There would be, when one finally penetrated closer to the mystery, the ox-dull stubbornness of people who knew something but lived in superstitious terror of it themselves and dared not even speak about it. With silence there would be the age-old defences of Africa against the white man—obstruction, underground intimidation, boycott on food supplies, queer sicknesses. And there would be, if one survived and persisted in trying to penetrate yet farther, Africa implacable, savage, diabolically ingenious in keeping hidden the sinister things that are African.

Soberly, and with a very hard expression, King led his safari through country that was new to him, scouting around in the neighborhood where he had picked up the crazed orderly. The caravan squelched through a sticky mud that less than a fortnight before had been the deep dust of the dry season. The procession was not now in a long snaky line, as it had come over that path, for each following man would but tread deeper into the sucking puddle left by the feet of his predecessor. Spread out like a line of skirmishers the men went, each one picking the best ground he could find.

It was the duty of the Masai, helped—for the present—by the *askaris,* to see that no man resorted to the simple African trick of dropping his load behind a thorn bush and slinking away out of the clammy wet to the shelter of the nearest native village.

Later on, when the safari would come into the really wild country of unfamiliar tribes—wherever that direction might turn out to be in this morass of nonexistent clues and obliterated paths—no persuasion or beating would drive a man of them beyond sight of the bwana whose white prestige protected them.

"From the direction of the sun's left side came the drum talk that pursued that man," said King. "Somewhere in that direction will be a village, and somewhere near the village a witch doctor. Perhaps I have that which will induce him to talk."

It was on the second day of the mire that the Hottentot pointed to the unmistakable signs of Africa in a donga whose steep sides they skirted. And "days" as applied to travel in this weather meant, not the twenty miles or so that King with his customary light safari covered, but a bare eight or ten. The donga, two weeks ago a dry sandy gash that twisted across the plain, was now ten feet deep with turbid water in which floated scraps of thatch and splinters of wood, the debris of a hut, and the carcass of an undernourished cow.

It happened every year. The rain came in its fury, the deluge tore away great slices of overhanging bank and with them huts, cattle byres, everything built too close; and every year Africa, callous, without thought, rebuilt in just the same feckless manner as it had always built.

IT WAS a big village, the usual sprawling mess of mud-and-thatch huts. The rain had lasted just long enough to wash away the accumulated smells of appalling African insanitation. King told the Masai to let the men run free to indulge in a holiday of the chitter-chatter and gossip of the road that is dear to the native heart.

In matters requiring wit rather than brawn it was the shrewd little Hottentot who served as a go-between for dealings that were not usual to white men. To him King gave an old brier pipe the bowl of which had been carefully carved with an intricate design.

"Go, little apeling," he told him, "and ferret out the witch doctor. Tell him that the Old One of Elgon cut that pattern. Perhaps this wizard is not so far but that he can read it and will exchange wisdom for a gift of a good blanket of many colored stripes."

The Hottentot returned in due course carrying the pipe wrapped in a banana leaf as an object worthy of reverence.

"It is a great magic in that pattern, Bwana. For the *tagati*, having seen it, was immediately well disposed. And, moreover, bwana—" the little man stood on one leg and clicked his tongue in awesome excitement—"he owns a *lebasha*, a finder of lost things, and he will let him turn his eyes into the darkness for you."

"A *lebasha*, hm? That's a hokum that I've heard of but have never yet seen. This may be interesting."

King was ruminative as he picked out a gaudy blanket from the trade goods. He numbered the ancient Wizard of Elgon among the first of the black men who had treated him white. That old pipe bowl, carved with whatever symbol it was of witch doctory, had won him entry to many things that white men never saw. This was going to be a new one.

The *lebasha*, he knew, was a clairvoyant, who by magical processes could be endowed with the scent of a bloodhound and could then pick up trails or trace stolen articles to the very door of the robber. What made the hokum interesting was that King knew certain unbelievable stories of such articles having been found. By all means the *lebasha* might prove to be worthwhile.

The magician lived in a clearing a mile away from the village. The tortuous path to it was hung with witch signs: skulls of animals; pointers; warning marks; grass curtains that nobody would dare to pass across the path. But these were now drawn aside. The symbols on the pipe bowl had opened the road for the white man.

The witch hut was surrounded by a thorn boma festooned with the usual emblems of magic—bones and snake-skins and dried embryos of unborn creatures, all the gruesome claptrap dear to African superstition. At the entrance stood an ebony figure, as stiff and as motionless as a statue carved out of the same wood and as naked as an idol except for a maze of painted designs. Only moving white eyeballs showed that the man was alive.

King looked keenly at the paint-smeared design. No leopard spots or wavy lines there. The cult that he sought was not there. But information that might lead to it perhaps would be.

King passed through the gateway. The Hottentot groveled after him. Within the hut, an enormous megaphonic voice boomed—

"*Jambo, bwana m'kubwa,* who has the favor of the Old One of Elgon."

King smiled a little grimly. He was too old a hand, he told himself, to be impressed by any skullduggery. Yet the performance that he now witnessed left him wondering.

The hut was illuminated only by such light as came through the low door, and by a tiny fire of cowdung on the bare mud floor that smoked acridly and hurt the eyes. A blanket-muffled figure squatted on a three-legged stool almost in the embers.

King knew the ceremonies of calling upon magicians. He stayed on one side of the fire and passed his gift through the smoke. The wizard took, but did not inspect it. He was shrewd enough to know that a man who knew so much of the proper etiquette would know enough to bring a proper gift.

A stool was in readiness on the near side of the fire. King squatted upon it.

"I come, wise one, seeking knowledge of a word and of the trail from where that word came."

"So much bwana's servant has told me, but the word he has not said. The seer into the dark is ready, the magic drink is ready. What is given to him to smell out shall be smelled."

The wizard grunted an order, and out of the farther gloom of the hut shuffled a youth. A thin, anemic looking creature with a witless look in his eyes and a nervous affliction that twitched one side of his face. The wizard raked a pot from the embers and poured from it into a gourd a liquid that stank of dead things.

King watched with cold criticism.

The boy squatted, gulped down the liquid and shivered. The wizard stroked his face with tense fingers and muttered incantations. The boy began slowly to rock on his heels. King saw that his eyes rolled upward in their sockets till only the yellowish whites were visible.

The Hottentot moaned in awe at the workings of black magic. King, coldly skeptical, commented to himself—

"Hm, a neurotic type, a narcotic drink and some sort of hypnotism."

The boy ceased his rocking motion and sat back stiffly at an impossible angle, breathing stertorously.

The wizard drew away his fingertips as if tenuous threads were attached to each. He whispered:

"He has gone into the place where the dead thoughts of men are stored. His eyes see into the darkness. Let bwana ask now what he will know."

"Ask him," said King, "whether he knows the word—*N'gamma*."

It was not the entranced boy at whom King looked. He watched the wizard keenly. But if the latter knew anything about the word whose significance had driven a man crazy he kept his composure with an astounding coolness. It was upon the boy that its effect was surprising.

He whimpered like a dog and cowered on all fours. He gave the exact impression that if he had a tail he would have tucked it between his legs.

"Ha!" said the magician. "He has found the word. It is a word of fear. He will smell out the trail to the place of that fear."

The boy breathed deeply; sniffed, in fact. Then suddenly he made a throaty barking noise for all the world like a dog, and scurried out of the hut.

"Come," said the magician. "We must follow fast."

THE BOY ran in a queer, dead sort of way, his head lolling forward, his body limp. King, catching up with him, noted with a distinct shock that his eyes were still turned up in his head. Like a sleepwalker the boy ran, seeing nothing, guided by some queer subconscious sense, avoiding obstacles and trees by inches. At intervals he threw up his head and barked.

In a straight line the extraordinary trail ran, for some two miles, till a donga intersected the path, filled of course with rushing, turbid water. At the donga's edge the bey stopped and howled mournfully.

Still he pointed with his hand in the exact direction of his course. Then he fell down and lay gasping and twitching in a convulsion.

King knew that it was said of a *lebasha* that in his assumed characteristic of a hound he could not follow a trail across running water; that at a stream the magic power left him.

"It is finished," said the wizard. "He can go no farther. Yet there where he points is the true trail, bwana. That is all. In this matter I can do no more."

King walked back to his camp through the thin drizzle, his head sunk on his chest, wondering.

"And what, wise little apeling, do you make out of all that?" he asked the Hottentot.

The little man shivered.

"It is a great magic, bwana!"

That night a drum tapped rhythmically. Fitfully it throbbed into the dark. It stopped. Then repeated. Then stopped again. Then repeated once more.

"And of that what do you make?" King asked of the little man who shivered in his blanket.

"Nay, bwana, it is a drum talking," said the Hottentot. "Of it I make nothing. Only it is not the same talk that those other drums spoke." Curiously the little bush dweller, so astute in other things, when magic was in the air remained truly African, foolish, frightened, witless.

"I make of it," muttered King, "that this wizard was in so far honest that this word of fear has no significance for him.

"He is not of that dark cult. Yet, true to the brotherhood, he taps information for such as may have interest to know that a white man comes seeking. There will be trouble on that trail."

IT WAS a credit to King's organization of his safari that with the morning's start only one man was missing. It was to be expected that on any hard and unpleasant trek men would desert at an opportunity like this in a comfortable village.

But the Masai took it as an affront upon his personal honor that even one man should have gotten away. He shouted threats and raged through the village, dragging frightened men out of their huts, shaking his great spear in their faces, and promising death and dismemberment if the fugitive were not delivered.

But to no avail.

"Let him go," said King. "Time is more valuable than one man. Give his load to an *askari*."

That was another source of shouting and argument. They were fighting men, screamed the *askaris;* they would not stand by and see one of their number reduced to the low estate of a burden carrier. It was exactly as had been foreseen.

The Masai charged in among them like a raving lion. They shrank from his fury.

"Fighting men?" he growled at them throatly. "Who among you is a fighting man? Let him stand forth and speak. Lo, I will fight him; shield to shield and spear to spear. Or, if he has a brother, let the twain stand forth. Or if a cousin or relative, let the family stand forth together against an *elmoran* of the Masai and let us see who has knowledge of fighting!"

Magnificent in his wide-flung challenge, tall ostrich plume and monkey-hair elbow-garters flying in the wind, the great fellow glared at them. His eyeballs rolled white; his nostrils twitched; the white scars of a hundred battles showed upon his chest and arms.

Of all fifteen *askaris,* no man, no family, showed any eagerness to put their claims to so heroic a test.

"So?" snorted the blood-hungry one. "Then we can talk. Thou, loud mouthed one." He took the selected man by the throat and shook him. "Thine is the burden today. Tomorrow it falls to the lot of the next loudest."

King affected not to notice all this.

"Up, up!" he called. "Up loads and away! What is this bickering? Time passes and the way is long before us. Up and trek."

He strode ahead. He knew that the safari would follow. A

boy showed him the ford across the donga. He followed down on the other side to a point opposite to where the *lebasha* had fallen to the ground after his weird performance. From there he set a compass course.

"Since no other trail is known to us," he said to the Hottentot, "this at least is a direction."

So in that direction he led the way. The safari strung out behind him, picking the best ground available.

Hardly a mile had they progressed when King stopped suddenly. A clucking noise of dismay escaped from the Hottentot. What lay on the trail was no sight for panicky porters. King threw up his hand and shouted back:

"Here is quicksand. Let the men make a circle to the right—a wide circle. Let no man approach this bad ground. Barounggo, come here and see."

The safari swung away in a detour. The Masai splashed up through the puddles, wondering what need his master had to show him a quicksand in a country where there were thousands of quicksands.

"Not a quicksand," said King. "But we've found your lost man."

The Masai looked and started. Instinctively he lowered his spear and crouched ready to meet an attack. But there was no hostile force in sight, no lurking figures behind bushes. Only a man, the porter who had been missing that morning. He lay face up in the thin rain, naked, his arms stretched out as if crucified on the sticky ground.

In dry weather the hyenas would have nosed him out before dawn. The steady rain flattened the scent. The body was therefore intact and the yellow clay design stood clear against the sodden black skin. A crude leopard spot on each breast and down the belly a line that divided to point to each thigh.

King's voice was hard.

"This is no thing for the eyes of the Shenzies," he said. "But

you two, who have made many safaris with me, my right hand
and my left, what counsel have you to offer in this matter?"

He wanted to know right then and there whether superstitious terrors of black magic were undermining the courage of
his henchmen, without whose loyal support he might as well
turn back from this sinister thing to which he had put his hand.

His right hand and his left. Both men's eyes shone. There
were times over late camp-fires when they argued with endless
acrimony as to which one was right and which left. Never could
they agree, and shrewdly King never told them.

"You, apeling, who have wisdom in the ways of the bush,
what say you?"

The Hottentot stood on one foot and scratched his knee with
the toes of the other.

"Bwana," he rendered his well considered verdict, "this is no
witchcraft here; but the doing, as we know by this mark, of
fierce men from a far place. Of men moreover—" he grimaced
with the preternatural wisdom of a very old chimpanzee—"of
evil men who have that which they wish to hide; otherwise they
would not leave a sign such as this to frighten us from the trail.
And when a secret is hidden—" monkey inquisitiveness chuckled from his wizened face—"it is honor to him who has the wit
to find it out."

There was no suggestion of turning back from this trail that
gave its stark warning that this was a phase of Africa not to be
meddled with. King ruffled his hand through the little man's
woolly hair, at which he, suddenly shy, chittered away like a
marmoset.

"And you, warrior?" King turned to the other.

"Nay, bwana," said the great fellow simply. "Shall strange
bush pigs do this to an *elmoran?* Painter folk who smear designs
with colors. Shall such people slay one of my Shenzies and go
unscathed? Let bwana give his order, and the safari shall
proceed."

King stood scowling down at the dead thing that had been

laid out in his path. Perplexity furrowed two deep lines in his forehead.

"I have never heard of any leopard society this far east," he mused. "And the leopard cultists don't paint; they use steel claws. What in all black deviltry is the meaning of this mark?"

Questioning the empty air brought no light to the enigma. King shrugged.

"At least it means that that queer hypnotized creature was right, that this is exactly the direction that we want to go. Let's go."

That was the only clew. A direction, no more. But a direction given by black magic and confirmed by a dead man. King held his compass to it.

THERE FOLLOWED days of dreary tramping through the slush. Progress was wretchedly slow. Long detours had to be made to find fords across the flooded dongas. Actual distance gained was sometimes barely a mile in a long day's hard going.

Porters fell sick. African natives, who are capable of enduring privation and poor food under heavy loads when engaged on their own futile affairs, revel in the luxury of sickness in a white man's safari.

Patiently King dosed them—a long line of complaints every morning. Quinine and cathartics were the stock prescriptions. King made them as nauseating as a Nairobi chemist had taught him. The men engulfed them and liked them. Medicine in all the horrible and revolting brews of native quackery was their heritage and was good for them in strict ratio to the price extorted by the quack. Free medicine at the hands of a white man was a luxury, and the whole staff vied for it accordingly.

Without the dosage their susceptible minds would have magnified their vaguely imagined ills into honest cramps and gripings. Discontent, sullen conviction of persecution and general disorganization would have ensued. So King held daily clinic and fretted for the squandered time.

Villages were few and far between. This was sparsely settled country. In the villages no information was to be picked up. Here was the blank ignorance that King had expected. To the stupid Algain tribesmen the word *N'gamma* meant nothing. And King hardly hoped to be able to work a witch doctor again. But he persisted on his compass course. That stark warning at the beginning had been evidence that he was aiming right; and no other course, no clew, was available.

There was some small compensation. The rain, after the first fury of the monsoon burst, slackened to intermittent downpour and drizzle. The sun managed to break through now and then to warm chilled bodies; though no day passed without its good six or eight hours of wetness. Clothes, despite slickers, were never dry. Blankets were soggy. Leather goods sprouted green fungus overnight; and worse, so did the loose cereals of the food supply. Maize, rice, beans, the staples of porter diet, ran to mold—which meant fermentation; which meant stomach ache; which meant more medicine.

Conversely to human misery, all nature rejoiced. Man pays for superiority over nature by having become a creature of artificial shelters. Without them he is wretched. Denied them for too long, he sickens. But nature blooms.

The burnt bush country that had been waiting for its first drop of moisture literally burst into exuberant green. Flowers leaped out of what had been barren dust patches without a speck of leaf in sight. Even the mimosa thorn sprouted pink rosettes of bloom that scented the air—and the long thorns grew inches longer.

Birds of gaudy plumage appeared out of the long leagues of nowhere and sang their derision of the rain. Insects hatched in their myriads and nearly all of them seemed to require human food. But game was scarce. It kicked its heels all over many hundred miles of green plain and drank where it willed.

Meat therefore was infrequent. And corn was moldy. And through all that misery nearly two score of African males had to be pushed along, cajoled, coaxed, bullied, carefully herded like beasts of burden. There was potent reason why people did not travel in the rainy season; why Africa, beyond rail and auto road reach, sits down and stagnates, isolated, for six months in every year.

DOGGEDLY KING pushed on. The direction was exactly eleven degrees west of North; and by compass bearing King held to it till his reward came in meeting with obstruction.

Native villages began to be vaguely helpless about finding fords. Food supplies were curiously unobtainable. There was no corn; there had been a famine; the elephants had trodden down the last season's crop; the villagers were starving themselves.

The restlessness of the porters was evidence that they were being slyly urged to desert. And desert some of them did.

King smiled thinly. This was the second phase of his quest that he had expected. It was proof that, while the common herd knew nothing about the dark mystery, they had been tipped off to impede the white man. A food strike in the wilderness is a weapon a hundred time more potent than in a civilized city. Africa was sullenly defending its secrets.

Against that stolid, unwavering defence many a white man's advance has helplessly wilted and come to an end; and that, incidentally, is one of the administration's strongest reasons for the employment of native police.

Barounggo stormed into the presence of local chieflings and flung down one of two choices.

"The *bwana m'kubwa*, my master, requires potio for his men. So and so many baskets of this and so many of that. If they be forthcoming swiftly, perhaps we condescend to pay. Otherwise we slay and take."

Of all peoples the African is perhaps more susceptible to lordly bluff than any other. And at that it was precarious guessing for those back country chiefs to determine whether the truculent great fellow were bluffing or not. It was a strong safari; the white man who ran it looked like a hard and determined individual; and the Masai was an awe-inspiring figure. Sulky orders were given, and women brought the required potio to the camp.

THE COUNTRY began to change. The open thorn scrub with its tall sentinel acacia trees began to close in. Trees in clumps began to be frequent: tamarisks, silk cottons, copals. The safari was beginning to come into jungle country.

King mused upon a phenomenon of his own observation in Africa—that it was the people who lived in the jungles, rather than the open dwellers, who seemed to have evolved the more diabolic forms of dark and fantastic cults.

He was out hunting for meat when he met the first of these forest men. With the Hottentot carrying the extra gun and four pole bearers to carry in whatever he might shoot, he was skirting the jungle fringe, himself in advance, treading like a cat. A man blundered into view before he knew that strangers were near.

Seeing them, the man gave a howl, dropped his pack and bolted back into the bush path. King called after him and set the Hottentot to shouting in the half dozen or so different languages that he knew. After a frightened silence the man hesitantly called back and presently was persuaded to emerge. A stalwart, quite intelligent looking man he was, and it turned out that he understood Swahili very creditably.

There were Boranna tribes in the jungle country, he said. He himself was journeying from his uncle's father's village—he pointed with his chin—two days' journey distant to his own village; he pushed out his lips in the other direction. His pack contained fish that he had netted in a jungle pool and mealie cakes that his uncle's father's second best wife had made as a gift to his own woman who was sister to—

King cut the man short. These African family affairs were always terrifically involved. He wanted to talk about other things. Yes, said the man, there was plenty of game in the jungle; he had passed bush bok only fifteen minutes back; but why worry about bush bok? If bwana were hungry, the man would gladly trade some of his fish and mealie cakes for a brass cartridge or whatever the white man would give him. In fact, he would trade all his fish and mealie cakes; for he could catch more fish and many women could make mealie cakes, while no woman could make a brass cartridge.

Altogether an obliging and ingenuous fellow; an unspoiled son of the wild. King asked him a few more questions about the beyond, of which the man knew nothing, traded in his mealie cakes for two empty shells and sent him grinning on his way.

Strictly enjoining his four men not to monkey with that pack and particularly not to become suddenly panicky and come clamoring on his heels, King with the Hottentot went into the dim jungle path to look for bush bok.

Bush bok were not so plentiful as the man had indicated; but natives always have the most fantastically inaccurate information about game, depending upon what they think the questioner wants to know rather than upon fact.

But meat was badly needed in the camp. Fish and mealie cakes were a delicacy; but after all, one native basket would not extend to any miracle of loaves and fishes for a whole safari. King crept quietly on, a long way farther than the fifteen minutes within which bush bok tracks should have been apparent.

The farther he went, the more perplexed became his expression. A couple of times he consulted his pocket compass. Finally he stopped. A phenomenon was here that required consideration before plunging ahead. It was through a cautious observation of things that did not just click that King was still alive. The Hottentot's cunning round eyes peered up at him.

"Does the pointing machine say what my feet have been thinking?" he asked, chuckling at what he knew would be a confirmation of his own observation.

"It says, little wise imp, that this path follows parallel with the jungle edge; and I'll bet you not fifty yards from it, just to keep out of the sun in hot weather."

"Aho? So that that man, who was not a fool, walking this path, would have known that we hunted along the fringe?"

King nodded, his eyes narrow with suspicion.

"And yet he pretended to be surprised—and I have seen no other path by which he might have come."

"Nor are there any bush bok. In such a path, bwana, there may well be a man trap, or men with spears hidden."

Why, King wondered, would a native pretend not to know that a white man was hunting parallel to his own path? Very cautiously, stepping on noiseless toes, King picked his way back along that suspicious path, pausing to listen, peering into every bush tangle.

It was with relief that he came into the open where the ingenuously obliging jungle dweller had blundered into view.

Nothing had happened. No attack; not a suspicious sound. The sun had broken through a ragged hole in the clouds. Steam rose from the wet grass, warm and pleasant and cheerful.

"*So-ss-ss!*" The Hottentot, standing frozen on one leg, hissed the warning note of a puff adder and pointed.

The plantain leaf cover of the native pack had been removed. King might have known that four greedy native boys would plot to steal a little—just a taste—of the delicacy and then cover up their little depredation. And of course that was just what they had done. They lay now, all four of them, half hidden in the long grass, twisted into horrible contortions. Death had not come easily to them.

"Aa-ah!"

King's long exhalation of understanding was almost as sharp as the Hottentot's hiss. In three long strides he stood looking down at the four twisted bodies—and seeing nothing but the racing pictures of his own thoughts.

So this was the place. That uncanny boy with all his hokum of smelling out the trail had been right. Right to a compass degree. Somewhere in this jungle happened whatever it was that had happened to Sir Henry Ponsonby and had driven his orderly crazy. The blind search had passed through the baffling belt of blank ignorance, through the outer defence of passive obstruction, and now this was the third stage: active opposition unhampered by a single inhibition of civilization. Africa fighting with every weapon of its dark imagination to prevent the white man from finding out what the white man must not know.

"Somebody who backs this thing is very clever," muttered King. "It just happens by the grace of God that I hike and hunt better on an empty stomach."

"And what," the foresighted little Hottentot wanted to know in advance, "is to be told to the remaining porters who have not already deserted about these four who do not return?"

"Hmph! Tell them just this," said King. "They will now stick closer than bush ticks. In this jungle we find trouble in many forms."

"Truth," clucked the Hottentot. "The skin inside of my belly tells me that here live the father and mother of trouble."

YET BOTH forebodings seemed to have been unnecessarily gloomy. King entered the jungle tense and alert against any treachery. With six *askaris* he took the lead. The porters, as many as were left of them, huddled behind. The Masai and the remaining *askaris* formed a rear guard, every man armed, watchful.

King knew the devilish ingenuity of man-traps, springy, bamboo things armed with hardwood spikes and set beside the trail, held by the most innocent looking liana vine triggers. Another kind might be set in the path, covered with leaves. Such a thing, sprung by a passerby, would rake the bowels from a man's belly, or a heavy knob would crash into his face. Another deadly trick was to tie venomous snakes beside the path. And what new devices there might be besides, nobody could guess.

Every forward step therefore was tested; every bush scrutinized. Progress was agonizingly slow. Nor was there any means of knowing which path might lead to the headquarters of the trouble or which might meander for miles to some unimportant hidden village.

"Presently," said King, "we shall hear the drums that tell of our advance; and we shall know at least the direction."

But there were no drums. Giant frogs boomed question and answer with deceptive regularity. A bittern kind of bird thrummed in a marsh with a volume worthy of a war drum. But no signals. Nor, as the party slowly progressed, were any man-traps encountered.

Of course, the obvious remedy for all this uncertainty was to waylay some jungle native, grab him and make him lead the advance. Even though he might refuse to betray the big juju village, he would know where the tribal man-traps would be located.

And it was just such a native that they caught—a tall fellow who came trotting along, singing lustily. Strangely enough, he exhibited no surprise at meeting a white man's safari creeping through the jungle. The surprise was rather on the part of the safari at the man's open-faced honesty.

Surely, he said. There was a big village barely a day's journey distant; and if the bwana were afraid of turning into the wrong path, he himself would be glad to lead the way for a small gift out of the bwana's generosity.

King remembered the cheerful ingenuousness of that other jungle dweller who had happened along with his mealie cakes and fish. Grimly he said:

"All right. Just three paces ahead all the time; no monkey tricks."

The man actually looked hurt. But the tempers of white men are always incomprehensible to natives. This man accepted the condition as the tantrum of just another queer white man and presently he was trotting ahead, chattering along over his shoulder in African good humor.

King thought to surprise something out of him.

"What do you know about the word, *n'gamma?*" he asked abruptly.

But the man displayed blank ignorance.

"Nay, bwana, I am but a cultivator of yams, and from them I make beer which I sell. I am no wise man who knows strange words. But in the big village is a *m'zungu monpéré*. He knows many strange tongues of many peoples. Without doubt he will enlighten bwana."

Well, that certainly seemed to knock the bottom out of a lot of things. A *monpéré* was a distortion of nothing less peaceful than *mon père*, handed down from the days of the early French missions. All missionaries, irrespective of race or creed, were *monpérés*.

A missionary was established at the big village. And it was there that King had been expecting to find the seat, the very home, of the black cult that was not afraid to lay hands upon white men. This thing was more baffling at the end of the trail than it had been at the beginning. Or was he off the trail altogether? King wondered. But then he remembered, not two hours' run behind, four men twisted into horrible shapes because they had stolen just a taste of mealie cakes and fish.

However, they all arrived at the mission station without mishap. The missionary was a Reverend Dr. Henderson, a Scotch Presbyterian. He was delighted to have a visitor and was, of course, the very soul of hospitality, as missionaries in the far outskirts of nowhere always are. He insisted that King should take up quarters in his own little bungalow. For King's servants he found room in his compound with his own black boys; and the safari he allocated among the huts of his converts, quite a little village among themselves.

"A dry hut and a few days of recuperation after this dreadful weather will set them all up," he said.

When all that was done and everybody comfortable he perked his lean face to one side.

"Let me see, er, Mister King," he inquired. "Is it possible that I have heard of you, Kingi Bwana? Er, might it be the same?"

King nodded.

"I hope the stories haven't been all bad."

The Reverend Henderson's wide blue eyes displayed almost alarm.

"Dear me, dear me. I sincerely hope—you know, Mr. King—er, you must forgive me. But it is said, as I suppose you must know, that where trouble is brewing, there Kingi Bwana is likely to show up. Nobody would travel during this season unless there were something serious. I do hope that nothing is wrong anywhere near here. Everything has been going along so nicely."

KING POSTPONED a discussion until the after-dinner prayers were concluded and the houseboys had distributed themselves among their huts within the wire fenced compound. Then over his pipe he told the missionary his story quite frankly, and concluded:

"I figured I was absolutely hot on the trail. But now I'm hanged if I know whether I'm not away off."

The Reverend Henderson was, of course, shocked at the recital.

"Oh, I hope so," he almost pleaded. "I hope you are wrong. In fact, I am sure you must be wrong. Nothing so dreadful could have happened here. Everything has been so quiet. And as for any juju cult—" He shook his head.

"But hang it all," King insisted, "I know I've been aiming right. There's been proof enough in the murderous interference. And it couldn't be much farther. That orderly of Ponsonby's could not in any circumstances have been running and hiding for more than a week; and it's just about a week's hard going from here in good weather to where I picked him up."

"Indeed? Good heavens, how horrible! They were here, of course. It was barely a month ago. As a matter of fact, Sir Henry was going to send me a runner from Lenia to return some books. But—er, well, somehow he failed to do so."

"Aa-ah! He was at Fort Harrington and he was here—and he disappeared. Hmm! Well, leaving aside my theory about a juju—which I don't yet give up—what about slave raiding?"

"My dear Mr. King—" Dr. Henderson spread out his thin hands deprecatingly—"you know very well that most of this slave raiding is propaganda put out by certain European powers that want to embarrass Abyssinia in order to gain trade concessions. We are just a few miles south of the border here, and if there were any such horrible traffic—"

"So? Just below the border, eh?"

"Yes, Bagawaiyo, this village, is on the old caravan route; and established in British Territory, I have no doubt, for security's sake."

"Aa-ah! An old caravan route? Right handy for running off a few men now and then."

"My dear Mr. King! I should have heard some rumors. Men, of course, disappear. Some fall victims to the jungle; some just go away in the haphazard African manner; and in the borderland district the percentage is always high. But I have been here two years now and I have heard nothing that might lead to suspicion of anything so dreadful as slave traffic. Nor did my predecessor leave any such notes. Oh, let me assure you that nothing that might call for official intervention has been going on here."

King remained silently noncommittal. He liked missionaries on the whole. Skeptically tolerant, he felt that their Christian endeavors at least did no harm and he strongly agreed with their civilizing influence—though that did not mean that he agreed always with the soundness of their individual judgment. And then again, regrettably, there had been, in the history of Africa, renegade preachers who actually made use of their influence and their cloth to cover relationship with the most objectionable kind of back country traders.

King reserved his comment. The Reverend Henderson went on:

"Let me tell you what we shall do. I shall send a note over tomorrow morning to the Reverend Leroy. He knows these people much better than you or I could ever hope to."

"And the Reverend Leroy is—"

"A colored brother. From Jamaica, I believe, or Barbados. I can not altogether agree with some of his dogma, and he can not agree with some of my theories of approach to the native. An educated black man, you know, is always apt to feel a little superior. But he felt the call to minister to his own race and he is doing splendid work. Naturally he is closer to the undercurrents of native doings than any white man can be."

THE REVEREND LEROY proved to be a splendid specimen of light negro, broad shouldered and robust, with a keenly intelligent face. He was meticulously dressed in proper clerical garb and he spoke educated English with a vaguely elusive accent.

He smiled broadly at the idea of juju.

"Not among these Boranna tribes. These people are two-thirds Galla blood. The Galla are fighting men, almost as ferocious as that Masai of yours. They are animists. There is some minor witch doctory among them in outlying districts; though none here.

"At worst, their function is rather the interpretation of the forces of nature, predictions of rainfall, birth auguries, luck charms; a mild form of sorcery that no sensible man can object to in Africa where so many more important evils have to be combated. Juju, on the other hand, is the most debased form of idolatry. Anybody who has made a study of Africa knows that the more virile fighting people, the Zulu, the Masai, the Galla, never went in for that sort of thing."

King grasped at once what Dr. Henderson had gently hinted at. Leroy was distinctly superior; didactic, one might even say. King had to admit that he ought to have thought of all those quite patent facts himself. It was true. Juju belonged among the debased Central and West Coast peoples. The men here were an upstanding, open faced folk. He laughed and said to the Reverend Leroy:

"Well, I figured I was hot on the trail. But you know your own people."

"Not my people, Mr. King." The preacher's voice was bitter. "I do not know my own people. My parents were taken away from wherever they belonged—as slaves—by white men. I have no people."

King felt suddenly quite queerly shocked. He had known slaves; he had seen plenty of them in his own day. Savages they had been, dull creatures of no understanding, quite possibly better off in their condition than at large, exposed to the diseases and dangers of their native state. Right in his own country he had known colored men whose parents had been slaves. Humble people they were, far from the country of their origin.

That had seemed different somehow. But to meet an educated man, a man of understanding, in Africa, at home so to speak, who did not know where was his home! That was shocking. King could understand the resentment that such a man could feel against the system that had caused his condition. The preacher was talking again.

"And now his Majesty's government is all in a pother because politicians in Parliament point indignant fingers at black Abyssinia about slave raiding. Let his Majesty's government turn its eyes closer to home to look for slaves, the Anglo-Egyptian Sudan, for instance. You know as well as I do, Mr. King, that slave raiding today is punishable in Abyssinia by the death penalty. It is possible, despite that law, that some bold petty chief may dash across the border now and then and kidnap a prospective servant or so. And as a matter of fact that possibility must account for some of the occasional disappearances that do occur. But slave raiding on any organized scale? I assure you, Mr. King, there is no such thing in this district."

King could not help but be convinced. Yet doggedly he asked the question:

"So men do disappear, eh? And if not slaves, what did Sir Henry Ponsonby find out before he, too, disappeared?"

That question remained a dark mystery. If Leroy could throw no light on it, then it was indeed one of the hidden things of Africa that would be likely to remain hidden forever. King was impressed by the intelligence and force of the man. The Reverend Henderson, good soul, was the acme of hospitality and helpful solicitude; but he was the type of man of God who would never be able to see his flock other than as errant children. Leroy, however, knew what he was talking about.

The Masai, leaning on his spear, stood scowling after his departing figure.

"A proper man," he growled. "A whole figure of a man. What need has he to be ashamed and hide beneath a copy of white man's clothing?"

The Hottentot impishly strutted in imitation, copying the play of the big hands, the swing of the clerical coat, choking in paroxysms over an imaginary collar.

"Be silent!" ordered King. "And cut that out, ape's offspring. He is a holy man."

"*Wagh!*" growled the Masai. "I would like to fight that one."

Both men curiously resented the black man's conversion to white man's ways and clothing. Perhaps it was that both sensed the attitude of superiority. King, smiling skeptically, wondered, if that were the general native reaction, what might be the pros and cons of the never ending debate in religious circles in Africa about sending native missionaries to their own people.

But that was an idle and transient cogitation. The dominating thought in King's mind was that here or hereabouts Ponsonby was last seen and from here or hereabouts his orderly had escaped as a shrieking lunatic. Yet two missionaries who lived and worked here both gave the district a clean bill of health. That made a dead end to the whole trail.

King felt as completely defeated as a chess player when checkmated. Yet the muscles of his jaws, bunched as he prowled a long beat up and down the compound. He refused to condemn utterly his own judgment; he had been too careful; he had thrown all his knowledge of Africa into this blind game of chess where dead men marked the dark squares as proof of correct play. Now the whole board seemed to have been snatched from before him. Not very hopefully he turned to the Hottentot who crouched on a tree stump like a gnome on a toadstool.

"What wisdom of the lower pit have you to offer, impling?"

"This," said the grotesque one with certitude, "is an emptiness where one must buy wisdom from a great witch doctor."

"Bah! The *monpéré* says there is no witch doctor here."

The goblin gave vent to a sepulchral croak of negation.

"The *monpéré* is a man who has two hearts and three open hands with which to give; but knowledge is not among his gifts. Buy wisdom rather of that great black one who has become a white witch-doctor. It is written in his face that he has much— if he will sell to a white man."

"Hah!"

King was startled at the accuracy of the little man's observation. What he implied was true. The Reverend Leroy's attitude was distinctly mistrustful of white men.

King was just a semi-official white man to him. For all that he knew, this white investigator was the usual kind: loftily misunderstanding the black man's crudely torturous viewpoint, didactically positive of the white man's law, a forerunner possibly of soldiers and machine guns. Perhaps the Leroy did know something. But if, as a black man, he had made up his mind that silence meant protection for black men, no argument that King knew would persuade him to speak.

No, the next move in the game must be King's, to find somehow another dark square on the board where something or other—another dead man perhaps—would be a clue.

THAT NIGHT the rain roared on the thatch roof with the muffled thunder of drums. King sought for circumstantial arguments to break down the Reverend Henderson's bland assurance of prevailing peace and innocence. All that King could produce were a hypnotized boy and some dead men by the way; against which the Reverend Henderson quoted two years of tranquil residence among a superior class of natives with a growing colony of converts.

Then King heard it—soft and sublimated through the rain, barely distinguishable. But King had been listening for just that sound for a long time. He sat up tense, his eyes blazing.

Thump-thump—thump-a-thump—a-thump-thump-a-thump!

"It is a dance somewhere," was the missionary's ready explanation. "These foolish boys will dance all night for the most absurd reasons, and in the morning they are totally unfitted to work on their cultivated clearings."

"What hut is there big enough to stage a dance in this rain?" King, skeptical, wanted to know.

The missionary was nonplused. The thought had not occurred to him. Kaffa the Hottentot knocked on the door with the silver ring that he wore on his big toe. Entering, his round eyes glittered with excitement. Words bubbled from his mouth.

"It is the same talk, bwana, that we heard before that no man of us could read."

"Hellfire!" King muttered. "I'll bet I can read it now. I'll bet it's a gathering signal. Excuse me, Padre, for cussing, but this is big news. That's signaling the gang for a night pow-wow because we're here. And, come to think of it, that same signal when we heard it before was calling the scattered search parties together after we'd picked up their man. By golly, this *is* headquarters. I knew it. I knew darn well we hadn't gone astray. And me, I'm going right out and find where the gang meets."

The missionary was flustered and fearful.

"But, Mr. King, that is impossible. Nothing like that could be going on here. And if it were, remember, I beg you, 'He that meddleth with strife belonging not to him is like one that taketh a dog by the ears.'"

"This belongs to me all right," said King grimly. "It's my *shauri* that I came up here to meddle into."

"But to plunge into a secret native gathering—and at night—would be extremely dangerous. My dear Mr. King, I counsel and implore you to wait till the morning."

King was impatient to the point of discourtesy.

"Aw, shucks! Don't be silly. I mean—I beg pardon—have some sense. What would I ever find in the morning? Your peaceful native village, as ox-dumb and quiet as you've always known it."

"Barounggo is ready," said the Hottentot. "He waits."

"Good," said King. "Let's go!"

The rain made a blurred patch of the shaft of light from the mission bungalow door—just sufficient to designate in dim outline the gateway through the wire fence. In a moment the three were out of it and in pitch blackness. King carried only his flashlight; a lantern would have been a stupid advertisement of their presence. The other hand held his Luger pistol, the safety catch thrown back.

He had no illusions about what he might be going into. His first meeting with the people who drummed that way had shown that they were fighters, and their warnings along the way were stark evidence that they were killers—to say nothing as yet of Ponsonby who had disappeared or of his orderly who had been driven mad.

"What weapon have you, Kaffa?" he asked. As for the Masai, King knew that he stirred nowhere without his great spear and that he scorned all other weapons; the voice of the Hottentot panted excitedly from the darkness behind him:

"I have in my waistband the short sword that I took from the Somali dog last year and in my left hand a knife and in my right hand bwana's second gun that shoots six times out of the box that turns."

"Hmh! Sounds almost like you're armed. Now what direction are those cursed drums coming from?"

Fitfully the throb and plunk of the drums eddied about on the gusty wind. Big voice and little voice, talking their message now from dead ahead, now from away to one side. Guided half by guesswork, King found a path and crept along it stealthily, flashing his light for the briefest fraction of a second at a time.

Once the ray fell upon a crouching something that snorted and crashed away in the undergrowth. A hyena howled fiendishly out of the blackness. Intersecting paths confused the way. All around the village, of course, was a maze of paths. King swore in perplexity.

The driving rain drowned out the drum signals for minutes at a time. When King was just about ready to concede that perhaps the signals were finished, the message transmitted, the elusive *thump-a-thump!* would drift in—but from where? King's ears were trained. But he could not place those drums.

By trial and error the three progressed, following a path till they were sure that the sound bore more to one side.

Not a native was encountered. Either the whole community had hurried to the rendezvous, or those who perhaps did not belong among the initiates knew enough to stay very properly in their huts when the juju drums talked. Even had King been able to catch a native or two, he knew that there would be no hope at all of getting the men to admit that they could hear the dread drums.

SLOWLY THE three floundered along, King in the lead with his momentary spark of light. He was not afraid of mantraps. So close to the village they would be a danger to any blundering native. Besides, he was sure the signalers had relied upon the heavy shower to cover their cautious messages.

All of a sudden a veering gust of wind carried the sound unmistakably from ahead, convincingly loud. Momentarily the rain ceased. King tingled with expectations of he knew not what; but he was on the right path to find out. He pushed on, as silently as a cat, by feeling the bushes on either side, the flashlight switched off.

His boot bumped into something soft that lay across the trail. It heaved up under his foot. King sprawled over it; but, falling, clutched at it. In a moment he found himself tangled with a muscular naked body that writhed under him.

"*Awo!* What happens?" came the Hottentot's whisper; and on the instant he flung himself into the tangle.

The Masai's great hands came diving down out of the dark and clutched at whatever he could find.

Now three men, it would seem, ought to have been well able to capture one, however muscular. But the darkness impeded them, and the muscular body for which they fought had been carefully oiled from head to foot. Inevitably the man wriggled free. He emitted a shrill whistle, and there followed the quick pad of feet running down the path. After that nothing.

Nothing at all. No further sound of human origin. The drums ceased abruptly; that was all. The wind shook the branches high above, and heavy drops plopped with leathery concussions upon soggy, dead leaves. Soaked to the bone, the three men shivered. Somewhere a jackal moaned its long preliminary note and its fellows took up the hellish chorus of low howls rising cre-scendo to high pitched shrieks. King knew that they sat in a circle round some garbage heap in the very center of a huddle of huts with their noses pointed skyward while they screamed under whatever fell impulse it is that causes jackals to congre-gate and scream.

"*Ai thuah!*" The Hottentot shivered. "Sickness will come of this night."

King pressed his flashlight button on and turned it upon himself and his two men. There were no hurts. The muscular oiled man in the path had carried no knife. Just a watcher, lying craftily low like a snake across the trail.

King shrugged. There was nothing else he could do.

"Somebody," he repeated his conviction, "somebody who is back of this thing is very damned clever indeed."

IN THE morning King was grimly suspicious of everything and everybody in this hidden jungle village that was given such a clean bill of health by no less than two resident missionaries.

He was determined to try to retrace his wanderings of the night. Somewhere at the end of the path, if he could pick it out from its crisscrossed intersections, was something; or at all events there had been something doing last night; something secret enough to occasion the posting of a watcher on the path.

Quietly he told the Masai to post unobtrusive guards to see that nobody left the mission, and he ordered the Hottentot to keep eyes and ears open for whispers and rumors. He suspected even this missionary. But, surprisingly, the missionary was eager to accompany him on his quest.

"If there is any underground wickedness going on, Mr. King—and your extraordinary experience of last night almost convinces me—it is my duty to find out about it and put a stop to it before it grows to something that will perhaps need police interference."

King smiled thinly.

"So you don't approve of a police investigation coming here, eh?"

The missionary flushed.

"Oh, don't mistake me, Mr. King; don't misunderstand me. There are some splendid and honorable men among the police; but some natives elevated to power, Mr. King— Surely you recall the text:

'For three things the earth is disquieted, and for four which it can not bear; for a servant when he reigneth; and for a fool when he is filled with meat.'

and I am afraid, I am very much afraid, that native constabulary fall all too often into both categories."

"Hmh! It seems that we agree on some things at least," said King shortly. "But how about the danger of butting into secret native ceremonies?"

"Am I not my brother's keeper, Mr. King?" was all that the missionary replied. "Come, let us go. I shall take my Jezebel for a run, if you don't mind."

King raised his eyebrows.

"My watchdog," said the missionary, and was immediately embarrassed at having to explain. "A female, Mr. King; and quite, ah—indiscriminate." It was probable the solitary wavering attempt at humor in that earnest man's life.

The rain had for the time being ceased. As King picked out the previous night's path by no more than memory of turnings he watched the shivering "dew-boy" like a hawk for the least indication of lagging or unwillingness. The dew-boy in Africa is a wretched youth whose function it is to go ahead and shake down upon his own naked shoulders the accumulated moisture from overhanging branches and bushes that crowd the narrow pathways. But the boy trotted ahead wherever directed without hesitation. The Reverend Henderson's faith in the peacefulness of his bailiwick was renewed.

"You will find no juju house or devil-doctor along here, Mr. King. This road leads past brother Leroy's little settlement and on to some old rock carvings, and there it comes to an end."

King was immediately keen.

"Rock carvings, eh? Crude sculpture and native cults often go hand in hand. By all means let us examine these rock carvings."

Reverend Henderson laughed.

"You are too suspicious. You won't be able to attach any blame to my people here on account of those carvings. They are many hundreds of years too ancient for that."

The trail, as King picked it out, passed along a low embankment on one side of which, rudely fenced by the haphazard intertwining of a skimpy bush fringe, was a wide, ready lake. King stopped, wondering whether he were on the right path; whether, if they had passed so close, the Hottentot with his extraordinarily acute senses would not have smelled the water. But he reflected that the heavy rain of the night might well have drowned out the dank odor of the lake.

But another matter was causing King to stare frowningly

and to whistle a tuneless air through his teeth. Gray-green, moss-grown, log-like things floated in the lake—swarms of them. The dog, Jezebel, bristled and growled at them; then barked in a frenzy of hate. Some of the nearer logs rose just the merest trifle higher and swung end-on; almost imperceptible ripples showed that they moved forward. The dog quickly tucked her tail between her legs and fled yelping.

Crocodile worship was the idea that was revolving in King's head. His mind seized upon and analyzed the pros and cons. He could conceive of horrific things connected with crocodiles and African imaginativeness. Orgies fearful enough perhaps to unseat a man's mind. Yet juju rites, as he knew them, invariably centered around some individual fetish, some enormous patriarch crocodile perhaps, but not a lakeful of them.

"Still," he muttered the practical question to himself, "what do they eat?"

"Fish," said the Reverend Henderson readily. "They have left no fish in this lake. The natives travel a long distance to another pool to catch fish. Possibly, too, they are cannibalistic and devour each other."

"Crocodiles aren't cannibalistic," King grunted his observation of nature lore. But "cannibals" was another thought that flashed into his mind; though he was ready to reject it almost before the Reverend Henderson, shocked, said:

"My dear Mr. King, you have seen the people, a fine upstanding lot. They are not the type."

"And yet—" King doggedly groped for a connecting clew— "Ponsonby disappeared and his orderly went screaming crazy."

His eyes were focused upon a little low-lying island that loomed ghostly through the drifting mists that steamed from the scummy water's surface. Miasmatic islands and gruesome fetish cults were another combination that linked darkly together.

The Reverend Henderson read his thoughts.

"The place is little more than a morass," he argued. "Or at

least so it looks to be; and the low scrub on it is not high enough to conceal even a shack, much less any sort of juju house. Furthermore, there is no means of getting to it through this infested water; there is not a canoe in the place, as you can easily assure yourself."

King was half convinced, barely half. A reptile-infested lake and a reedy island offered nightmare possibilities to the devil-ridden African mind. Decidedly the lake must be investigated further. Grudgingly he conceded:

"You sure give the place a clear alibi. But answer this: Hut groups, you say, are all around in the bush. This is a well trodden path, well used. Why have we met nobody in pretty near two miles of it? It doesn't smell natural to me. But I'll bet you we'll find something not so healthy at the end of it. Let's get along and take a look at those rock carvings."

The missionary was complacent.

"I doubt it, Mr. King. Indeed, I venture to doubt it. I have been here for two years and my predecessor for five, and we have not found the soil unfruitful to our labors."

King grunted. To him the argument was not so convincing as the more practical one of lack of canoes and sheer excess of commonplace reptiles upon which to focus a cult. Yet a shock was coming to disturb the missionary's equanimity.

The dog, Jezebel, was running ahead in the path, nosing and scuffling in the underbrush. She turned a corner and pattered on. There sounded a whirring twang, an agonized yelp, and the body of the dog hurtled back into view as if it might have been one of those gruesome living projectiles that used to be fired from Roman catapults.

T H E   D E W - B O Y uttered a strangled shriek and shrank back into the bushes, his eyes goggling with horror at the thought of what might have happened to him. King leaped to the corner, his pistol drawn. No human being was in sight; but standing at the edge of the path, still gently quivering, was a springy bamboo, to the head of which, at waist height, was lashed a chevaux-de-frise of sharp hardwood spikes. Had a man pushed against the innocent looking tendril of vine that now hung from the adjacent bush, the instrument would have smashed full into his unprotected stomach.

King stared at it, and his mouth pinched down to a grim line. He nodded, acknowledging to himself the answer to the question he had but a few moments ago fired at the missionary.

"So that's why we met nobody on this path. Tipped off. Every man, woman and child in the village—except maybe the Reverend's converts; else that dew-boy would have known. And every African one of them kept the secret— The path I went over last night. And they knew damn well I'd trace it today. Clever. Hellishly clever."

King went back to the Reverend Henderson, whom he found gulping dry-eyed over the body of the mangled dog, incredulity and horror in this thin, ascetic face. Any vague part that the unhappy missionary might have had in King's all-embracing suspicion was dissipated at sight of his genuine grief and amazement. All that King found within himself to say rather gruffly was—

"Well, I guess this has been something of a revelation that big juju is afoot somewhere."

The Reverend Henderson rose from his knees. He was trembling.

"Revelation indeed, Mr. King. 'The sorcerers and idolaters shall have their part in the lake.' But what does it mean? What is this abomination of desolation of which I have known nothing in all my two years?"

King's voice was grim.

"It means just Africa, Padre. Things that white men—and maybe some black men—mustn't know. So my advice to you is to go right back to your mission."

King knew that he was at close grips at last with the sinister power, whatever it might be, that had eliminated Sir Henry Ponsonby for coming too close to its secret. He knew that all around him were savages who knew about that power—some of them without doubt a part of it, ready to carry out its ruthless commands as soon as it should judge its time to be ripe. But beyond that he knew nothing. He was up against one of the dark things of Africa. It behooved him to go very carefully. He did not want to be hampered in retreat by a frail and not very practical missionary.

But the Reverend Henderson was suddenly determined.

"Not alone, Mr. King, not alone. If this means some horrible form of witch-doctory I must find out about it and crush it before the police—before a worse thing shall befall. I can not hold with Brother Leroy's tolerance of what he calls the milder forms of sorcery. I'm coming with you. And, as a matter of fact, we shall pick up Brother Leroy on the way and convince him about the seriousness of this evil."

King shrugged. He had had experience of the obstinacy of these righteous men when they felt that duty called. He had no time to waste in argument just then. The dew-boy, after his narrow escape, was quite useless. He chattered and his knees trembled. King pushed him to the rear and himself led the way, cautious, alert in a strange territory. But there was no other man-trap. Shrewdly enough, the setter of the one reasoned that if the first should fail every succeeding step would be so carefully inspected as to render others useless.

A pattering of feet sounded behind them. King tensed, prepared for anything on that path. Then he relaxed.

"It is only one man," he said. In a few seconds the little Hottentot appeared. He carried King's rifle and ammunition pouch.

"Bwana," he panted, "the order to stay behind must be forgiven. For it was thus: Barounggo and I held conference, and Barounggo said, 'I smell blood in this place. Death walks upon crafty feet. Go thou, therefore, to the bwana and carry his gun. I stay and keep guard and I utilize the time in exercising these worthless *askaris* in the use of shield and spear.' So, bwana, I came, and if it was an offence I await rebuke."

"Huh!" King grunted. "Barounggo is always smelling blood." But a smile cracked his hard face. "It was no offence, apeling. But wit is needed here rather than shield and spear. Be watchful and absolve no man from suspicion."

BROTHER LEROY'S settlement was not so extensive as that of his confrère. Evidently his converts were not so numerous. The mission house was a neat little square building of adobe and thatch, thickly whitewashed. Straggling about it were a collection of round huts; and a short distance away a very large circular one surmounted by a cross, the three points of which were rounded off with gleaming ostrich shells.

"His chapel," whispered the Reverend Henderson, "though I deplore any pandering to native superstition in permitting their ideas of decoration. I can not help feeling they are grafting on to Christian teaching some pagan significance of which we are not aware, a practice which, alas, we have to combat in all conversion."

The Reverend Leroy was standing at his door. He came forward to meet them, and at the Reverend Henderson's serious face he laughed with a superior condescension. There was a certain derision in his tone.

"I know he is telling you about my ostrich eggs, Mr. King, no? Though I have assured my white colleague that in black Abyssinia—which was officially Christianized by the Alexandrine Monk Frumentius while my good friend's own naked forebears were still slinging stones at the Roman wall across North Britain—he will find all crosses decorated with ostrich eggs. But—" he became serious—"I hear that you ran into some secret ceremonial or other last night."

King's eyes narrowed.

"How do you know?" he asked bluntly.

"One of my little flock had some story about it. He did not know what it was all about. Local magicians, you know, don't let our converts into their doings. But it is noised abroad that you stumbled over a watcher."

"Yeah? Why was there a watcher? That's what I want to know," said King.

The Reverend Leroy shrugged.

"Obviously to keep the uninitiated away. Or—"his smile was malicious—"Kingi Bwana is known in Africa for prying into the more secret little native doings."

To which King grunted:

"Huh! Well it was a darn sight more than little doings, and I'm going to find the juju house where all this hellery centers."

"Oh, you won't find any juju house around here." The Reverend Leroy was positive. "There's not a hut in the whole district big enough to house any secret gathering, excepting—" he laughed—"my colleague's chapel and mine."

Again there seemed to be a blank wall of impossibility against which King knocked helplessly. Juju ceremonies, as he knew them, were inconceivable without some central home of horrors, some dark, skull-festooned temple of gruesome superstition. The only thin hope of a clew to the enigma that was left to him seemed to be the rock carvings.

The Reverend Leroy flouted the idea of danger lurking beside the path; and to prove his faith he insisted upon leading the way himself. He swung along with great, careless strides, and as he went he lectured learnedly on ancient sculpture in Africa.

Without mishap they came to a low bluff of outcropping granite upon the face of which crude figures had been chiseled in outline, like the inexpert drawings of a child upon a blackboard. Some were so worn as to be indistinguishable, some almost intact. Monstrous distortions of gods or devils they seemed to be, depicting the baser human attributes. Some were appallingly obscene. All conveyed the impression, so startlingly common to primitive religious statuary, of dreadful thought in their inception.

One in a surprisingly good state of preservation particularly attracted King's interest. It depicted an enormous serpent that seemed to be engulfing a whole line of human victims in a row. With stark realism a series of bloated swellings showed the passage of the bodies down the creature's gullet.

Another group pictured some sort of ceremonial. The monster seemed to be dead. A priest of some sort, decked in trappings of bones, performed an invocation while naked men beat their heads upon the ground in grief and veneration. Out of the dead body, phoenix-like, a crude outline of its spirit rose and towered above the worshipers.

King stared at the things, fascinated. The Reverend Henderson, though he had seen them before, shuddered.

"A singularly fearsome conception, even for Africa, is it not?"

King continued to stare in frowning silence. Then—

"So fearsome," he murmured, more to himself than to anybody in particular, "that if a man were to see such a thing in real life, I could well imagine him going shrieking crazy.…"

THE REVEREND HENDERSON stared at him round eyed, incredulous that so fantastic a horror could have any basis in truth. The Reverend Leroy had the greater callousness of his heredity. He dismissed the gruesome possibility with a large wave of his hand and discoursed expansively upon ancient serpent worship, showing a wide knowledge of the subject, tracing the venerable cult through earliest Europe and back to Africa in Egyptian sculpture.

But King was not listening to him. He was poking at some mud-spattered, fluffy substance with the toe of his boot. When the dirt and rubble was kicked away it turned out to be a little heap of feathers—chicken feathers that had once been white.

"Hmh!" King surveyed them blackly. "Looks like somebody don't think those pictures are too ancient to appreciate a little attention."

The Reverend Leroy's assurance was jolted. He stared at the feathers, his eyeballs white in his dark face. Then he found an explanation.

"Some superstitious savage, I suppose, making a luck sacrifice to the ancient gods. I must confess I did not know that any such practice existed here."

King was suddenly overcome by the feeling that this deserted scene of an ancient cult was dangerous ground; that eyes watched from the jungle. His skin tingled with a sense of impending hostility and with it of imminent discovery of something profoundly important.

Then he got it. The Hottentot's dry coughing attracted his attention. The little man's eyes caught his and rolled furtively in the direction of the Reverend Leroy. King's carefully casual scrutiny could making nothing of it at first, till, looking back at the Hottentot, he saw the cunning little face move almost imperceptibly sidewise. Carelessly he stepped aside himself; and then he saw what had been screened from his view by the great bulk of the black missionary—a symbol cut into the rock: two leopard spots and a wavy line that bifurcated at the lower end.

King's pulse pounded suddenly. But he forced himself to concentrate his interest upon the sculpture of the monstrous snake. He made vacuous talk while his mind raced.

"A fearful thing, as you say, Dr. Henderson. Fascinatingly so. A thing to which I must certainly devote more study."

"Yes, indeed." The Reverend Henderson shuddered. "Sir Henry Ponsonby, too, was very much interested in it."

"Aa-ah!"

This time there was no disguising King's emotion. All of a sudden, like lightning breaking through a black thunder cloud, a gleam of understanding lighted his eyes, and then his expression closed down on it, scowlingly introspective. Suddenly he said:

"Let's go home. This is quite the most horrible thing that I have come across in Africa."

On the way home he sent the Hottentot in front with his pistol, the Reverend Henderson in the center, himself bringing up the rear. He was more alert and watchful even than when he came, suspicious of more man-traps.

The only observation that King made as he went on his scowling way was:

"I had hoped to find Ponsonby somewhere, but—"

The Reverend Henderson gaped at him wide-eyed as he panted alongside.

"But what?" he whispered the nervous question.

"I don't know," said King shortly. A thought struck him and he gave the Hottentot some instructions. The little man's face contorted with wise understanding as he turned back on the path.

THE REVEREND HENDERSON slumped in his stiff, handmade chair, amazement, incredulity and utter dejection in his expression. His world was crumbling about his feet. A delegation of his flock, headed by his chief convert, a presbyter of his church, had come to him and had urged him to flee from that place.

They were afraid, they said. They had been warned, furtively and in quick whispers, by relatives who did not belong in the flock that the devil-devil of the place was angry with them.

When their minister, gravely reproving, had reminded them that their Father in heaven was all powerful to protect them from the power of the devil, they had replied with African literalness that, yes, they believed that, because their good teacher had so taught them; but heaven was far away and the devil-devil was here in their midst.

That was the first shock to their pastor. But they went on to worse. This was not the pastor's devil in far away hell who was at constant warfare with the Father in far away heaven—about men's souls in the future and that vaguely understood thing called sin—but a very imminent devil-devil who snatched up men's bodies right here and now and caused them utterly to disappear.

This was awful. It was nothing short of idolatry. What did

they mean? Their pastor stormed at them. What stupid superstition was this about witch-doctory or—he turned miserable
eyes to King and he used the hated word—juju?

Not witch-doctory, said the delegation; nor juju. "When juju
killed a man the remains were always fearsomely displayed as
a mark of juju's power. The body was found, or the horribly torn
skin was draped over somebody's thorn fence, or at least the
skull grinned from a pole in some fetish grove. But this devil-
devil devoured men, hair, bones and hide; there was never a
trace. Nobody knew who might be gobbled up next; the strongest men and the bravest warriors disappeared as silently as any.
The drums talked; the men went; that was all.

The missionary was appalled. Not so much at the bizarre
superstitions as at the revelation that such superstitions continued to exist among his Christianized flock.

"But why—" he wailed—"why am I hearing this now? Why
in all my two years of ministry here have I never heard anything
about these pagan beliefs?"

At that the converts' expressions became wooden, and they
remained dumb.

King gave the answer.

"Because, my dear Padre, you have never until now butted
into the secret doings of Africa. You have been content to gain
your converts and to lead them according to your lights; and
the dark outside has left you alone. But now, as your Book so
aptly says, you have meddled with strife that doesn't belong to
you and you are in the position of one who has taken a dog by
the ears."

Curtly he demanded confirmation of the chief convert. The
man had talked with King's safari men. He knew that this
bwana was not one to be put off with evasions. Yes, he admitted, hitherto the devil-devil had confined its attentions to the
unconverted herd; but the converts, feeling secure under the
white preacher's protection, had been content. But now they
had been warned by frightened relatives that the devil beast

was about to turn its anger upon them. So therefore they came to their pastor and wanted him to pack up and flee from the place.

And they meant exactly that. To up and go, no matter where, to any far place out of this particular demon's range. To an African, of course, it is nothing to pack his few pots and other belongings into a bundle and leave his mud hut that he could rebuild somewhere else with no expenditure except a little labor. That was what the whole panic stricken colony was ready to do.

"Yeah," said King through set teeth, "that's how secret Africa works. Frighten off your men with ghost stories, and the white man has got to up and go with them or be left stranded. That one is the oldest and the easiest of tricks to pull off and the hardest for the white man to combat. I tell you, Padre, my whole safari would be bolting, gibbering through the jungle right now, except that my Masai stands over them with his spear and threatens to pin the first man to the ground like a beetle."

He tried to extract some particulars of the devil-devil from the converts; but quite quickly he was convinced that they knew nothing. They themselves, of course, were not initiated into the mystery; nor were most of the other people. Only a few men and some women of the village were let in on this thing; and nobody knew exactly who they were. The devil thing existed and devoured some dozen people every month—at that a long whistle escaped from King—but that was about the sum total of the common knowledge.

"Well," King told them grimly, "I, personally, am going to kill this devil-devil. So get out and tell your friends that." He turned to comfort the Reverend Henderson, who was now a wilted and piteous figure of dejection.

"Why?" he kept moaning to himself. "Why have I not known? In all my years of labor among my people I have not learned to know their hearts. I have been filled with pride of mere numbers. I thought I was leading them out of their blindness to the light without ever realizing my own blindness. 'They made me keeper of the vineyards, but mine own vineyard have I not kept'."

Deliberately King began to jolt him out of that self-reproachful introspection.

"Of course, I'm the Jonah who has brought all this on to you; so I'll just take my crowd and get out. I'll camp—by golly, I'll camp bang in the middle of the village square and call on this secret society to do its stuff in public."

The Reverend Henderson was properly shaken out of his mood.

"Oh, by no means, Mr. King," he hastened to insist. "Such a thing is not to be thought of. In any case they—it—whatever this diabolical business is—have marked me down for destruction because they feel sure that I now know as much about their foul secrets as you do. And they know—as you know, Mr. King—that I inevitably abhor their every thought and deed and that I am bound to fight them with you."

KING'S BLACK frown twisted to a wry smile at the stoutness of the frail missionary's spirit.

"I wish I could think you understood exactly how tough a proposition this is, Padre. What your boys just said bears out what you yourself have maintained all along—that these people of fighting Galla stock are as a general type above the grosser forms of African cults. Only a few, the more debased individuals, are initiates in the devilish thing. Further—" he pointed a sudden finger at the missionary—"it bears out what I've been telling you about those sculptures and their meaning. This devil-devil thing devours without a trace—hide, hair and bones, *like a snake devours.* It all fits exactly."

The Reverend Henderson, pale, almost gasping, fought away the incredible horror with nervous hands.

"But such a thing is impossible, Mr. King. It is insane. Those sculptures are hundreds of years old. Nothing could live that long."

King shook his head.

"Some of them are old. The place is undoubtedly old—a good place to graft a new cult on to. But the rubble that I kicked up over those chicken feathers wasn't old; not weather-worn; the chips were sharp edged."

The missionary stared at him, trying to digest the implication.

"That symbol," said King. "Two spots and a wavy line cut into the rock; the same thing smeared with paint on the crazed orderly's chest. Not leopard spots; but the two eyes and the forked tongue of a snake."

The missionary stared in horrified silence.

"A clever man," King went on with awful conviction, "could easily chip out those snake pictures. He could scarify them; he could rub down the edges to make them look old. He could tell his fanatical gang any miracle story of how they got there. And the man who heads this thing is very clever indeed."

Against his conviction the missionary's mind rejected the hideous thought.

"I can not believe it, Mr. King. I will not believe that any human being can be so close to the devil as to feed human victims to a—" A tremor of shuddering choked his voice.

"In Africa," said King, "the devil is sometimes very close to the surface."

"But—" the missionary still refused to accept so awful a possibility—"but such a thing would be physically impossible. No snake, however monstrous, could—" He was unable to put the thought into words.

"I don't know," mused King. "I'm guessing in the dark. But I know this. I have seen in Nairobi an East Indian snake charmer feed six large rats, one right after the other, into a four-foot python no thicker than my wrist—and you could see the bulge of each one of them in its gullet just like in the stone picture. So a big snake perhaps—maybe a thirty-foot python—"

A choked sound came from the Reverend Henderson's throat.

"Merciful God forfend! Stop, Mr. King. For pity's sake, stop. I can stand no more. I can not; I will not believe such diabolism. But even if—" a ghostly ray of hope came into his ashen face— "even if a devil incarnate should organize so fiendish a cult, the physical impossibility remains. I know very little about snakes; but I understand they feed not more than once a month or so. A dozen disappearances in every month, then, as my converts said, could not by any stretch of even your imagination be accounted for by your horrible theory."

Relief came into his face. He even ventured to smile—in ghastly manner, it is true. His lips parted and his eyes lost some of their horror.

"Yes," King was forced to admit, "there you have me guessing again. Something doesn't fit. It's baffling. It's like no juju that I ever came across. But I'm almost hoping that I can find a lead to something. I've sent for that relative—brother or whatever he was—who warned your boys. Maybe he knows more than he told. I'm going to work a great magic on him, and he will, if he knows, lead me to the headquarters, the temple, the witch-house, or whatever it is, of this devil-devil cult."

The missionary stared at him. Since this hard and restless man had come into his life unbelievable phenomena of Africa had opened up before his dazed vision. He was prepared to expect anything now. Still he repeated the conviction of his two years:

"I am afraid, if your plans for destroying this horrible thing hinge upon finding a juju house, you are foredoomed to failure. I know my district, Mr. King. I assure you that within a radius of a day's journey there is no native building large enough to house a gathering of a dozen men."

King insisted:

"Somewhere is a headquarters, a big witch-doctor, a juju grove, something I'm going to find it. I've *got* to find it, him, them. Without that we're up a bare pole. We know that a hideous thing happens. To destroy it we've got to know where it happens. Let's have the man in."

THE RELATIVE who had known enough about the dark business to warn his convert brother was ushered in. He proved to be a stupid looking hulk of a man, very frightened just now and inclined to be obstinate.

"Good!" muttered King. "The dumber the better." Sternly he said to the fellow, "I seek information. I desire to be led to the house of the big witch doctor."

Immediately the man's face assumed an expression of ox-like dumbness. His eyes stared white. In a mumble he began the conventional rigmarole—

"Nay, bwana, I am a poor man, a cultivator of—"

"Good," snapped King. "That means you know at least something. Therefore, by means of the witchcraft that I now put upon you, you will tell. Look now upon this fetish box. It was given to me by the Wizard of Elgon. The Old One. The Wise One. The strong witch-binder. The One-eyed who reads men's hearts. It contains a fetish older than age, wiser than wisdom, stronger than strength."

King flashed the dread box before the man's popping eyes. It was a little flat box of metal, golden in color, impressed with a fishbone design of fine lines having a mirror-like clear oval in the center. It contained a safety razor. King intoned some more mumbo-jumbo.

"The fetish that no man may look upon and live is the fetish of the lion's heart that is strong, of the eagle's eye that sees afar, of the ancient serpent's brain that knows all things. Now, therefore, by the power of this fetish that I shall press against the back of your head where the hole is through which the life cord enters, you will lead me to the witch-house of the big witch-doctor."

The man goggled at the potent thing that glittered in King's hand. Fearfully he backed away from it.

The missionary stared at King as horribly fascinated as the native.

"What? How can—? Good heavens, what mad thing are you doing?"

King darted forward and clapped the cold metal against the nape of the native's neck. The man groaned like a stricken ox and sank to his knees. From behind him King grinned at the missionary.

"Magic not so black as it looks, A simple little psychological hokum. I shove this great oaf before me, pretty well at random. Wherever he goes willingly I know I'm away off; where he hesitates I know I'm on the right path; where he instinctively shrinks, I know I'm hot on the trail. Tactile telepathy, the scientific sharps call it. It's no more than keeping a sharp watch on a man's reflexes. Surprising how often it works. So if this frightened fool knows anything he may betray it. I'm leaving Barounggo on guard, and I told him to draft in your boys too. Ordinarily I'd not bother about juju by daylight. African juju works in the dark; it's got to use the dark to inspire the fear on which it builds its power; but I don't know what I may run into in this devilish business. I'm taking Kaffa and half a dozen *askaris*."

King's first random cast in his essay at witchcraft was in the general direction of the rock carvings; and immediately he knew, from the native's unwillingness, from his readiness to turn into side paths, that he was on the right track. Of course, the success of the trick was cumulative. The more often the man was steered into a path that he would have avoided, the more he was convinced that he was inexorably under a spell.

Unlike the previous occasion on that path, villagers were encountered, at which King grunted satisfaction, for it meant that, this move on his part being quite unexpected, no man-traps had been planted in the path. The natives who passed stared at the spectacle of a badly scared man being dazedly propelled by a little gold box in the hands of this strange white man who had descended like a tornado into their village.

The Hottentot shrilled abuse at them.

"Away, away, monkey folk! A great magic goes on here. Not for common jungle people to see. Away!"

The common jungle people covered their mouths with their hands that evil might not enter and hurried by.

Passing the big reedy lake, King stopped. It was inviting. It had the attributes of sorcery. Green scum, slimy algae, floating reptilian heads. He scowled at the low island, half a mile out, drenched in the warm vapor that rose from the water as soon as the rain ceased. A stage setting for witchcraft. But, as the Reverend Henderson had pointed out, the bushes that grew on it, though lush and dense, were certainly not more than six or eight feet high, and certainly there was not a canoe hidden anywhere along the lake shore—King had sent a searching party out to make very sure of that.

The unwilling guide squatted on his heels and chewed a sort of a contented cud. He was betraying no knowledge of wizardry there.

KING LEFT the place with a last longing look and pushed the man on, a half step behind him, keeping a firm grip of his arm with one hand while with the other he pressed the magic box against the back of his neck.

Immediately he felt the fellow's reluctance. King tested him out on a side path, deliberately steering him into one. The man's relief was obvious. King muttered at him:

"No. The fetish in the box tells me no. It says that this is not the path. Beware, foolish man, how you try to hoodwink the fetish that sees into the inside of men's heads. The witch-house of the big witch-doctor is where the fetish wishes to be led."

He shoved the man back on to the trail that led toward the sculptured rocks.

The Hottentot clicked his tongue against the roof of his mouth in awe.

"*Tla-awo!* It is indeed a strong fetish. For the man's knees are loose with fear, yet he leads the way."

Which was just what the wretched fellow was doing. His resistance to King's push from behind was beginning to be as unmistakable as his fear. King shoved him along, tingling with the expectation of success. If he could find the witch-house, the focal center of this cunningly hidden cult, his problem was solved. He would resort to simple strong-arm methods to break it up. That would mean a fight; somebody would get hurt; and there was no certainty as to who might be hurt most.

King waxed profane under his breath. Let him find the master mind who pulled all these strings from the security of his anonymity which he maintained by fear; that was the snake to scotch; the rest would be easy.

And then came a denouement that knocked his hopes high through the clouds that hung gray above him. King's profanity turned upon himself. Fool, he called himself, dolt and worse, for ever imagining that he understood the twists of the native mind.

Approaching the Reverend Leroy's settlement, the guide's reluctance became frantic. But inexorably King pushed him on, headed for the rock carving beyond and—he grew tense with expectation—some dark den of witch-doctory in the jungle beyond that.

And then the man, coming abreast of the Reverend Leroy's big circular chapel hut, bleating with terror, stopped there and goggled at the building as if the devil himself might emerge at any moment.

King stood dumbfounded. He knew from the wretched guide's abject limpness that, as far as he was concerned, this was the end of the trail. It was the Hottentot who voiced the complete deflation of their bubble that had seemed to soar with such buoyant hope. He spat.

"Awah, thuck-a! The fool has led us to the prayer house of the black man who has become a white witch-doctor."

And it was just that. The big witch-doctor, King had demanded; and who might more properly fill the role in a foolish savage's eyes than the burly black missionary?

Then the man moaned and cowered to the ground; for, as it might be verily a demon emerging from his den of mystery, the

massive form of the Reverend Leroy loomed through the dark
doorway of his chapel.

"Hello, Mr. Kingi Bwana," his voice boomed. "An unexpected visit, eh?" Then his face lowered angrily. "Why, what are
you doing with that blockhead M'bangra in the charge of an
armed force of *askaris?*"

He volleyed some guttural sentences at the man in a hybrid
tongue that King did not know. They seemed half to reassure
the groveling wretch; for he rose, and a thick grin began to
replace his terror. Still half fearful, he shambled away.

"Those Gubkani tribesmen are all fools," the preacher explained, still with a trace of exasperation. "Some of his people
are of my flock, and this dolt pesters me perpetually to set them
free of the spell that he feels sure I have put upon them and to
let them return to their pagan practice of dog meat sacrifices
in order that the ants may not devour their yam crop.

"But come in. Wait just a moment till I lock my chapel door,
and then won't you come into my modest home and let us
resume our most absorbing little excursion into serpentology.
I have been looking up and marking some references which I
am sure will interest you."

King morosely shook his head.

"I'd be a poor sort of guest today, Reverend. I've been con-
gratulating myself that I was on the road to finding out something about the Ponsonby mystery; but I've just received a severe
kick in the slack of my self-esteem.

"And I'll tell you without being ashamed; when I'm out in
this sweet district that you boost as being so peaceful I don't
like to allow too much time for any smart hellion to fix up a
little surprise for me somewhere on the way back. Thanks all
the same, but I'll be getting along."

IF THERE had been any people among those who had
noted King's trip and were therefore planning some ingenious
deviltry along the return path King would have fallen an easy
victim. He stalked along, his head sunk on his chest, seeing

nothing. Precautions were left to the Hottentot who scuttled in advance with the alert suspicion of a monkey.

King was immersed in his own dark thoughts, building extravagant theories, analyzing, tearing down.

He had been so full of confidence, so sure that he was on the right trail. And he was half sure still. That man had been so genuinely terrified, so desperately afraid that he was being bewitched into betraying—what? A colored missionary? Bah!

There was that blank wall again. That baffling checkmate. King thought he had discovered a forward move in the game; but the crafty opponent had every move covered. There seemed no move that King could make. He had explored every trail his mind could visualize. And here he was baffled, confused.

Yet—King swore—exactly what had that doltish native been so afraid of? What did he know, or think he knew, that he was so fearful of betraying in a Christian church? Of course, savage superstition might conjure up the most bizarre interpretations of Christian theology; but—

"Well, hell!" growled King. "One thing is damn sure; and that's that the other side has got to make the next move. My play is to watch and to miss nothing."

The only rational question that he evolved out of his long cogitation was to ask the Reverend Henderson—

"Have you ever been inside of Brother Leroy's chapel?"

"Why, er, no," said the Reverend Henderson. "He is not very orthodox, I am afraid, and—"

"What do you know about a hut just back of the sculptured rocks?"

"I, er—I didn't know there was a hut there. You see, it is rather in Brother Leroy's diocese, so to speak, at the other end of the village, and we don't like to be unduly inquisitive about one another's doings. I suppose it is just a native hut."

"One hut," said King. "Alone. Nothing else anywhere in sight. Does that sound honest native to you? I sent the Hottentot scouting yesterday after we had looked at those rocks, and he discovered it behind the bluff."

The missionary gazed at King with new apprehension.

"Was—is it big? Large enough to—"

He leaned forward, afraid.

King shook his head.

"Too small. Barely a one-man hut. Perhaps a prison. I'm going to see; and I want one of your boys, one who can lead me quietly by back paths where we'll meet nobody."

The missionary rose with determination.

King knew without asking what was in his mind. He wondered at the spirit that drove so sensitive a man to go out and fight this dark fearsome thing.

"All right." He shrugged. "But we must hurry. I didn't want to be caught out after dark; and I don't want to take any fool *askaris* because that devil-doctor is smart enough to catch one of them and play the same psychological hokum that I tried.

"If I can help it he mustn't know what tree I'm shinning up till I'm ready to raid his whole gang."

THE CONVERT was a shrewd enough black youth. Leading the two white men out of the back of the mission grounds, he chose winding back paths, barely used, overgrown with vegetation. Only once did they meet anybody, and then they heard singing as he came and they squeezed into the bushes till he had passed.

The hut was small, smaller even than King had expected, and not especially concealed. In fact, it rather flaunted itself on a little grass-grown eminence behind the sculptured bluff. Heavy jungle surrounded it, but the little hillock stood clear. King stopped warily at the jungle fringe and eyed the scene; and, doing so, his mouth twisted in disappointment. He had been hoping almost to find a prison cell. But even the missionary could see that the place was quite unfrequented by humans. The grass grew lush and untrodden; not a path led to the hut.

"The perfect site for a juju hut," said King, whispering in the stillness. "I don't mean a gathering place; a witch-hut; it should be hung all around with bones and claptrap and should be full of magic gimcrackery. But nary juju sign is there; the place is barren. Queerest witch-doctory I've ever come across."

He crouched low in the grass and wormed his way up the hillock, the missionary crawling less expertly behind him. Nobody seemed to be keeping guard over the place; no spears whistled out of the still jungle. Crawling round the hut, King pointed silently to a trail.

Five inches wide it was, as mathematically exact as if cut by a machine, and stripped as clean of the last vestige of grass as if shaved with a razor right down to the bare soil. From the jungle it came, an uncanny Lilliputian road that wound round an outcropping rock in one place and tunneled under a fallen tree in another; always exactly the same width and always swept clear of blade and twig. Right up to the wall of the hut the little road came, and there at a crack in the adobe it finished.

"Soldier ants!" whispered King grimly.

The missionary's eyes grew large.

"You mean—the man is dead?"

King refrained from any needless answer. He crawled on round the wall; and when he arrived at his starting place there was another queer discovery about that silent hut. It had no door! Unbroken by any sort of entrance, the wall circled it.

The missionary knew enough about Africa not to ask any foolish question. His face was haggard.

"Entombed alive! May God have mercy on his soul."

"One thing about rain-soaked adobe," said King shortly, "is that it cuts like cheese." He pushed his ready pistol back into its holster and drew out his hunting knife. Big chunks of the sticky material fell out before his silent attack. Soon he was at the bamboo core. He slashed away the cane lashings and wrenched away half a dozen poles at once. The inner lining of mud and straw was drier and harder. Working quickly, he undermined that and then a heave of his shoulder pushed in the whole section. The dim interior was exposed to his view.

The atmosphere within was not so foul as might have been expected—the thatch roof allowed for a certain seepage of air. King squeezed through the opening, the missionary with set face behind him. The hole was wide enough to admit some light; quite sufficient to see the gleaming white of a skeleton.

It was not the skeleton that both men had feared to find. On a raised pedestal of bamboo framework, it was a startlingly beautiful skeleton. Composed of innumerable fine bones in exact pairs on either side of a sinuous spinal cord; semicircular tapering bones, for all the world like a gigantic centipede. Round and round they coiled in a mountainous pyramid and at the very apex lay a flat skull, broad nosed, as big as a small shovel.

King had seen snake skeletons before; but it was the monstrous size of this thing that appalled him. As wide as a man's body was the spread of those curving rib bones. The length of the brute he could only guess; but his estimate made it at least thirty feet.

"Good Lord!" he muttered. "A snake like that could do it easy."

"Do what?"

The Reverend Henderson knew perfectly well what was in King's mind, but he dared not let himself accept the thought. King put words to it.

"Just what the rock picture showed—gulp down a man, or maybe more."

The Reverend Henderson covered his eyes with his hands.

"Incredible," he moaned. "Incredible."

King stared at the awesome thing, marveling at its size and symmetry. He had never been repelled, as some people are, by snakes; and this thing was really an extraordinary work of art in its interlaced curves that mounted up and up in constantly decreasing circles to its apex. Picked meticulously clean by the ants; not a bone displaced; everything intact; a perfect museum specimen.

Only the head. King stepped closer. The broad skull that caped the apex was cracked; cut apparently by some sharp instrument; and that, explained the death of the reptile.

"So that's it," said King. "This juju business is a snake worship with human sacrifices. Just like I thought. This was the god. Something killed it; and this is its shrine, walled up, inviolate, so nobody could monkey with it even if he dared."

"Incredible," murmured the missionary again. "Incredible."

King from his closer position saw what he had overlooked before. He thrust his hand between some of the curving ribs and brought away a small object, a small circular thing some four inches in diameter, with a dull sheen.

"Incredible, you say? Look at that. D'you know what that is? That's a native bracelet; brass; the only part of a victim that a snake couldn't digest. And look in there; that'll be a nose ring. Proof enough, I guess. And there's—"

King stopped short and, regardless of sharp bones, plunged his hand into the mass. He gave one close look at what he found, and it seemed that the sun tan paled from his face. He gripped the thing in his fist and stood tense and silent.

"What—what is it?" The Reverend Henderson asked in a quavering voice.

King opened his hand. What he held was a piece of gold dental bridge work.

The Reverend Henderson shrank away from it and covered his eyes once more. No words came from him; his whole body shuddered.

"I guess," said King very grimly, "we've found poor old Ponsonby. Let's get away from this ghastly place."

THE REVEREND HENDERSON slumped in his uncomfortable chair. It had been a strenuous day for him. His eyes were closed against the light from the little kerosene

oil lamp upon the massive communal table that almost filled
the rest of the room; yet weakly he insisted upon denying the
existence of further evil in the district where he had labored
for two years. King strode up and down on the other side of
the table, stopping only to fire arguments at him.

"So that's how the thing must have happened," King summed
up. "Ponsonby found out too much. They grabbed him and put
him up for sacrifice. The orderly was marked. 'Dedicated!' he
kept babbling. Maybe he saw the thing happen; maybe, if that
rock picture is true—and it has proved up so far—he was next
in the line; one of a string to be 'devoured without trace'. Good
Lord, that would drive any man crazy! We don't know how he
ever got away; but I tell you, Padre—" King pointed his finger
at the missionary and his thumb at his own chest—"you and
I, we've found out too much. I'm not trying to scare you; but
you've got to be careful how you go around on your business,
visiting your sick and all, alone, away out in the bush like I've
seen you do."

The Reverend Henderson let his head fall back against the
wall.

"Thank God I need have no fear. The hideous thing is dead
and this wickedness has ceased. Lacking their frightful idol,
the cult must decline. With God's help we can stamp out the
last vestiges that still cling."

Skeptically King expected no immediate help from any deity
to stamp out a ferocious cult that had flourished until a short
month ago—the time since Ponsonby had disappeared. He
knew the tenacity of African superstitions. For any evidence to
the contrary the cult was still going strong.

"I tell you, Padre," he argued, "dead cults don't set man-traps
in the bush to murder people who are investigating them."

"Vestiges," repeated the missionary stubbornly. "The idolaters
remain. Their god is dead. It is my function to deal with idolaters."

"But, Padre, that thing has been dead a month, by all indications; and your own converts have told you that eight men disappeared within the month."

The Reverend Henderson pressed his fingertips wearily against his eyelids.

"Dead snakes do not eat eight men," he insisted. "Nor, for that matter, as you yourself have agreed, could a live snake eat eight men within one month."

King swore under his breath.

"There you've got me, I'll admit. I don't understand that part of it—yet. But all the same, maybe they've got a new snake. This gang is a darn sight too active to be hanging on to the memory of a skeleton. What do you know, now, about snakes in this district? What's the current talk about big ones?"

Slowly the missionary removed his fingers from his eyes and stared at King. By sluggish inches one hand traveled down his face and dragged at his lower lip. There had been such tales, many of them; but he had taken them with the white man's customary grain of salt. With reawakened anxiety he nodded at King.

"Aa-ah!" King pointed his finger impressively. "Then I'll bet they've got another someplace. Don't argue with me, Padre. There's no trick to catching and caging a big snake. I know. I've caught 'em for zoos. Anybody who knows how can catch even a thirty-foot snake—let alone the possibility of anything bigger existing in these jungles. I tell you, Padre, this cult is alive."

THE REVEREND HENDERSON covered his eyes again and bowed his head in his hands. He was too physically weary to find further arguments.

King was full of determination.

"We know half the mystery now. We've found out what this devilish business is. We've got to find out who is the clever devil and where he operates." He bit his teeth together. "And when I find him, by—" He did not complete the sentence. "One move he's got to make. One false move in his game, and you pray to your God, Padre, that I don't slip up on my end."

The next move in the game that was growing so dreadful in its uncertainty was made with a bold suddenness that even King had never expected.

Midnight had barely struck when a frightened convert came in, wet and glistening, out of the rain; and before the missionary could prevent it he clasped his knees and bowed his head upon his shoes. Moaning, he reported that his wife's brother, the one who had given warning about the devil-devil and had been put under the fetish by King, had not returned to his hut; that his womenfolk had waited and waited and had then inquired at neighboring huts and had finally searched the jungle paths; but had found no sign of the man. He had, in fact, disappeared without trace.

King whistled a thin note of alarm and sprang to his feet. He snapped out of the morose abstraction in which he had been sitting. The table in the room, designed for communal gatherings, was an immense thing built of great hand-hewn planks two inches thick and supported by sturdy treetrunks for legs. King banged his fist upon it so that his rifle and cartridge belt, lying upon the farther corner, rattled.

"By God!" he swore shamelessly. "The fellow did know something. I knew it. He fooled me, taking me to Brother Leroy's; but somebody saw him leading me. The word went to headquarters. He was recognized as a possible source of danger and was removed. Slam, just like that." He crashed his fist upon the table again.

The missionary's white face stared at him. His lips moved in unconscious habit of prayer, but no spoken words came from them. King paced the room like an animal in a cage.

"Somewhere," he insisted. "Somewhere is a key to this hellish business. The man can't be so clever that he leaves never an opening. Somebody must know something—if I could but catch such a one and beat it into his thick skull that I'd protect him from this devil that has them all scared dumb and blind. By golly, I'll tear this village apart hut by hut. Somebody will show me the key."

The Reverend Henderson sat with his hands folded.

"I hope so, Mr. King. I pray so. We walk in darkness and the shadow of death. O Lord, enlighten our darkness."

In answer to which the thin rain whispered on the thatch and heavy drops chuckled in the puddles below the eaves.

King prowled back and forth, grumbling to himself like a bear.

A houseboy stood trembling at the door. A man had brought a message, he said.

King sprang at the boy.

"Where?" he demanded. "Bring him in. Who is the man?"

But the man had not waited. He had come in the rain, the boy said, secretly, his face covered with a cloth so that nobody should ever be able to say who he was. He had whispered his message and he had fled.

The message was that if indeed the fierce new bwana was not afraid to make war upon the devil-devil and to deliver the people of the village from its devourings, then let him know that the black drums were talking even now in the place of the rock carvings.

King made one long stride to snatch up his rifle. The next step carried him to the door. He called:

"Kaffa! Barounggo! Quick! Six good *askaris!*"

He swung round to the missionary.

"Sorry I can't take you, Padre. I don't doubt your nerve; but this is a matter of speed, and maybe a stiff scrap in the dark. Watch out while I'm away. One thing is, if that gang is busy doing juju at the rocks, they won't likely be coming raiding here. By golly, maybe this is that clever devil's false move. Ready, Barounggo? Away! Away!"

THE RAIDING party came into the vicinity of the rocks without having stumbled over any greased watchers or having sprung any man-traps. It had taken time; for even on the most circuitous route King had been infinitely cautious.

The rhythmic drone of the drums had long since ceased. But a dull glow of light glimmered through the bushes. A voice mumble-jumbled words. Other voices moaned a responsive chant.

King reached his hand into the wet darkness and drew the Masai close to him.

"How many of these four whom you have picked, if we see what I think we may see, will stand and not run?"

"Nay, bwana," the Masai whispered back. "Have I not picked them knowing that death stalks in the night? The six will stand."

"Good. Listen then: If we are discovered and attacked, let no fool run bleating into the jungle, but stand back-to-back. So may we win clear. Forward now, more silently than snakes."

On their stomachs the men wormed through the dripping underbrush. King squeezed his face through a tangle of scrubby roots, and the dim view that he achieved offered him the first cause of elation that he had found since he had started on this quest. It was the small number engaged in the gruesome rite. Not more than thirty dim figures moved in the light of the torches that sputtered in the rain. It bore out what the converts had said—that this dark cult was restricted to a carefully chosen band of initiates; and that, of course, also accounted for the secrecy which it had been able to maintain.

The ceremony, whatever it was, had proceeded well on its way. King could see only that the votaries squatted on their heels in three irregular lines before the low granite bluff upon which were carved the serpentine figures, and that they swayed in unison to their moaning chant.

Facing them with his back to the rock stood an enormous black man painted and made up with all the grotesque imagery of African art to resemble a devil. White circles enlarged his eyes; great white teeth were painted on to his lips; goat's horns added to his height; necklaces and armbands of bones hung about him. Flanked by two torches in the hands of deputy demons, he presented as fearsome a picture as the most debased superstition could conceive.

The devil-doctor mumbled some sort of litany, and the congregation swayed on its heels and chanted its response. King could catch only the jumbled rhythm; he was too far distant to recognize words. Quite clearly the ceremony was being conducted with a careful regard to quiet secrecy in the rain and dark. It had progressed to a point at which it became startlingly clear that the fantastic devil personification was not by any means the object of veneration; he was no more than the high priest of rites that were more gruesome than himself.

Sacrifices apparently had been made. Feathers again. King could distinguish white feathers at the demon priest's feet, wet and bedraggled in the rain. Now a single soggy boom sounded from a hidden drum. The devil-doctor raised his arms above his head. He loomed gigantic in the smoking torchlight.

Then King tensed to the word that he had trailed through so many dark and twisted ways; the word that had associated itself with fear beyond human reason.

"*N'gamm-a!*" intoned the devil priest with a deep inflection that boomed like a drum.

"*N'gamm-a! N'gamm-a!*" wailed the congregation.

The blacks heaved forward on their hams to bow their heads to the ground. In that position they remained, faces in the mud, moaning and groaning the dread word; and then a movement commenced over the brow of the granite bluff above the priest's head. A movement that drew a startled gasp from King and caused him to snatch his pistol from its holster.

Spasmodic gulps and shufflings in the brush beside King were evidence that the others had seen the fearsome thing too. Then a warning growl from the depths of the Masai's belly, and the shufflings stilled.

Over the rim of the rock the head of an immense snake began to appear. Broad and flat, the size of a small garden shovel, it hung there motionless: then it turned its neck to look this way and that.

"*N'gamm-a! N'gamm-a!*" groaned its prostrate votaries. Their bodies were contorted in Negro ecstacy; their voices rose to a clamor.

Immediately, like some demoniac bandmaster, the devil-doctor shushed and toned down their ardor. Blood-chillingly careless of the great head that swayed above him, he devoted his whole attention to quelling the hubbub of the worshipers. Slowly the head swung down to him.

Stiffly. Too unnaturally stiffly.

And then King's tension escaped from him in a long, windy whistle. He could see that the thing was manipulated by men from above. The great head was a mask; the body was a hollow of woven grass, painted in flowing triangles and circles.

Grotesquely the thing twined and swayed in imitation of a vast serpent. Its neck arched high; it curved down to nuzzle at prostrate men. In the dim torchlight it was horrifyingly life-like. It slid down off the bluff. With gruesome realism it opened its great jaws and made as if to engulf a man whole. Its devotees beat their heads upon the ground and moaned its dread name:

"*N'gamm-a! N'gamm-a!*"

It smacked its lips and moved on to another victim.

WATCHING THE fantastic ritual, King knew that these men were not engaged in any exaggerated play-acting; they were reproducing something that they had seen, something that they knew to be true. A thought flashed to him, a bold idea which he turned over in his mind as he lay. He surveyed the scene, the numbers. Scowling, he calculated distances and possible obstacles. Then his tight lipped ghost of a smile hardened on his face and he wriggled backward from his position.

Feeling in the dark, he found the Hottentot and the Masai and drew them together. To them he whispered his thought.

"Look you now. Those are men, full already of a fear that they make in their own minds, unsuspicious of danger, feeling themselves secure from observation. Moreover, worshipers; weapons not to hand. If therefore we rise suddenly out of the dark with a great outcry and a shooting off of the guns that

these Shenzies have brought, it is in my mind that in the confusion and the aimless running we may capture that devil-
doctor."

He waited to learn whether the idea was too entirely reckless
to stand the judgment of his two henchmen. The Hottentot
was the first to assimilate it.

"And that one being without doubt the chief," he whispered,
"so would the head of the serpent be crushed."

"We be eight armed men," said the Masai gravely. "Let us
rush upon them shouting our war cries and slay before they
find their weapons in the dark."

With that much assurance of cooperation King was encouraged. The object to be gained justified the risk. Cautiously he
gathered his men and gave his instructions. They were all to
burst out together with all the uproar of a surprise attack, yelling,
calling upon imaginary hosts, shooting off guns. King and his
two henchmen would make a rush for the devil-doctor; the
others would act as supporting interference wherever they saw
fit. If attacked, they would get their backs to the serpent rock
and fight it out.

The very boldness of the plan was the reason for success more
complete than King imagined. Secrecy of personnel was the
basis of the fear by which this dark cult ruled—anonymity and
the silent suddenness with which it snatched away its victims.
It was the tried and tested method of any secret police. And
should fear alone be insufficient to deter prying eyes, should
some bold investigator elude the watchers of the outer ap-
proaches, the cunning organizer had foreseen even that and
had drilled his people accordingly.

At the first shout of the attack the giant devil-doctor roared
an order. Immediately every torch was plunged into the nearest
puddle. Black darkness blotted out the scene. No man of the
worshipers yelled in aimless African confusion; only the fast
pad and splash of running feet betrayed flight.

King charged forward in the darkness. Naked bodies lurched

past him. He collided with one man and flung his arms around him. The fellow was too small; it could not be the burly witch-doctor. He hurled the captive from him and plunged on. Ugh! He barged into another and recoiled from the collision. An answering grunt came from the darkness and a heavy blow thudded on the side of his head. Ears ringing, he ducked low and lurched for the man's waist.

Another grunt answered the impact of his shoulder. Power-ful arms gripped and whirled him around. His own clutching hands felt dangling festoons of ornaments. His heart surged with a fierce exhilaration. This one felt more like it. This must be the burly devil-doctor himself. But King had a fight on his hands. He locked a leg behind the other's knee to trip him; but the ponderous defence to that was a blow that descended on the back of his neck and had him clinging dizzily.

"Bwana! Bwana! Where?" came the voice of the Masai.

"Here!" grunted King. "To me! No spear play. Hold him."

King tore one arm free and repaid the punch by hacking down over the other's kidneys. That fetched an answering grunt.

The Masai joined the struggle.

Like a bull the big witch-doctor plunged and heaved between them. In the thick blackness no one knew whom he held or whom he hit. King, straining mightily against muscular limbs as hard as his own, was aware of the thud of heavy feet reced-ing. His earlier surge of exhilaration reversed itself to a plunge into bitterness as he realized that he was wrestling with his own Masai.

The footsteps died into the bush. Far rustlings still sounded here and there. In the amphitheater before the rocks was only the sound of groping men. King swore loudly into the night and fished his flashlight from his hip pocket. But that had been thoroughly crushed in the fight. It took time to open up a waterproof matchbox and by the light of carefully cupped sticks to survey the damage.

King held in his hand a length of necklace composed of teeth and other symbols of sorcery. The Hottentot had a man's dirty loincloth. The others had nothing. The Masai was worst off. He bled freely from his smashed nose.

"Upon that one," he growled, "will I yet lay my hands and rend his bowels from him."

King had a guilty recollection of having planted a full blow upon somebody's nose in the dark, but of that he said nothing.

"Home," he ordered. "And fast. That devil is clever enough to organize an ambush on the way."

I T WA S dawn when King arrived at the mission. In spite of his failure he was keyed up with elation. He had been at grips with that elusive devil-doctor, and ideas had been racing through his brain.

"Padre," he told the Reverend Henderson, "you've got to help. Oh, I know you've been doing your utmost; but it's your converts who've got to help; and you've got to make them. I guess you know by this time that black men—the very best of them— know things and talk things that you never dream. I've known it all along. Now nobody can tell me that your converts don't know a few more things that they've never told. They've been scared witless. But already they've spilled more than they've ever whispered in all your two years; and you've got to make them tell more; or if they don't know, they've got to go gossip in the village and find out more.

"As smart as this devil-doctor is, some one of his people must have talked a little to somebody. I've got the beginnings of suspicions, horrible suspicions. But I've got to know more before I dare make a move. I've got to have a key; and to find the key I must have some native help. We're at a stage where this thing has gone beyond white man's sleuthing.

"What natives will never tell us they'll tell each other; and I want you to send your boys out to rake up information. I want you to do it right away. This cunning devil-doctor knows now that we're on to his game, and we must act fast before he can think up some new hiding—or maybe he's bold enough to take the offensive on a large scale. This is war now, Padre. I'm going around to see about the morale of my own crowd. You go and see what you can get out of your converts. Tell them we'll protect them; get that scare out of them."

KING'S PLANS and exhortations took up his whole morning. The men were badly frightened. Talk of magic and devil-devil had been spread insidiously among them; and not a man of them knew just how or by whom. This one had heard that such a one had said, and so-and-so had been told by somebody else; and that was as far as King could get.

Heard what? Said what? But nobody knew just what. There was a devil-devil that devoured men. That was all. And there was the stark proof of the man who had dared to give a warning and had immediately disappeared.

There was no arguing against that, no cajoling. King cursed in helpless fury; but he knew better than anybody else the effectiveness of Africa's age-old weapon against the white man. With the exception of his two staunch boys he knew that the rest of his men were useless, ready to run at the first sight of a painted face in the night or the first blare of a ghost gong.

He came into the house, very serious. The things that he muttered to himself were through hard-clenched teeth.

The Reverend Henderson was dejected.

"I could learn almost nothing. It is my honest belief that my people don't know. The secret has been too fearfully kept among its votaries. It is generally known that a secret cult exists, and my one consolation for not having learned of it is that the villagers have scarcely dared to talk about it among themselves, not knowing who in their very midst might be a member."

He flung out his hands helplessly.

"Verily, Mr. King, as it is written in Revelation, we are face to face with that old serpent which is the devil. This is one of those manifestations of evil that the good Lord in his wisdom permits from time to time for the trial of men's souls; and—"

"My Lord!" insisted King in his desperate impatience. "Were

you able to learn nothing? Couldn't you get even a hint out of them?"

"Only," said the Reverend Henderson, "that this word, *N-gamma*, or whatever it is, seems to be the individual name of the devil-devil and that the cult is that of a horrible demon called by the curious name of Dumbell."

"What's that?" King whirled and gripped the missionary's arms so that he winced. "What was that name?"

"Dumbell," repeated the missionary, his pale eyes wide with apprehension at King's vehemence. "As nearly as I could gather from them, just Dumbell."

"A-a-ah!"

King slowly let go of the missionary's arms and drew away from him. He was suddenly very calm. A hard grin that had long been absent from his face came back to it. His chest and shoulders expanded with the throwing off of a weight.

"The key!" he whispered. "At long last the key! And it fits! Hell, why couldn't I stumble on that before? But here in Africa where it doesn't belong! Good Lord, who will ever understand Africa?"

His finger pointed his conviction.

"Padre, do you know what your boys' Dumbell is? It's Dambala, the serpent god of voodoo. And it all fits. It fits everything—and it's going to shock you harder than anything yet.

"Voodoo doesn't belong in Africa—and that accounts for the discrepancies that couldn't jibe with juju. Voodoo is dumb African superstition transplanted by the slaves to the West Indies and there enlarged by the sharpened imaginations of the slaves' descendants, embellished, built up away beyond crude juju into the fantastic horrors conceivable by black men who have been taught all about the Christian's devil. Those feathers! White roosters are sacrificed in voodoo rites. Those goat's horns that the witch-doctor wore—the emblems of a voodoo priest or *papa-loi*. Every item of it fits. Gosh, why couldn't I tumble to it before? But who'd have thought to find it in Africa?

"And the man. Educated. Talking English with just a trace of an accent. Clever enough to organize this thing and to run it the way it's been run. Hounded out of his own island, maybe, by the local police. Now hold steady, Padre. All that you know about Brother Leroy is that he came from some West Indian island."

"Mr. King!" The Reverend Henderson sprang to his feet. "The Reverend Leroy is a Christian missionary! He has been doing a great work; his converts' devotion to him is a—"

King brushed him aside.

"Yeah? Who told you?"

His conviction was growing on him.

"A missionary of what? He was vague even as to his denomination. What converts? How many? Just the brothers of his cult. Most of the people here, as you yourself have pointed out, are a good bunch of fighting men, too straightforward for crazy horrors. And the only two buildings in the district big enough to house a gathering, as he had the nerve to point out—golly, how he must have laughed—are your chapel and his. And that poor devil of a man who disappeared led me straight to his. And you've never seen inside of it. It fits, I tell you. Every last little bit fits." He flung away and paced the floor with long strides.

The Reverend Henderson stood staring at him miserably. The accumulation of facts was inevitable. He could find no excuses or explanations. King whirled on him again with outthrust finger.

"And I'll tell you what I'm going to do. I'm going to raid that chapel! Oh, I know the trouble he can make for me with the government if I'm wrong. I'd have to leave the country; my reputation would be blacker mud than this whole business is black. But—" he continued with determination—"I'm going to raid."

His eyes blazed with exhilaration and the excitement of discovery. His stride was a nervous prowl as he laid his plans.

"Tonight. As soon as it's dark. I'll take men enough to fight his gang off. I can muster enough of them for that."

The Reverend Henderson sank back into his chair. His slender body shrank into its hard angles. It's hand-hewn African hardwood engulfed him. He looked very frail and small. His world as he had known it had crumbled to black dust.

I T W A S dark when King and his picked party slipped away from the mission. Men had been sent scouting the nearby paths an hour in advance to hunt out any possible watchers. No warning must be permitted to reach that clever adversary. A thin drizzle made the night black.

More roundabout than ever, King made a convert lead the way. The farther they progressed, the deeper grew King's frown; for, as once before, no villagers were encountered.

"Warned off," growled King; and to the convert, "Feel out every foot for man-traps even this far out. In spite of all precautions that devil suspects something."

To the Masai—

"Pass the word down that if we're attacked in ambush the torchmen will light up instantly, stick the torches in the ground and every man take cover."

No ambush, however, was encountered. But a drum throbbed dully. King drew the Hottentot to him.

"The same signal, apeling, is it not?"

"*N'dio bwana.* The signal of gathering. By some magic he knows and he gathers his men."

Going with infinite caution, the raiding party came finally to the so-called mission settlement without having encountered mishap or man-traps. They had made a complete circuit and stood grouped now at the edge of the clearing on the far side.

The straggling huts loomed shapeless among the banana leaves; the patter of rain upon their wide surfaces was the only sound. High above the general mass was the dimly outlined dome of the chapel with its ostrich eggs against the sky. All of it was menacing, as if silently waiting. Not even a dog barked.

At an African village such a phenomenon was cause for suspicion. But the Hottentot said with callous matter-of-factness—

"A snake god, if its taste be not entirely spoiled, will at a pinch eat even dog."

King marshaled his men according to a simple but effective plan. He and the Hottentot with a brace of torchmen were to rush the chapel. The Masai and the rest were to act as outside defence.

"Watch more carefully than ever in your lives," warned King. "That cunning devil is up to something. Now Kaffa and I go first, and the rest of you deploy out around the building. Quietly if we can. Barounggo, if by chance they are all inside, waiting in silence, upon my call charge your men in. Come ahead."

It was with something of misgiving that King found himself before the dark recess of the chapel door; he had met not a soul in his cautious crawl and he did not know what peculiarly hellish thing his adversary might be up to. The door, of course, was locked. King took a long breath. So far, good; but now for whatever might be inside.

Nothing was to be gained by waiting. Already the dark forms of the Masai's men were shaping up behind him. He drew back, felt the distance and lunged his shoulder at the door.

It was built of massive, hand-cut planks, but it was set in a frame of bamboo and adobe mud. The whole thing tore out under his impact. He lurched into the darkness, sprawling over the wreck of it. Immediately, mindful of spears waiting at the entrance, he rolled over and over to the middle. The first thought that flashed to him was that he encountered no furniture, only a bare mat floor. He heard feet dash in behind him. On the instant he was on his own feet, tense in the blackness.

No spears. No breathing of crouching men. A match sputtered to a pitch torch and shortly its smoky light flared and revealed emptiness.

No benches, no chairs, not even the crudest kind of church furniture. The big circular floor space was bare—a meeting place for naked men, that was all. But piled against the walls was an assortment of other things that proved King's suspicion.

At any moment he expected to hear the uproar of conflict outside. Hurriedly he swung the torch round the walls. The adobe surface was ornamented with crude anthropomorphic designs, most of them obscene like those on the sculptured rocks. Predominant was the symbol of the eyes and the forked tongue.

Hanging from pegs thrust into the adobe and in untidy piles upon the floors was a collection of all the gimcrackery of African witchcraft coupled with the paraphernalia of voodoo—bones, animal skulls, dried embryos, woven grass masks with painted eyes; and with them goatskins, horns, bladder-rattles and phallic objects.

In one corner, black and shiny with use, the drums, a pair of them—big voice and little voice; the black drums that only an hour ago had been talking a message of deviltry into the night.

But it was still something else that King sought. Quickly he made the circuit of the great room, kicking away piles of skins, lifting floor mats, peering behind the raised altar. It was a den or a pit of some kind that he hoped to find; some sort of cage or something that might house a big snake. But nothing of the sort came to light. Only the hanging objects and the disorderly piles ranged along the wall.

Still no sounds of conflict came from outside. King went to the door. His spearmen stood in an irregular line before it. Torches had been lighted, and they sputtered in the rain. The untidy hut groups stood silent, the open spaces between them empty.

The Masai's big shoulders loomed up from the direction of the little whitewashed house. He laughed as he reported:

"We have been fearing shadows in the emptiness, bwana. They have gone. By some devil's trick they knew that warriors came. The drums spoke the signal, and they have fled."

But King could conceive of no such tactical error on the part of so shrewd a man as Brother—or to name him correctly—Voodoo Papa-loi Leroy. He was filled with a very wholesome suspicion of that man's every move.

"More likely," he grunted, "the drums signaled the gathering for some devil business in the woods."

"*Kss–ss–ss!*"

The Hottentot snatched a torch to peer at a trail on the ground. The men stooped to look and clapped their hands over their mouths. Ox-eyed, they stared at it and fearfully they cast glances over their shoulders into the shadows.

From the door of the voodoo house the trail ran, a smooth swath in the moist ground. As thick as a man's body, it wound away into the darkness. The Hottentot whispered the thought that awed all of them.

"Such a trail is made by a snake. A snake big enough to devour men. The very father of all snakes."

King scowled down at the wide track, deeply impressed by a great weight. An involuntary chill crept up and down his spine. What new and incredible trickery was this? Naked footprints showed alongside the wet spoor. King gnawed at his lower lip. Was it humanly possible that a monstrous thing like that could be trained? Could it be herded along on a sacrificial hunt with its attendant ghouls pattering on swift feet alongside? In the drizzly dark of that deserted and silent voodoo den he was ready to believe any diabolism of Papa-loi Leroy.

"Up! Up!" he ordered. "Home! And by the shortest route, To hell with mantraps—they'll be set the other way anyhow. Get going. The very devil is abroad this night."

N O T A soul was encountered on the path; though in places it wound among outlying clusters of huts. Never had a trail been so deserted. But the Hottentot, pattering ahead with a torch, testing, literally nosing out the trail, announced—

"Men have passed this way before us; and with haste, stopping not even to reset these empty traps behind them."

Men. In haste. On the trail that led to the mission. Apprehension began to reach cold fingers toward King's heart.

Never were hut groups so silent; not even the glimmer of a dried dung-fire showed between the chinks where the rain had eroded the mud plaster. But that, King knew, was to be expected when the black drums had given warning that juju walked in the night.

King's apprehension as they drew near to the settlement became certainty when that, too, showed no signs of life. Not a light shone from the little mission house; there was not a sound.

"Something wrong. Come ahead! Barounggo, watch out for ambush."

He dashed forward. His gun had been ready to his hand throughout that jungle trail. No challenge came at the mission gate from the *askari* whom he himself had posted. In two leaps he was across the compound. The mission door was an open black shadow.

"Padre." King called through the four rooms. "Padre, are you all right?"

Not a sound. Running, King kicked open the back door. Beyond the empty rear compound the convert huts stood dark and silent. King snatched a torch from the nearest man and raced to a hut. He kicked the door down.

Within the hut, huddled with blankets over their heads, were men. Cursing, King kicked them till, howling, they found their feet.

"What happened?" King stormed at them. "What hell's business has been here?"

White eyed, they goggled at him.

King took the nearest one by the throat and shook him.

"What happened? Speak, idiot, damn you, or I'll beat your dumb face in!"

Then they all gave clamorous tongue at once. Men had come—men with grass masks over their faces. Not men—devils. They had slain, the *askaris*, or the *askaris* had run away; they did not know. The devils had seized the *monpéré*, their master, thereby proving that their power was greater than the *monpéré's* god. Those who had not been seized had barricaded themselves in their huts or had fled into the jungle.

King leaped to other doors. Without prelude he kicked them down. Within were other cowering men. King kicked them too. They knew nothing. Nobody knew anything. Masked devils had come; that was all.

King swore into the night. The Masai's dark form bulked beside him. Imperturbably he reported;

"Seven we find slain. Two will live. The rest—" He shrugged his shoulders. "A full day will I expend in administering beatings."

"Up!" shouted King. "Up! Beat those frightened fools to work! That devil had the same thought to raid here while we raided there; and his is the greater gain. Up and after them, and we may yet come in time."

"After them indeed," said the Masai. "But where in this night? If one of these fools upon whom that good man has wasted his labor had but the wit to follow and bring word—"

King had an inspiration.

"The lake!"

He revolved the thought in his mind and his eyes glowed. He nodded his conviction. "Yes, the lake! There can be no place other than that island."

"Awah!" Even the Masai recoiled at the prospect. "A fit place, indeed, in the midst of that evil water, for a devil serpent that devours men. But, bwana, without a canoe how could even that devil doctor do such a witchcraft?"

"That trail!" King was running to the mission. "The trail that led from the voodoo-house door. It was not a giant serpent. It was a canoe dragged along by men. That's where that cunning devil kept it hidden. To work! Beat those men to work!"

The Masai roared among the shivering converts. With kicks, blows and pricks with the point of his spear he set to herding them into the mission-house. How, without a second canoe, anybody might traverse that crocodile-infested water, he had no idea. But his faith in his master was immense. If the bwana said he would go to the island, no matter what the difficulties, no matter what the odds might be when he should get there, to the island he would go. Without asking questions the great fellow collected and bullied the men to whatever work it was that the master planned.

King was heaving at the great community table; that ponderous thing of solid planking and young sapling legs.

"Of this we make a raft," he shouted. "Swift, swift, every man! Ropes, axes, chairs, beds, whatever there is! Kaffa, set two men to rip boards from somewhere and thin down shafts to make paddles. Speed! Speed!"

The table was a good ten feet long, and solid. Beneath it, just under the edge, ran a stout six-inch horizontal strip to give bracing to the legs; it was a veritable coaming for a boat with the table upside down.

For a breathless moment King thought of felling trees and hewing logs, but the immediate shade trees of the mission were hardwoods. To go hunting through the jungle in the dark for something lighter was not to be thought of. Time was important.

There was no knowing what awful, unholy, gruesome rite might be progressing on that island.

Ruthlessly King smashed chairs, cupboards, all the meager furnishings of the place—anything that would float—and lashed the lumber thus obtained lengthwise along the table top. Heaving with half a dozen men, he turned the thing over. Furiously swinging an ax, he knocked the sturdy legs flying. They, too, went under to add buoyancy.

TIME SPED inexorably; but so did the making of the raft. A mass of ropes and planks and odd firewood, it was finished faster than anything that had ever happened before in that part of Africa.

"Good enough," panted King. "It'll hold together. Now, then, get under it, every man! Hoist! Edgewise through the door, fools! The shotgun, Kaffa. It'll be a murderous weapon at close quarters; but this is a murderous business. Away! Away! Axmen ahead to clear the path! Speed! Speed!"

Supported by every man who could put shoulder to it, the cumbersome raft went lurching out into the night.

At the lake edge King stared in the direction where he knew the island should be. No glimmer of light came from it. No whisper of sound. It seemed that, if men moved on it at all, they groped their way in some nameless ritual of the deeper hell. Coupled with the blackness of night, the rain roared down upon the water's surface with a sudden fury that drowned out all other sound.

Gingerly, wary of the water's edge, the men pushed the raft in. It floated high. King's quick estimate was that it would carry five. That would be, besides himself and his two henchmen, two others.

But which two? Explosive grunts and staccato croaks came from the dark water. Who of those shivering men would be willing to go? And of what value would frightened men be in—in whatever it might be that would be met on that fearsome island?

It was no time for speculation. King pounced upon the two men nearest to himself, irrespective of whether his own or converts. He pitched them bodily on to the float. For half a mile they had to drive that cumbersome thing through reedy water; he wanted stout arms for paddles; he could not stop to pick fighting men. Speed! Speed!

He jumped on board after them. The raft lurched. The two men screamed. The Hottentot was already there. The Masai heaved mightily against the raft, wading knee deep to give it a good send-off. Then calmly he swung aboard.

"Crocodiles," he said coolly, "are more fearful even than these jungle people; they do not come where much noise is. Think you, bwana, that those devil men will fight?"

King did not at once reply. He drove great straining strokes with his crude board paddle. Things other than paddles splashed out of the darkness ahead. The raft gathered way. Once it bumped jarringly against something that grunted. Something swished and hit the water with a slap that sent a wave over the six-inch gunwale. A man groaned.

"Speed!" growled King. "Speed!"

"Even rain like a waterfall," panted the Hottentot between strokes, "is not without its virtue; for thus will the devils not hear our coming."

"And at least," said King with a grim satisfaction, "this time they will not be expecting any interference."

The low island loomed ahead, a blacker shadow upon the black water. King strained his eyes to distinguish a possible landing. Before he could adjust his sight to distances the raft grounded softly. The rain's fury was abating; but its patter upon leaves drowned out all sounds of the hurried scramble ashore.

A narrow fringe of weedy beach encircled the island. Beyond that were the bushes that could be seen from the main shore— dense, tough, a veritable wall. Stiff thorns against his groping hand quickly convinced King that passage through it would be a matter of machete work.

From within the wall, from the very belly of the island, there now sounded above the patter of the rain, like a bass accompaniment to it, a low, booming rhythm. Too low to distinguish words; but King had listened to that emphasized rhythm before.

"*N'gamm-a! N'gamm-a!*"

When he had heard it before it was a prelude to the appearance of the great stuffed snake above the sculptured rock. Here on this island, what?

"Hell! There must be a path someplace. Quick!"

In a frenzy of anxiety they stumbled along the beach, which was littered with flotsam and driftwood, holding on to each other to keep their feet. The two extra men followed only because they dared not remain behind. A black shadow that lay like a log across the way grunted and scuttled into the water.

"The hell with them! Come ahead!" King whispered fiercely.

Other shadows slid away from their advance. The island was small and roughly circular. They had scrambled round perhaps a third of it when an immense shadow loomed ahead, full across the path.

Huge and black, disdainful of a handful of stumbling men, it refused to move.

King's hesitation was only momentary.

Muttering something about hell, he ran at it and jumped high. Clearing it with room to spare, he landed, turned and stood his ground, laughing hysterically—but determined.

It was the dugout canoe.

Hauled well up, its nose stuck into a dark tunnel that opened through the tangled bush wall.

"*N'gamm-a! N'gamm-a!*" The low rhythm sounded clearer now. At intervals came the terrifying drone of a devil's litany.

King plunged into the path, the Masai at his heels. The shrewd little Hottentot waited a moment and then his soft, insistent, whisper came from behind.

"The canoe would hold perhaps ten men, bwana."

"*Hau!* Perhaps then they will fight," growled the Masai.

"Perhaps," amended King grimly, "it has made more than one trip."

FORGING AHEAD by touch, King pushed his face into thorns. The rain drowned his sharp exclamation. The tunnel had suddenly zigzagged; and immediately King knew why. It was to hide the light. Ahead was a glow.

In a half dozen long, cautious strides King stood at the end of the tunnel; and all at once he understood the whole devil-begotten secret of the island. He understood why no structure was ever visible from the main shore, why no lights were ever seen—the dense bush tangle, of course, accounted for that. But structure there was, and no imagination was necessary to tell King just what its grisly significance might be.

The tunnel debouched into a space cleared of bushes, like the island, roughly circular, perhaps some sixty feet across. The structure in the center of the clearing was nothing more or less than a wide cage, a glorified mousetrap in which victims awaited whatever death their captor decided upon. The victims in the trap were the missionary and two of his converts. Just what form of death their captor had planned was not as yet apparent.

The cage was constructed of stout bamboo poles driven into the ground a few inches apart, braced with crosspieces and strongly lashed with split canes. A flat top covered it, just above man height, similarly braced and lashed. A quite unescapable cage; in fact, an arena.

And like an arena, it was lighted. On little bamboo shelves, screened from the rain by matting, burned wicks of twisted bark floating in clay saucers of grease. Outside the arena, at intervals all round its circumference, stood men, black, stark naked, perhaps a score of them. They jigged a shuffling step to accompany the droned litany. Their responses fell in cadenced unison:

"*N'gamm-a! N'gamm-a.*"

That ominous word had meant fear wherever King had met it. The last time it had preceded the appearance of a serpent god.

Fear was upon the jigging men now, though not the abject, face-in-the-mire reverence of the rock ceremony.

"Something queer about that," was King's immediate suspicion as he stood tense in the black shadow of the passage, on tiptoe to explode into action just as soon as he should know what and how.

He could have reached out his shotgun and touched the man directly in front of him. He felt almost as if the man must hear his breathing. But the fellow's whole attention was focused upon whatever it was that was happening—or going to happen—behind those bamboo bars. Farther down the line King could get a view of faces. They, too, were keyed to a pitch of expectant excitement that left room for observation of nothing outside. Blubbery lips trembled, eyes goggled white, features twitched. Brutal faces all. Debased. Like the faces of gorillas—or of devils.

And then it came to King why these people were not all bowed down to the mud at the word, *N'gamm-a*. This spectacle was not worship. It was sport.

Worship might come later. But these men were waiting for something to happen, some horrific thing that would glut that appetite for blood which was the necessary prelude to voodoo ecstacy.

Whatever it was that was coming, the Reverend Henderson inside the cage knew as well as did the fanatical audience. King could see him between the bamboo bars. He was upon his knees, his hands folded before him, his lips moving. His thin body was naked. Smeared upon his breast with yellow ocher was the symbol of the serpent eyes and the forked tongue. Hope had left him. He was praying.

King thought gravely that so must other Christians have prayed in an arena long ago as they waited for the lions.

As for the converts, terror had bereft them of all voluntary motion as well as speech. They lay on the ground, caked with mud; at intervals their bodies twitched spasmodically; their eyes rolled in their heads. Then King saw that dirty cloth gags covered their mouths.

It was on the farther side of the cage that all eyes seemed to be so hypnotically fixed. Vision there, through a double line of bars and against the smoky grease lamps of that side, was not so easy for King. He could make out the big form of the voodoo *papa-loi* who droned the monotonous chant to which his lesser devils kept time. Beside him seemed to be a multiplicity of bamboo stems adjoining the cage, a sort of supernumerary cage, as it were; though its function remained vague.

The *papa-loi* waved his arms high in impious imitation of invoking a blessing, calling upon the spirit of his demon god to manifest itself before its people. And from the slavering excitement of its people it seemed that they saw something; that the god *was* manifesting itself.

Then King saw it too, and his heart came into his mouth. Having once discerned it out of the smoky gloom, he wondered that he had not picked it out before. Connecting the supernumerary cage with the arena cage was a square black hole, a sort of trapdoor, high up, just below the ceiling. Out of this hole protruded a frightful head, enormous and flat, the size of a garden shovel. Motionless, it hung there. It might have been a wooden mask. But then a great bifurcated tongue licked out and flicked slowly up and down, tasting the air.

"*N'gamm-a! N'gamm-a!*" intoned its jigging demons. Their nostrils twitched; they licked bubbling lips.

Unhurriedly a length of thick neck slid out of the hole and hung there hesitantly. This way and that the broad head turned to look—exactly as had the wooden one at the rock ceremony.

"*N'gamm-a! N'gamm-a!*" The rhythm speeded up its tempo. The stamping feet sent a tremor through the ground.

The cold-eyed devil-devil seemed to be satisfied with its scrutiny. With effortless ease a vast body began to flow out of the trapdoor. The great head arched gracefully down to accept its sacrifice.

The enormity of their effort brought stifled groans from the gagged converts. Their spasmodic jerking threw them bounding and skittering across the arena mud. The missionary, with the superhuman moral strength of a stout soul enclosed in a fragile body, remained on his knees and prayed to his God.

King's jump carried him right up to the bars of the cage. A

naked body stood in his way. A back arm blow hurled the man sprawling. King shoved his shotgun between the bamboo bars and let go both barrels at once.

The great head and neck disintegrated into a red mass of streamers and ribbons. Like a vast rubber cable the body that had protruded jerked back into the hole. An agonized howl came from a naked man who had been watching the show from directly behind. A brief space of silence was caused by sheer astonishment. Then a vast writhing and a rending of wood from the supernumerary cage—and hell's pandemonium.

Shocked beyond all reasoning by the apparition entering their confident security, the devil-worshipers' single impulse was to bolt around either side of the trap to the protection of their *papa-loi*. There they milled, a yelling mass, in the narrow space between the cage and the jungle wall.

"After them!" yelled King. "Don't let them get set!"

The Masai shouted his ferocious war cry of stabbing spears:

"*Ss-ghee, ss-ghee!* The devil-doctor is mine, bwana," he pleaded as he ran. "He who smote my nose is mine."

GIVING THE devil his due, credit must be given to Papa-loi Leroy. Bellowing rage and encouragement, he launched himself from the platform on which he had been standing and pushed a wave of his men before him. King found himself engulfed. His gun was knocked from his hand in the first rush. Hot, naked bodies pressed upon him. They shrank from him as from a materialized ghost; but sheer pressure of numbers in that confined space forced them on to King. Foot and knee and fist, he fought with yelling men who clawed at him more in fright than in battle rage.

He saw the Masai wading shoulder deep through screaming men, his great spear flashing redly as it rose and fell. But those were only obstacles in his path.

"Wait for me, Rainmaker," he shouted. "Hold fast, thou great one. *Hau!* Art thou running from an *elmoran* of the Masai among all thy demons?"

The terrific flailing of an enormous body in the supernumerary den began to burst the walls apart. Sections of bamboo flew in the air. With a splintering crash a whole side fell out. Something like a ship's hawser swept the feet from under the milling mob. A huge coil writhed high and fell crunchingly. Men howled beneath it and leaped frantically to avoid it.

King began to realize that the hands that beat at him were weaponless. With relief he remembered that these men had come as spectators to a sacrifice; weapons, if any, would be stacked somewhere; probably left in the canoe. How long before somebody would gather his wits sufficiently to go for them? In desperation King put into practice every low, man-maiming trick that he knew—knee to the groin; elbow twisted till the bone cracked; rabbit punch. Men fell howling away from him.

It came to him with a sickening feeling that in all this confusion there was no sign of the Hottentot. Perhaps the little man had gone down. Under his feet King felt himself treading upon his gun. Risking everything, he fought down to get at it. Men howled and piled themselves on top of him. From somewhere outside of his own fight King heard a shot spit viciously. He heaved up out of a mound of men to see Leroy, a pistol in his hand, struggling over surging heads to bring his arm down and point it again at the Masai. The Masai roared and plowed through a barrier of bodies.

"There's for thee, father of devils!" he shouted.

The great spear licked out in a full arm lunge. A foot of it suddenly stuck out of the voodoo-doctor's back. He disappeared in the screaming mob; but the shaft of the spear with its monkey-tail tuft waved drunkenly in the air above their heads.

Seeing the Masai unarmed, a wave of men threw themselves at him, howling like the devils that they worshiped. The Masai went down; but from beneath the bodies his indomitable shout came:

"*Whau!* That was a stroke! Wait, devil's offspring. Wait but till I get my weapon again."

His voice was muffled. His breath came gaspingly. King wrenched free and swung his gun to waist height. He fired. Men writhed away, shrieking. Other men, finding King's hands engaged, clawed at him from behind. King swung round and fired blindly. It seemed that the whole pressure before him disintegrated. Only groans came from about his feet. He saw the Masai surge up out of a sea of men, his spear in his hand. The men yelled and broke before him.

The Masai had no inhibitions. Armed or unarmed, enemies were before him, men who did demoniac things. They fought against his master. His business was to slay them.

Before the threat of his spear they broke and ran. Shouting, he chased them. Round and round the cage he chivvied them. Some in their desperation dived for what they hoped might be thin spots in the bush tangle and there they stuck. They were speared. Some broke partially through. The Masai reserved them for a later hunting. Some climbed monkey-like to the top of the cage.

King smashed his fist into the face of the last man before him and was free to run and catch the berserk Masai by the arm.

"Have done! Cease, slaughterer!" he shouted and shook the man out of his red fury. "There is work. Cut me the cords of this door with your spear and let us get the *monpéré* out of this. Put him in the canoe under guard of those two cowards who would not follow; and then we must go and look for Kaffa."

The Masai was immediately sober.

"What? Is the little man gone? The apeling with whom I have had my daily quarrel? *Awowe!* Then will there indeed be a slaughter. Speed, bwana; he may yet live."

He sliced his spear blade against the fastenings of the cage door and plunged in with King. The skulkers on the roof scuttled away like spiders. The missionary had fainted. King took the frail body up in his arms. The Masai followed with a grease lamp.

At the tunnel's farther entrance dark forms sprawled on the beach. A goblin figure perched on the prow of the canoe. He started up and lifted a short Somali sword. Then he clucked.

"*Whah*, bwana! I thought it was another of them. One came like a fool, not looking, bellowing for weapons. Him I slew. Another came. Him also I slew. Yet another came. Him also—"

"Shut up!" said King. "Murderers twain have I for servants. Here, get the *monpéré* into the canoe."

"*N'dio,* bwana. But softly, bwana, softly. Spears are in the canoe and knives. Show a light, thou great oaf of a Masai, that we do not lay him upon sharp edges."

King held the lamp above his head and watched his incongruous pair tenderly handle the missionary between them. In the shadow he was not ashamed to let the hard lines of his face soften in appreciation of two black men who stood more staunchly by him than many a white man might have done. But bruskly he shook sentiment from him. His voice was gruff.

"Carefully now, carefully. Otherwise the gifts that it was in my mind to give for a little blood spilled in the right time and place will be forfeited for clumsiness. Come now, Barounggo, ungag those rascals and kick them to their feet. Then swiftly away from this evil place."

"And those others, bwana?" The Masai voiced disappointment. "Those devil men who have temporarily escaped? It would be a hunting like rats in last year's straw, bwana. Shall those evil ones go free?"

"They shall stay right here," said King grimly, "till we come and collect them in our own good time. If they hunger, let them eat their own dead, as do all devils. If they don't like this den of their own making, let them swim. Come, let's get going."

ONCE AGAIN the Reverend Henderson sat in a chair of stiff, hand-hewn hardwood—brought from Brother Leroy's "mission." King swung his legs from a sturdy table, late of the same place. The missionary was pale and exhausted; but his spirit remained unquenchable. King's grin was that of an archangel who has well and truly executed a major readjustment of the universe.

"So that just about cleans up that," he said. "They were pretty well tamed when I went to fetch them off their island—what was left of them. A boot at the exact psychological root of their tails and a sight of something to eat brought out a whole basketful of confessions. The mystery is very simple—I mean about their snake's impossible appetite. I should say Leroy had a complex about slaves; he couldn't forgive the white men who had run off his own parents; so when he got into trouble in Jamaica over his voodoo stuff he came over and started a slave racket right here in British territory, knowing that the Abyssinians would be blamed; and to cover up disappearances here he organized his Dambala devil cult and had them believing that it got *all* the victims. The slaves marched up into Abyssinia and turned them over to the borderland chief, who took them quietly through Jubaland to the coast, where Arab dhows picked them up for sale in Hadramaut.

"A right smart lad was Brother Leroy. He was making a pile of money out of his game and he sent it all away to the coast; must have banked it somewhere; though these poor dupes, of course, couldn't understand anything about that."

"Thank God for that," said the missionary piously. "And did you find out about—about that unhappy orderly?"

"That too. They put up a scrap, he and poor old Ponsonby. The gang was afraid they'd upset the canoe in the middle of the lake, so they were tied up. But the orderly seems to have managed to pick up a *panga* knife in the dark and concealed it somehow. The snake got Ponsonby and was kind of taking things easy, sniffing around the other. It was then that his mind cracked. He howled and gibbered something awful, they said. It must have been a ghastly business. But he managed to cut loose and, gone berserk, he took a tremendous swipe at the snake's head with his knife; didn't kill it outright, but that's what it died of later.

"Of course there was a tremendous confusion, what with the snake thrashing around in the cage and the worshipers struck dumb. And then the orderly, still howling horribly, burst through a rotten spot in the cage wall, hacked down a couple of men in his way and got clear away in the canoe. That's why they just had to go after him to get him back. The *N'gamma* died a couple of days later; so they put it away in its little hut to lie in state, and Leroy had his men out and caught the new one within a week. They tell me there's a warm water pool where the snakes come to shed their skins."

The Reverend Henderson was silent with closed eyes. Several times he shuddered. At last—

"What are you going to do with them?" he asked.

King knew that the missionary was thinking of men, not of snakes. Frowning in troubled thought, he kicked his boot heels together

"I don't exactly know. If I take them in to Nairobi they'll be officially tried and hanged as accessories. Yes, hanged. Just for being dumb African fools, dupes of the devil Leroy, crazed by mumbo-jumbo. And then'll be more trouble."

The missionary opened his eyes and looked up.

What could be worse than the hanging of men? King nodded.

"Yes. Official trial will mean witnesses. You and me and dozens of these people. Investigations of local conditions. Police. Tribal punishment for not reporting the thing. Fines. Impressing of the prestige of the colonial government."

"Oh, Mr. King—" the missionary cried appealingly—"cannot that be avoided? Is there no other way?"

King nodded again.

"Sure there is—if your conscience will let you collaborate with me in throwing a little dust into the eyes of his Britannic Majesty's colonial government. A quite simple way. I can let Barounggo cuff their ears and give each of the gang a swift kick in the nether loincloth—in public—and then turn them loose. Their bad influence will be busted for keeps, and their own people will twist their tails plenty. And you can start all over again with a lot of knowledge that you didn't have before.

"I shall report to the governor that no slaves were being raided from Abyssinia—which is true; that Ponsonby was unfortunately killed by a snake—which is also true; that I have killed the snake—which is the truest thing you know.

"I shall write that report, and I shall keep away from Nairobi for a year—go exploring in Abyssinia maybe; lots of things in Abyssinia I've never seen. And you—" King pointed his finger at the missionary—"you will stretch your conscience and write an enclosure to my report to back me up with your O.K."

The Reverend Henderson remained silent, his head against the hard chair back. For a moment he was silent, his eyelids closed in thought. Then softly he murmured the quotation:

" 'Therefore shall I save my flock, and they shall no more be a prey.' "

He sat resolutely upright.

"Mr. King," he gave his conviction, "it is my sincere belief that in this case the end justifies the means."

Weeks later, when the governor read that report—scrawled on a sheet of mission copybook paper—he told a scandalized secretary—

"File as officially accepted."

He drummed his fingers on his desk. Slowly a wise smile spread over his august features.

"Good man, that Kingi Bwana chap. Saved us no end of native trouble and military expenditure—and he always thinks we don't know. Some day I must catch him and find out what really happened."

WARDENS OF THE BIG GAME

THE BIG elephant danced in his rage. He charged in thunderous short rushes, wheeled and thundered back. He flung his trunk high and screamed brazen blasts of fury. He stamped the dust to a yellow smokescreen. He tore up tussocks of dry grass and thorn bush and lashed them to shreds against his own horny knees in a giant frenzy of destruction.

Two white men and two black stood frozen in their tracks and watched him. Nothing separated them but two hundred yards of open veldt scrub.

King, big-boned and lean, frowned at the awesome spectacle through dust-rimmed eyes. With an adroit motion he juggled a stem of grass across to the other corner of his mouth and grunted:

"Plenty mad, isn't he?"

"Terrific." The district commissioner whispered. "I hope to heaven he doesn't wind us."

King nibbled his grass, tight-lipped. "He may not wind us in this heavy air. But he'll sure as hell wind that native village we left dead behind us."

The district commissioner moved his head in slow inches, desperately careful to attract no attention to their precarious position, cautiously surveying the immediate landscape for its scanty trees.

A fleeting grin cracked the caked dust from around King's wide mouth.

"Elephant eyesight isn't that good," he said.

"I think," the commissioner hazarded, "we might make that mimosa tree in a mad altogether rush."

King flashed one quick eye at it.

"Easy," he agreed. "But the native village will still be right back of us. And this big boy is mad enough to be considerable catastrophe to the heathen."

"Terrific!" The commissioner murmured again. "I wonder what so infuriated him?"

The grin passed from King's face. Only the lean, brown hardness remained. Angry disgust was in his voice.

"I can see from right here what's made him mad. Wait till he swings around and I'll show you."

The commissioner hissed a sudden intake of breath. "By Jove, he's got it! Watch him! He'll be down on us. Good Lord!"

It was true. A wave of sultry air, pregnant with refuse, crept up behind them and rippled the grass tops away out toward the angry beast's orbit of rampage. Instantly it stood tense, its ears flared immensely forward, its trunk high in the upper stratum of odors above the dust.

"Good God!" the commissioner repeated. "Run for the tree!"

King swung his rifle sling from his shoulder. Quite coolly he looked down to his feet and shuffled his boot soles to see that he stood on no loose rubble. His eyes began to narrow down in cold alertness and he eased a cartridge from the magaaine into the chamber of his big Jeffries .475.

One of the black men, a huge fellow, decked out with knee

and elbow garters of monkey hair in all the superb nakedness of a Masai Elmoran, took a horn receptacle from the lobe of his ear, tapped snuff from it upon his great spear blade and sniffed it in a splendid gesture of confidence in his master.

The elephant was striding in enormous uncertainty, ears like fans, trunk stiff before it, questing the vagrant airs with massively vengeful purpose. Even at that distance its snorts of expelled air came like a steam exhaust.

The commissioner became suddenly official.

"Kingi Bwana, there's no need to shoot that elephant. We can still make the tree in safety."

King sighted for a moment along his barrel to gauge the sun glimmer on his sights. He lowered the weapon.

"Go ahead, if you want to," he said. "And better jump. 'Cause when he comes he'll make it in fifteen seconds flat."

"Mister King!" The commissioner was officially formal. "I forbid you. You deliberately refused an elephant license when we started out. If you unnecessarily shoot this beast I shall be compelled to fine you the government penalty of a hundred pounds."

King grinned, his eyes warily fixed upon the gray mountain of rage.

"I believe you damn tape-bound officials would do just that thing," he said cheerfully. "All the same I'm going to shoot it. For two reasons. One is that stinking native village behind us."

"Good God!" That realization broke through the commissioner's agitation. "The women will all be in their huts at this hour too. Shoot it from the tree then."

As before, the grin soured on King's face.

"You know damn well nobody can shoot a charging elephant from up in a tree. Not dead. Head on is the only possible shot. This poor beast has suffered enough already. That's the second reason. I'm not going to let it carry away a lot of useless lead."

The other black man, a Hottentot as small and wizened as the Masai was huge, clucked a quick warning.

"*Angalia, Bwana.* He has picked the scent. He is coming."

The gray mountain screamed its rage once more and charged down straight for the little group of puny humans. King shuffled his feet again and stood, his mouth and eyes thin, parallel lines.

Fifteen seconds! But to the commissioner they hammered in the agonizing rhythm of his slow, crawling pulse. Incredible man, this King, taking a blood-chilling chance like this. All on account of some inexplicable sentiment about that murderously charging beast having suffered something or other.

The thunder of its feet vibrated on the ground. An avalanche of hurtling flesh and billowing dust, it rushed enormously nearer. All ears and reaching trunk and wicked little red eyes.

But the commissioner held his ground alongside of King.

"Shoot! For God's sake, why don't you shoot?" he heard a cracked voice reiterating; and vaguely he realized it was his own. And coolly King's voice:

"Fifty feet is plenty good."

The mountain loomed immensely above them. A scream like a locomotive warning blasted the air.

KING LIFTED his rifle to his shoulder, held it a second, and fired. Its roar cut the scream appallingly short. The elephant's fore legs stiffened to the full ton impact of the .475 bullet. The barrel feet plowed parallel deep furrows in the ground. Slowly, like huge brakes applied, they came to a stop. The gray bulk swayed, fell over on its side as a mountain falls.

Through the choking dust King was grinning tight-lipped at the commissioner. The commissioner was aware of his own voice again, high pitched and dry.

"Good God! Why didn't you shoot sooner? Lord, the thing was almost upon us! Is it out of sheer bravado that you do these things, Kingi Bwana?"

"Fifty feet," King repeated the rule. "There's a space no bigger than your open hand between the frontal bones to aim for."

He led the commissioner forward. "Look now." His voice was dark with anger. "See why he was so mad? Tearing around that way? He'd never have bothered us else. Poor brute."

At first the commissioner could notice nothing amiss. Then it came to him that the fallen beast had only one tusk. The other—where the other had been—was a mess of splintered ivory and a pulp of raw flesh.

"Good heavens! What a ghastly mess! How could a thing like that happen?" the commissioner wondered.

"It could happen," said King grimly, "only from a rifle bullet. From a bullet fired by a man who has skill enough and nerve enough to creep up close enough for a side head shot—and who could then be drunk enough to miss. So think that over. That's why I brought you all the way to this place when you said you wanted a big-game hunt. I wanted you to see what kind of thing was going on in the far ends of your district."

"But—but, dash it all, my dear fellow—" The district commissioner was bewildered—"how—who would be so lunatic as all that? Besides, no elephant licenses have been granted in this district. This is all under strict conservation."

King laughed harshly.

"Sure, it's under conservation; marked off on your maps and

listed so in your office by an ex-Tommy clerk. You'd fine me a hundred pounds if I shot an elephant without a special permit or in defense of human life. A good ruling. The game needs it, and every decent white man is all for it. A nice piece of legislation—but do you know how many, many loads of first-grade scrivelloes and prime hard Mohammed Ali the Banyan trader shipped out of here last season? All new ivory too; no old buried stuff from some back-jungle chief's hoard."

District commissioners of East Africa are lords paramount over territories as large as many an American State and control the destinies of several hundred scattered white men and a few million blacks. They represent the might and majesty of empire. But the D.C. took the thrust at official routine functioning meekly. His half mutterings were defensive.

"Huge district—not very accessible outpost—some confusion since Patterson's death. And the new game warden was—"

King's incisive interruption shocked him out of his excuses for the unwieldiness of imperial administration.

"And what did Patterson die of? What did your office record say about that? Dysentery, they wrote it down, I suppose. And I'll bet they commented in a neat, round hand, 'inaccessibility to competent medical attention', and 'much to be regretted,' et cetera and what not."

King shoved his hands deep into his breeches pockets and stood wide-legged, frowning moodily into the far heat haze. His voice darkened with his face.

"Well, maybe it was. Dysentery is easy enough to get, God knows. Only that Patterson knew as much about dysentery as most of the medicos around here; knew it at first hand, like I do. And in the 'confusion' after his dying, two tons of ivory went out of here."

"Good God!" The D.C. stared at him, wide-eyed. "What frightful thing are you hinting at, Kingi Bwana? What do you know about Patterson's death? If any crime has been covered up you must—"

King flared out at him.

"Aa-ah! I'm not one of your damned policemen. None of all this is any of my business. I'm not even one of your people. Just a 'bally Yankee safari conductor', as more than one of your snooty colonists has tried to rub it in on me. I don't know a durn thing about it. I've never seen any of the crowd running this racket; they're too smart. I know only what you white rulers of the land laugh at—native talk, gossip around my camp-fires, chatter that comes to me just because I'm not one of you, because I don't high-hat my men. I've shown you what's going on. Now sic your new game-warden onto it."

The D.C.'s face clouded to match King's.

"Ah, the new game-warden—Young Ponsonby." He shook his head helplessly. "I wasn't at all keen on his appointment. But his people are very influential at home. A younger son, you know, something of a scapegrace. So they shipped him out; and—-I'm afraid he has never known what a real job means."

He shook his head again over the difficulties and entanglements of official expediency.

"Well—" King had no trace of sympathy with anything official—"that's your hard luck—and his. Or maybe it's all yours. Anyway, he isn't camping out along the lone water-holes, running his chance of getting 'dysentery'. He's playing polo at his headquarters station and dancing attendance on your civil surgeon's newly imported flapper niece. Aa-ah, blaa! What's the use?"

King blew his indignation from him windily through his high-bridged nose. Then he shrugged and grinned.

"That's more native gossip. You don't have to believe any of it. It's none of my affair. But I've shown you this much; and it's up to you to halloo your young scion of Milord Whoozis on to attending to the job his influential folks sent him out for. And you can tell him, as my best tip-off, that he's up against one wise and tough *hombre* that's the leader of this crowd. You don't know it yet, Commish Bwana, but I'm telling you, gang methods have arrived in your colony. This is a crowd that's out to scoop the cream of its filthy racket, and it's not only defenseless game they'll shoot on sight."

"Good Lord, Kingi Bwana, you talk in the most casual manner of the most desperate things! Why, if anything were to happen to young Ponsonby, relatives would rise upon their hind legs in the House of Lords and would demand an investigation into the whole process of government in this colony."

King remained callously unimpressed. For things to happen to foolish white men was their fate in Africa. Other white men would replace them.

"Probably be a good thing for us common herd in the colony if something would happen to him. Maybe you could put in a warden who'd protect the game. You'll need a man who knows the country, who's as clever as a leopard, and who has half the nerve in all Africa to buck this crowd."

The district commissioner took King by the arm.

"Kingi Bwana," he told him with rueful conviction, "you are a masterless man and a blasphemer of sacrosanct things. You talk to me in a way that some of my subordinates would give a month's pay to hear. Take me back to camp, and keep on talking. I need some help. But easy with your mechanical robot legs; my knees are still limp from watching that terrific brute charge down on us."

King fell into a long stride that doubled the commissioner's labored ones through the stiff bunch grass.

"Sure, I'll help you. I'll tell you all I know. Two tons of ivory the Banyan trader smuggled out in his last load. At a pound sterling per pound, London market, that stacks up into money enough to attract some brains into the racket. There's plenty of your ex-soldier land-bounty settlers who have brains and don't figure to ever make that money out of honest farming in their lifetimes. And maybe your office clerks have notes on some of them who they think won't stick at anything. Sort 'em over. Stick your shiny new game-warden on to sleuthing them down."

"I'll need more help than that, Kingi."

"I can give you some more, at that. From camp-fire gossip I figure there's some half-dozen of them in the game; and from tracks that I've seen I can tell you that this particular guy who's shooting around here treads his right foot pigeon-toed. But you don't have to worry about him. No man can go fooling around elephants with a bottle on his hip. An elephant will get him all right. No guessing about that. You don't have to worry about any of them; they're just shooters—maybe man-killers too, if they're interfered with. But you must concentrate on the big shot who's organized them. He's the man to get before your warden gets 'dysentery'."

The D.C. stared at King as at a man who speaks of horrific things without turning a hair. Which, as a matter of fact was exactly so. Like all white hunters, the griefs of government officials were no affair of King's; they drew fat salaries to compensate them against the hazards of pioneer living that the lone hunter man had to accept as a part of the mere matter of keeping alive.

"You talk casually, my Kingi, of apprehending miscreants whom it would be dangerous to approach and against whom it would be extremely difficult to prove anything."

"You *make* it difficult," King snorted in his disgust. "You minions of the law and order want proof that'll stand in one of your courts. Baloney! These guys are rustlers pure and simple. You've got to send your man out to round 'em up and treat 'em like rustlers."

The D.C. walked half a mile in silence. Then he said:

"Kingi Bwana, you've told me the kind of man I need for this job. I know just one such man. I appoint you chief game-warden of this district with all the salary and emoluments that go with the position."

KING STOPPED dead in his long stride.

"Me?" he crowed his derision. "You want me to shove my face into this gang racket? And write reports and keep mileage

records and fill two pages of your office file with a long story
every time somebody takes a shot at me? No sir-ree! Not me!
I'm a free man. I'm contracted to you for another two weeks,
and then I'm my own boss, and I don't have to write letters to
anybody's office clerks and have 'em write back and ask why I
didn't mention how come I fired away twenty-three cartridges
'stead of my allowance of twenty."

King spread his shoulders and breathed deeply, crinkling his
nose to the sultry air.

"Nossir, Mister Commissioner. You can't appoint me any
bloated government plutocrat with a dinky office in Malende.
I'm a conductor of safari. 'To conduct Mr. G. Williamson and—
or—his party,' my contract reads..... 'to lead him to hunting
grounds as detailed in permit.... to protect him at all times
from danger contingent to, or arising in connection with,
sport,'... and so on and so on. I know your government contract
form for white hunters by heart, if you don't. It's hard and tough
enough on hunters; but you can't buy me into government
servitude."

The D.C. trudged another quarter-mile, immersed in
thought. Then:

"Two more weeks is it?" He smiled wickedly. "During which
you must conduct me wherever I want to go; and, 'should client
be unable, for any reason, to conclude the term of his contract,
balance of term must be paid, as agreed; but the hunter shall
hold himself at the disposal of client'—or words to that effect,
You see, my insurgent Kingi, I happen to have read some of our
official forms. Therefore—" the smile became diabolic—"you
will conduct me to my headquarters and leave me there. You
will then repair to Malende and take the new game-warden
out in my place. And you will exert every care to protect him,
etc. etc."

All the cocksure independence vanished from King's de-
meanor. He looked almost frightened.

"Aw now, Commish Bwana," he pleaded. "I don't want to

sheep-herd this milk-and-white dude of yours around the thorn scrub. Why, gosh durn it, he hasn't even had time to get sunburned yet; and, from what I hear, he's steadier holding a tea cup than a rifle, and his blood is so blue there can't be any room left for red."

The D.C. was inexorable—and serious.

"You, my Kingi, are a masterless man who will never understand, nor appreciate, the needs—nor duties of colonial administration. The youngster must be broken in."

"But I'm telling you, Commish, this is a mighty unhealthy district for game-wardens during the next couple months. You'll be sending your son of your best old families to get well slaughtered."

"You, my Kingi, will exercise every precaution to protect him at all times, et cetera, et cetera, as your contract reads—and to the best of your ability too. I think it says."

"The hell with the needs of your colonial government," growled King. "You're out to get me murdered, keeping my contract."

"Yes, Kingi Bwana. My office is full of complaints against you from angry officials who clamor that you flout all constituted authority. But you keep your agreements. Two weeks with you will be very good for young Ponsonby. I shall write him a confidential order by runner."

MALENDE, THEREFORE, saw a disgruntled Kingi Bwana and his wizened little Hottentot servant looking for Ponsonby while the compact safari camp waited in charge of the great Masai a mile or so outside of the settlement.

Ponsonby, if not in his quarters, would likely be in the club. It has been said that where as many as three Englishmen are there will be a club. In these outlying district stations in East Africa, which have perhaps not more than half a dozen official residents, but are nevertheless centers of a far-flung white settler population, there is always a club; a frame building consisting at least of a billiard room, a mixed bridge room and maybe one or two others, but principally of a wide veranda in which cold fizzy drinks can be served to tired white men in long cane chairs.

Ponsonby was there, a tall young man, impeccable in a tussore silk suit. He had a petulantly aristocratic face; not weak, but distinctly spoiled. King, dressed in a faded khaki shooting coat and shorts, efficient bush clothing, eyed him with distaste.

But Ponsonby was traditionally hospitable.

"Oh, Mister King, is it? What will you drink? I've been expecting you. The D.C. wrote me."

With a certain resentment he took a letter from his breast pocket and handed it to King. Couched in the farcial formality of colonial officialdom, it "had the honour to inform him" that he would consider himself under the orders of Mister King until further notice; and it "remained his obedient servant," the district commissioner.

King's thin grin came out. Good old D.C., making things easy that way. And, in a time of stress it seemed that he was not so afraid of influential relatives.

But King slowly tore the letter into little pieces and dropped them into an empty glass. He looked very steadily at Ponsonby.

"I don't work that way," he told him. "I don't like to take orders from any man; and I don't expect anybody else to like them. If a man can't work *with* me I'd just as soon not have him along."

Ponsonby's angry eyes lifted over his glass rim in a dawning surprise. This, coming from this hard-looking man, required time to assimilate. Embarrassed by a national incoherence under emotion, he mumbled vague sounds that resolved themselves into. "Umm, er, awf'ly decent. Ah—have a drink, what? And sit."

But King drove uncompromisingly to the point for which he had come.

"How soon d'you figure you could be ready to start?"

"Well, er—I was hoping to play against the Planters next week; but—"

"Yeh, I guessed somp'n like that. But how soon would you figure on getting down to your job?"

"Why, er—" Ponsonby's pink-and-white English complexion, untouched as yet by African sun, flushed. His petulant mouth bit down on his speech. "Damnitall, since you put it that way, I'd say any time you're ready."

King shook his head.

"I'm ready now. But I'll say tomorrow at dawn for you."

He was not making it any too easy. But he explained: "The D.C. tells me you'll be needing to cover as much ground as you can. So I've cut out porters and I'm figuring to travel by light truck. Cramped, but we can make it all right in this dry season, and I'll he able to show you at least a couple of the water-holes in two weeks' time. After that, if you're going to tackle the job, you'll have just six weeks to work.

"If you want to throw in with me you'll need your oldest clothes; and I'll have no room for an extra camp boy. You'll find mine more efficient in the bush anyhow. We'll not be picnicking."

White men in Africa become accustomed to their own servants. Some—the more sartorially inclined—grow to be quite helpless without the dark familiar spirit to whom they relegate their intimate personal needs, down even to the matter of pulling off their boots and stockings and finding their toothbrushes. And in the confusion of a safari camp—Good Lord!

It was unfortunate that at this strained moment another white man lurched up the shallow veranda steps. A broadly built, untidy looking man, scrubby-chinned; the very antithesis of Ponsonby's perfection. A hardy type of outlying settler. Dust, and a pistol strapped to his belt, showed that he had just come in from the bush, and his brusque shoving past King was evidence that the road had been long and conducive of liquid stimulant.

A rough and uncouth denizen for a club that sheltered a Ponsonby. But in little district clubs where white men are few membership rules must of necessity be broad. Ponsonby had a hot answer ready for King. But his British trait of keeping his personal affairs strictly personal choked it down to a short, "How do," to the stranger.

But the settler man seemed to have an alcoholic chip on his shoulder. Ponsonby's cool dressiness, in contrast with his own dusty workaday costume, aroused a latent class resentment. He stared red-eyed at the young man.

"Ho!" he said, and there was a nasty edge of insinuation in his Cockney twang. "The nice new gaime-warden a-settin' cushy to 'is tea with nothin' ter do."

Ponsonby remained seated, aristocratically calm.

"Attending strictly to my own business, thank you."

"Ow indeed. It's many o' the likes o' us would wish we 'ad such a heasy business."

The man's rudeness was quite uncalled for. But King could understand the antagonism of a hard-working planter, or whatever the man might be, to the easy security of an official. He stood impartially aside. This was none of his business; and it was an unexpected opportunity to observe how this foppish young man would react to insult.

Kaffa, the little Hottentot, who had been squatting, blanket-swathed in the broiling sun, stood, up and began to scratch himself with the sudden vehemence of an infested ape—with quite unnecessary vehemence. King knew that the cunning monkey's eyes missed nothing and he knew his habits well enough to understand that the little man wanted to attract attention to himself. He moved to the veranda rail to watch him.

The Hottentot postured and scratched grotesquely. Always down toward his right foot. His bright round eyes, instead of watching his own activities, flitted to his master's and then to the belligerent stranger.

King under lowered lids looked the man over. And then he got what he had missed in his absorption in the argument.

The man's right foot turned pigeon-toed.

King's eyelids flickered and went narrow. That track that he had seen around by the water-holes where the elephants drank had been pigeon-toed. Nothing very unusual in that; but that, too, had been the right foot. Still nothing very unusual. Any man who knew tracks knew that many people had that idiosyncrasy in one foot or the other.

Nothing very definite to go on—not by any means "evidence" of anything at all. But—

King watched the man. He still remained aloof. Coldly aloof. He was no nursemaid of pink-cheeked officials—not yet. The man was rough and powerfully built—maybe dangerous. If he should perhaps beat this game-warden so that he might not be able to travel with tomorrow's dawn it was still none of King's affair—might save him a great deal of bother.

But all his faculties were focused on the man, on his every action. Alcoholically quarrelsome—that would fit in with the unknown hunter. Unprovokedly belligerent against a youngster who, far from giving offense, had merely been polite—could it be for no other reason than that this was a game-warden, as had been Patterson, who died of—whatever it was?

So absorbed was King that he did not hear what the man said. But Ponsonby was slowly getting up. With nice care he set his glass down. Half turned from the man, he said in a politely conversational tone:

"You wouldn't want to repeat that, would you?"

Instantly the man did. A foolish word of little meaning; but one which the convention of the English public schools has ruled to be a fighting word.

Ponsonby walked up to the man, quite slowly, buttoned the lowest button of his silk jacket, and hit him squarely over the mouth.

Inexpertly, but with the well-bred heartiness of one going through a necessary ceremony, as much as to say:

"Now, come what may, we must fight."

The blow rocked the man back on his heels; more on account of its surprise than by its force. But it was sufficient to gash his lip.

It brought no ceremonious response from him; no gentlemanly squaring off for formal fisticuffs according to amateur rules. The likes of him had not been brought up in that school. Moreover he was just on the edge of being drunk, and in that condition he seemed to be a man of a demoniac temper.

WITH THE first spurt of blood from his lip he screamed an incoherent noise and tugged at the pistol at his belt. Ponsonby stood paralyzed at so startling a reversal of everything proper.

But there was nothing new and unexpected in this sort of thing to King. He jumped like a great tawny cat, reaching for the man's pistol hand. His grip closed on it; and the maniac instantly turned, snarling, upon his interference.

He was burly and thick-muscled. But his own surprise was coming to him. He swung ferocious blows with his free left hand at King. The pistol, shoved high, fired through the veranda ceiling. The man, gibbering rage, pushed in breast to breast and tried to match his strength against King's to force the gun down. King let the man struggle, till, presently finding his opportunity, he dragged the imprisoned arm over his shoulder, slipping his hip under the other's body and heaving him cartwheeling over the low veranda rail. The gun remained in King's hand.

The man fell on his head in the dusty marigold bed that bordered the building front, where he rolled and sprawled ruinously.

Instantly in a gorilloid rush the Hottentot crouched over him.

"Do I slay him, Bwana?"

King shook his head. "We are in the presence of the *serkali* that rules such things by law; not in the bush."

The man struggled to his feet and wobbled round the angle of the house.

"A man," King commented after him "not hampered by any inhibitions Looks like he fills the bill. But we can't prove a thing on him. Nor he isn't smart enough to be the big shot. Anyway I'm glad I know what he looks like."

He swung round to Ponsonby.

"What," he asked him bluntly, "are you going to do about him?"

Ponsonby faced King as though rebutting in advance an accusation.

"I could turn him over to the sergeant constable for attempted felonious assault with a deadly weapon. But I won't. This is my private affair."

A thin gleam of approval came into King's eyes. Slowly he began to nod.

"Maybe," he ruminated half aloud. "Maybe, dammitall, you have the makin's."

Of which Ponsonby could understand much less than nothing.

"So then," King continued. "Let's get back to what we were talking about. My guess is that you were in half a mind to tell me to go to hell. And to help you make it up I'll tell you that, if my next guess isn't away off, this club member of yours is only a sample of what your job means."

Ponsonby's brows went up in well-bred disgust. To affect nonchalance was his hereditary creed.

"If my blighted relatives insist that I must live in a land where my club fellows are like this, I suppose I shall have to bally well learn to save my life for myself. And really—looking at your methods—I'm sure I couldn't find a better teacher. So let's let it stand for dawn tomorrow—and er—thanks, old man."

"It's funny stuff," said King, "but sometimes it has the makin's."

"What is? What has?" asked Ponsonby, mystified and wholly serious.

"Blue blood," said King. "But you won't understand. Like your chief says, I'll never understand the duties of colonial administration—something mixed up with a holy thing you Britishers have, called the service of empire. But I'll take your drink now, and sit. There's a plenty of more important things for you to understand about this business—like, for instance, keeping alive during your next few weeks. Patterson was a good man; but they got him."

It was a modest little *safari* that King had arranged for the breaking in of dude Ponsonby. Almost meager—and purposely so. This was no pleasure trip for millionaire sports who bought with their lavish money all the luxury of tent boys and cook boys and personal boys and canned delicacies and a moving-picture man.

King had clients like that too. They came and they got their trophies—or King got them for them—and they went home and told their tales of hardship and danger. Good people; gold mines necessary to the existence of licensed white hunters.

But this was a serious business of finding out whether a man might be fit for the job of protecting the game. King was at no time a nursemaid for incompetents. If his own time and effort must go into the thing, make or break must be the result.

So the outfit consisted of a simple ton-and-a-half truck. Most of the space was devoted to five gallon drums of gasoline and to necessary spare parts and supplies. The big Masai and the Hottentot clung where they could on top of the pile. With them, aloof and very superior, huddled a Nairobi native who rated himself as an auto mechanic and considered therefore that he should do no other work. But the other two knew better than that.

Ponsonby rode on the driver's seat beside King. King, a stubby pipe stuck into the corner of his mouth, maneuvered the car in and out between the spiny mimosa trees and around—or through—the dongas, steep-sided gullies left by the fury of last season's rain. His eyes scouted far ahead and, with a certitude quite incomprehensible to Ponsonby, picked out a route that never caught him in a blind alley of impassable thorn.

With a quick motion of his lips, he shifted his pipe, as if it might have been a cigar, to the other side of his mouth so as to speak to Ponsonby on his left.

"Your chief stuck me with this job because I showed him something. I'm going to show you something worse."

"Yes? What is it?" Ponsonby gasped between spasms of jolting as the truck climbed stiff grass tussocks and slammed down into the dusty hollows.

"You'll see." King bit angrily on his pipe. "We'll set up camp presently and then we'll have to walk a while. That polo outfit your oldest clothes?"

"Oh, quite. That is to say, my oldest sports clothes."

King smiled his anticipation. They left the car in the shade of an acacia grove. The mechanic's function was to act as watchman and to see to it that there would be sufficient dry fire-wood collected by the time the others came back.

The four of them set out on foot. The Masai, magnificently naked, led. Low thorn bush rasped against his legs, leaving dusty white scratches upon their rough hide. Then came King, in pigskin leggings and shorts, his own bare knees as horny as the Masai's. Behind him were Ponsonby and the Hottentot.

Fine dust swirled from the thorn scrub as the men's legs brushed through. It caked with the sweat that drenched their clothes. Down steep gully sides; along sandy bottoms where leopard tracks preceded them for aimless miles; up gravelly banks; more thorn scrub.

King's ears told him of Ponsonby's progress behind him. Not looking back, he remarked:

"Kinder tough on those shiny riding boots, isn't it?"

"Why, yes," Ponsonby panted. "But it's worse on my riding breeches."

"Uh-huh," grunted King. "Figured so."

Not till half a mile further did he look back. Ponsonby's shiny boots were furry with tiny nicks; the closely tailored breeches had shredded clear away; the knees were raw and bleeding.

"Holy gosh!" King surveyed the spectacle. "Hell, I didn't know those valuable things were that fragile. You should have yelped before this."

Ponsonby was grateful to stop. "I—er—well, the rest of you seemed to be getting along all right; and so—er, so I—"

King's grunted commendation was enigmatic to Ponsonby. "The blood comes redder'n I thought." From his frayed shooting-coat pocket he produced a pair of long strips of closely woven cloth. "I've seen this happen before," he said caustically, as expertly he wound them, puttee-wise, round Ponsonby's lacerated knees. "But durned if I've ever seen such frail and fancy pants. This'll slow you up some; but it's not far now."

A few minutes brought them to a litter of scattered bones; only the heavier ones intact, the rest—and amazingly thick ones at that—marred and cracked by the tremendous teeth of hyenas.

"ELEPHANT," SAID King shortly to Ponsonby's stare. "And worse than what I showed the D.C."

He pointed with his toe to a great flat plate of bone.

"Shoulder blade. D'you notice anything damnable about it?"

"Why, er—I suppose these are bullet holes."

"Yep." King's voice was throaty with anger. "And could you guess what kind of bullets would make a neat row of holes like that all in a line?"

"I should almost say—good God, you don't mean to tell me that was a machine-gun!"

"Right! You're damn right. And that shows you the filthy kind of crowd this is."

"Why, good Lord!" Ponsonby was genuinely shocked. "How

foully unsportsmanlike! That's—By Jove, that's as bad as shoot-ing a fox."

King flashed a look at him; but the man was staring in re-pugnance. King agreed with him dryly:

"Yeh, as bad as shooting a fox in your country. And the way I understand you view-halloo people look at it, that comes pretty near worse than shooting a man. Which it is, 'cause a man can shoot back. You've got the right idea, fella. Damned if I don't believe you've got the makin's."

He scowled moodily at the splintered bone.

"It takes guts and it takes skill to drop an elephant clean with a rifle. One of them, we know, has at least the guts. But the rest of the filthy gang cut loose with artillery. And—" he swung round to look squarely at Ponsonby—"it's a whole game-war-den's job to stop 'em."

Ponsonby stared at him, pale and wide-eyed. He sucked in his lower lip and bit on it so that it went white. Then he nodded.

"If you'll help me."

King's grin broke slowly over his face.

"Well, I'm stuck with the chore for two weeks," he agreed. "Come on back to camp and I'll tell you what we're up against. I'm guessing a good deal; but here's how I lay it out."

With unsparing detail as they went along he outlined his theory.

"This gang, the way I figure it, aren't hunters, all but one of 'em. Not even farmers. Town riff-raff that survived the war and took their bonus in land grants—Colonial Empire that your government preached 'em. Well, they came out and went up against drought and locusts and tsetse fly, and they hadn't the experience nor the backbone to pull through."

"Yes. A lot of them came back, soured and sore, and went Red."

"Some of 'em stayed. Back-alley rats; misfits in the big open country. Then the game conservation department down at Nairobi decreed a rest period for this district. Complete prohibition except for certain over-stocked species. A durn good thing. Every decent white man conformed. Till now some smart gent has figured there's a quick clean-up in ivory and hides. He organized a gang, and they've already got some. But the next few weeks will be the cream."

"Why more than any other time?"

King scowled across the heat haze as at a mirage picture that curled his nostrils in disgust.

"The tail-end of the dry season. The smaller water-holes are drying up. Game will be concentrating around those that are left—places like Unduli Pan and Magimagi. Everything—elephants, rhino, antelope, everything there is in Africa all in one place; all thirsty; and, even when they're scared away, all bound to come back. With the first break of the rains, they'll scatter all over the landscape; but until then, the last six weeks, they're like tied hand and foot. That isn't hunting any more; it's murder. These swine aren't hunters. But the war taught 'em how to use a machine-gun. They'll clean the district like a stock-yard. Ivory, horns, hide, anything that has a commercial value."

King's picture was starkly repellent. The prospect of his share of the "duties of colonial administration" opened up more grimly before Ponsonby with each new thing that he learned about it. Still the tradition of his caste to make light of danger was uppermost. He contrived a wry smile.

"By Jove, that reminds me I've never been so dead for a drink. And d'you know, my people pulled strings and sent me out to this job because they said I was doing no good at home, and here would be nothing to do and plenty of sport."

King added the last inexorable detail.

"And there's nothing to stop 'em—except the game-warden."

Ponsonby walked on in silence. "And Kingi Bwana," he amended.

King's answering grin was twisted.

"Yeh—for two weeks. And a sweet chore I'm stuck with. Poor old Patterson is proof that this crowd isn't sticking over anything in their way. And there's a good half-dozen of 'em; maybe more." He strode on, scowling. "There's just one hope we've got. These are town crooks; cunning rats, but they don't know the bush. It'll be bush lore against machine-guns."

Ponsonby's question was a despairing cry for help.

"If you feel the way you do about the game why can't you stay for more than two weeks? The D.C. would pay—"

King's hand suddenly on his shoulder stopped him. The camp was in view, the truck showed through the trees, all quiet and undisturbed. But King was peering at it with alert suspicion. With silent pressure he guided Ponsonby behind a tree.

THE GAME-WARDEN, with his new sense of the danger that surrounded his office, tingled to a sense of caution. His voice dropped to a whisper.

"What is it?"

"Funny," King muttered. "Something queer there."

"What is? I don't see anything."

"Look just to the left of the truck. That tall bird."

"That stork sort of a thing? What is funny about it?"

"That's a greater bustard. The best eating on the plains; but much too wily a bird to be so near the camp if there was anybody around. Camp is plumb deserted."

Ponsonby felt his pulse begin to pound.

"You think— What do you think might be the matter?"

King's deft shrug threw his rifle-sling from his shoulder as the weapon smacked neatly into his hands.

"Durned if I know. But I'm taking no chances in this game. You stay right here."

King's quick look called the great Masai and the Hottentot to follow him.

"We're going look see."

"But my dear chap. I can't hide away like this. This is my business and it's my duty to—"

"Duty be damned," King hissed at him, his eyes never off

the distant camp. "You stay right here. My contract calls for me to protect you to the best of my ability and so on and thus next. It's your people made the rules. My reputation as a *safari* conductor can't afford to take risks."

Yet he was already on his cautious way forward, skirmishing from tree to grass tussock to further thorn shrub, the natives like dark shadows behind him. Abruptly they disappeared from view. Ponsonby was left enormously alone with the hot silence of the empty African veldt. A silence empty of all visible, yet full of things that moved, prowled, slunk, unseen.

Danger? Tragedy? Death? What? A silence that dragged on to slow aeons.

Then the far snap of a pistol shot. Ponsonby's tense nerves twanged like taut wire. He looked for an instant eruption of struggling figures, of more shots. But only the bird leaped convulsively high in the air with a flutter of wide wings. Then King's tall form moved beyond the car; shouts rang out. He saw the flash of the Masai's spear as he moved through a patch of sun.

Then presently a dark form came scurrying back through the bushes—the mechanic. All the forms merged into a group. The mechanic gesticulated excitedly.

When Ponsonby panted up King was tersely questioning the boy. He gibbered and gesticulated with white rolling eyes and outthrust liver-red lips.

"What did this white man look like? What did he say?"

"He was tall. Yet Bwana, not so tall. He was bearded. That is to say, bearded not more than four of five days. He was dressed like—like a white man. He demanded drink. He beat me near to death, Bwana. But I escaped and fled into the bush."

That was the only thing that was definite. A white man had come in a quarrelsome mood and, African-like, the boy had bolted into the bush.

King shrugged his helplessness. "There's Africa for you. Dumb, blind, panicky. Damnation! I wish it had been one of my own men. Kaffa would have outwitted him and Barounggo would have speared him."

"What—who do you think he was? What did he come for—and not stay?"

King barked a short laugh. "This is Africa. No white man's movements are secret. Particularly not yours just now—and mine. Still, if one of them had the nerve to come, why wouldn't he stay to make his play? A friendly visitor would have stayed." His eyes flickered suspiciously into the surrounding bush. "That crowd wouldn't hesitate to bushwhack us."

The Hottentot who had been scurrying around, questing like a dog, yelped his sudden find.

"Ha, Kaffa. Good apeling. What hast thou?" King hurried to him.

The little man was squatting over a patch of ground free of grass. With a skinny finger he pointed. Among the boot tracks in the dust were two within striding distance of each other—and one of them turned pigeon-toed!

King swore softly. On hands and knees he groveled with the Hottentot to find confirmatory trail. He went back to Ponsonby whistling tunelessly through his teeth, his eyes very narrow and hard.

"Trailed." He gave him the cold news. "Trailed from the moment we left Malende." And with grim meaning: "The game-warden is out on the job and the gang is losing no time. Still, what the devil was this play?"

The color ebbed from Ponsonby's heated face, but he said: "Quite complimentary, I'd call so much attention, what?"

"Your friend," King told him. "Pigeon Toe. He demanded drink. That about identifies him—though, damnitall, any man would do that after a hike through the bush."

That suggestion reminded Ponsonby of his own need that the excitement had temporarily driven from him. He reached to the rickety camp table upon which stood a sparklet syphon and a half full bottle of whisky.

"Aa-ah!" The ejaculation rasped from King's throat and he snatched the bottle. "Perhaps that's the answer."

Ponsonby raised his eyebrows. "What is? Dash it all, I never met anybody so full of surprises."

"You'll get your plenty," said King "before you get home—if you ever do. What I just said: to reach for a drink would be the first thing any man would do, coming in from a hike; and he wouldn't stop to investigate much." His own narrow eyes bored cold gray into Ponsonby's wide blue ones. "Maybe that's how Game Warden Patterson got his—dysentery."

"Good God!" This came close enough to home at last to jolt the nonchalance out of Ponsonby. His affectation of languid interest was charged with white-eyed horror. "Good God, you don't mean—"

King nodded slowly.

"Patterson never got whatever it was that he died of by accident. He knew too much about Africa to take chances with impure water or anything like that. I guess that was his whole trouble. He was on the job and he knew too much."

GENERATIONS OF tradition ebbed back out of Ponsonby's past to steady him. He swallowed a few times and licked dry lips; but his voice, when it came was natural—not drawlingly humorous, but sober.

"That's a frightful suspicion to have against any man. They may be poaching and all that—beastly unsportsmanlike and so on. But this—Good Lord, this would be murder."

"Maybe, brother, maybe. But I'm taking no chances. I never take chances." King up-ended the bottle and let the liquor gurgle onto the thirsty ground.

"Don't do that!" Ponsonby reached for the bottle; but too late. "Ah, pshaw! Now we'll have no evidence. We may know who the man is—might even identify him with the tracks, with the native boy's identification in a court. But we have no proof of anything on which to convict him."

"Yeah?" King rasped his impatience. "You'd want to drag a

man like that into a court, would you? Just like your chief. You people are so bred to law and order that you can't understand you're up against a crowd that'll stop at nothing. You're not safe in your tight little island now. You're in big country; hard country; and let me tell you there's some hard men in the outlying corners of it."

Ponsonby was willing to concede much to this man who seemed to know so exactly what he was about. But his tradition of lawfulness was as difficult to disturb as any other. He mumbled something to that effect.

"Listen." King seated himself on a camp chair and filled his pipe to help him reason patiently with tradition. "This is none of my affair. I'm in it for two weeks, and then there'll be nobody gladder than me to get out in a hurry. But if you want to live you've got to get this straight."

He flipped a grub-box key to the Hottentot and ordered him to bring a fresh bottle of whisky with an unbroken seal and some of the bottled soda that he carried against the contingency of finding a water-hole too befouled by animals for use. He lit his pipe and growled through the smoke.

"Listen. Take this much flat, without argument. Like I told the D.C., gang methods have arrived in your colony. Town rats with machine-guns organized to a racket for some quick money. The only one who seems to know the bush is this Pigeon Toe; for which you be good and mighty thankful."

Ponsonby was all agreement.

"Granted, my dear chap. I believe everything you say. So I must—we must arrest them and—"

"*We* must?" King blew derisive smoke. "You can't drag me into any official heroics. Listen some more. In my country we used to try to arrest our gangsters and bring them to the law. Our officers were shot down in their scores by gunmen whom they didn't know but knew them by their uniforms—just like this crowd whom we don't know, knows you—and me, durn it. Our gangs had a swell time; they came to pretty near run the country. You Europeans jeered at us about it. But we've learned. We're figuring at last our officers are more valuable than our gangsters, and at last we're giving 'em a free hand to take no chances. So we're getting the gangs. You want to arrest these rats and haul 'em to a law court. O.K., that's maybe your 'duty of colonial administration'. Me, I figure I'm more valuable than an ivory poacher. That's one reason why I'm getting out of this mess when my two weeks are up. So if you want to quit and go home, now that you know what it's all about, that'll release my contract; and nobody gladder."

The exposition of the situation was cold-blooded and unsparing. King watched Ponsonby shrewdly. Make or break. King's interest was in a warden competent to guard the game. Either this youngster would come through or break.

Ponsonby's eyes were hunted. They looked at King—not at the man; at the picture of his words; a hopeless picture of lone-handed inexperience against he could not quite visualize what, but something ruthless. He fingered his rifle nervously. His eyes wandered over the landscape, the vast trackless bush, miles upon miles of thorny shrubs—under any one of which a man's bones might lie and dessicate and never be found. His eyes came back to King. His lip was white under his teeth. His voice dry.

"Perhaps we—we would get something done before your two weeks are up."

King's slow smile crept up behind his eyes and slowly he nodded.

"Perhaps *we* could," he agreed this time. "If you don't plumb throw away your life on fool chances. And here's something that'll maybe help your conscience."

He pointed with his toe. His eyes that had followed Ponsonby's roving gaze had focused themselves warily on a far point in the bush. Narrow again; and alert as a leopard's, they watched something. His toe pointed to the smudge of moisture where he had emptied the bottle. An insect lay on its back amongst the sparse grass roots at its edge. Specks that were ants remained unwontedly still. Eyes less observant than King's would never have noticed them.

"Would you consider that sound evidence that somebody had been interested in doping the new game-warden's drink?"

Ponsonby stared, white-faced, as what had been suspicion became cold certainty.

"And if a man came skulking around the bush after that, would you consider it lawful evidence that he was the man, come to see how it worked?"

Ponsonby nodded, puzzled. "Any court would consider it highly circumstantial."

"And if he had a gun would you count it a good bet that he had no inhibitions about finishing what he started?" King's hand was stealing round behind his chair to where his rifle leaned.

"Why yes, I certainly—. King, what is this you're driving at?"

King rose softly to his feet and edged behind a tree, his rifle ready.

"Then you better take cover; 'cause there's somebody who fills the bill snooping round back of that tambuki grass belt."

PONSONBY FOUND himself behind a tree—not through any conscious volition of his own. His pulse pounded in his head. The stark conditions of his job were piling home on him with a vengeance. He knew all the desperate emotions of the hunted.

"Have we permission, *bwana?*" The Masai, lying flat on the ground with the other natives below the bush screen, rolled fierce, eager eyes to his master.

King nodded. The Masai laughed softly and, bending low, ducked into the scrub. In a moment his great form was lost to view. Not a motion of bush tops showed his passage.

The Hottentot threw off his blanket. Beneath it was revealed his extraordinary shape, as naked and as muscular as a chimpanzee, armed with an immense Somali knife. He scuttled off in another direction, spreading out to get the marauder between them.

They were amazing to Ponsonby, these men, pitting their steel and sheer jungle craft against a firearm that lurked cautiously somewhere out in that grass belt.

He stared out at it from behind his tree with a tight prickly feeling of tragedy hanging imminent and inevitable. Whichever way it went, somebody would die. He had never seen violent death before.

The distant grass moved. Cautiously a rifle barrel emerged; then a head and shoulder. Tragedy was unfolding itself before his fascinated gaze. Which of those stalking men would it pick? He wanted to yell a warning.

And then his heart came up into his mouth. The rifle was pointing, not at some unseen thing in the bush, but in his own direction. Good God, at himself!

The primal instinct of self-preservation was older than any tradition of lawful process. He threw up his rifle and fired. Out in the tall grass a khaki-clad arm flung into view. The rifle flew from it. Both disappeared. A thin yellow haze of dust floated up.

Ponsonby's rifle remained at his shoulder, stiff and rigid. He stared out at the slowly settling dust, hypnotized by the suddenness of what he had done.

King's voice broke through the dizziness that buzzed in his head.

"Damned if he hasn't got the good makin's." Like a faraway picture, out of focus, there was King walking toward him.

"You've been learning somewhere or other to shoot off a rifle, feller."

"Why yes, I, er—I've done some—Have I killed him, d'you think?"

King was radiating good will. "If you haven't, the Masai will—unless Kaffa rounds him up first. But I think you've got one dumb bushwhacker out of the gang. Let's go see. But careful; he may be smart enough to play possum; though, by his clumsiness, I doubt it."

They found both the natives squatting over a huddled shape in a faded khaki uniform.

"It is not the crooked-footed one," the Hottentot announced. "But his gun is of the best kind and he had nine cartridges and a hunting-knife, not so good; but some good tobacco, and—"

King cut short the itemized list. "Yeh, I guessed it wouldn't be Pigeon Toe. He'd be too smart to be got so easy. This is some dumb gorilla who didn't know so much about the bush; just mean enough to be a killer. It's our luck the rest are like him. It's Pigeon Toe that's really dangerous; though even he isn't the big shot."

He turned to his two henchmen.

"Take up the trail and read the story of it swiftly before dark." To Ponsonby he said: "If we don't have to up and run for it, we'll let our good mechanic bury this. If we do have to, the hyenas will attend to the evidence of your lawlessness as efficiently as they did to Patterson."

Ponsonby stared at him. He was constantly finding cause to stare at King.

"You wouldn't run away from them?"

"If some half a dozen more like this gunman would be around somewhere? Would I durn well not! I've got no duty of administering your colony. I'm guiding you through the hoops; and I've never had a client killed on me yet."

He led the silent Ponsonby back to the camp. His heart was warming to this youngster whose aristocratic relatives thought he was coming to no good at home.

"Don't pull such a long face about it," he told him. "That was a nice piece of shooting you did there: fast and clean. That leaves one less gunman to get."

Ponsonby reverted to his despairing cry of a while earlier.

"Two weeks is a desperately short time. I'll be lost like a babe in the woods when you go. Dash it all, why can't you carry on if you're so keen about saving the game?"

King was more disposed to explanation of his actions than he had been.

"I told you one reason; I'm not hiring out as a policeman to buck this mob according to your law-book of rules. I'm too plain scared of them."

"Don't spoof." Ponsonby said. "This is serious."

"Well, I am too." King insisted doggedly. "But there's another reason. I'm tied up. Contracted to take Major Devanter of Malende on *safari* as soon as I'm through with this D.C. deal."

"I might have supposed you jolly well would be," said Ponsonby miserably. "I've heard it said that Kingi Bwana is a valuable man. But I didn't know that this Major Devanter was a sportsman."

In the emphasis upon the title there was a subtle censure of those ex-wartime officers who clung to their rank in civil life.

"He isn't," said King. "He's a rank tyro. But it seems he's wanted to for a long time; and he contracted me early this spring. I'd have preferred to take him some other time; but no other time would suit him."

"Con-demnit! *Must* he have you? He's an old-timer here. He ought to bally well know you wouldn't let him go round shooting the water-holes at this season."

"Guess perhaps he does know. But he doesn't want to shoot here. He wants to go way out Tadyeni way after sable antelope. A damnfool trip I think; but I can't let him down." King grinned mirthlessly. "It's one of your good governmental regulations that a white hunter breaking contract can have his license revoked and can be 'fined or otherwise disciplined at the discretion of the local administrative officer'. That would be you."

"He might release you." Ponsonby did not sound very hopeful.

"I can't ask him. He's made all his preparations months ahead, fixed his business for a holiday, got his licenses, bought outfit and all. That's the reason for your breach of contract ruling. Maybe you could persuade him—or maybe the D.C."

Ponsonby in turn grinned without mirth. Here was this King man, despite his stout insistence of not letting himself be dragged into an official conflict, actually suggesting possible ways and means.

"I wonder," he said. "Maybe the D.C. could. This beastly thing seems to be of sufficient importance for any decent white man to forego even a long-planned trip."

"Wire the D.C.," King decided quickly. "Send a runner with the message to Lembu. That's the nearest line. If he can't twist the sacred regulations to get around Devanter, you'll just have to bow to 'em humble and buck the racket on your own."

Ponsonby looked at King with the dull hopelessness of one upon whom judgment has been passed and whose hope of reprieve is slight. But he made his voice say:

"Be a jolly little party, I expect, while it lasts."

"That," King nodded sententiously, "is the compensation you must pay for the privilege of belonging in a great empire and having duties to impose the white man's peace upon the empty back bush. The gods of Africa don't make it easy for the white man. But I've managed to last. Keep your nerve, and maybe you will too. But you'll have to have help. You can apply to headquarters to have some constabulary assigned; and by the time the six weeks' slaughter is over the order will maybe go through. I'll have Barounggo round up some men for you—not servants; fighting men. Ha! Here come the two of 'em now. I bet you Kaffa has all the news like it'd been written in a picture book."

THE HOTTENTOT screwed up his face and shut his eyes tight. In a singing monotone he began to recite the story, actually as though repeating the pictured word from memory.

"Bwana, there were two men, the crooked foot who came first to the camp and put the *muavi* root juice into the whisky bottle—"

"What's *muavi?* How does he know?"

"Sh-sh!" King hushed Ponsonby. "You mustn't break the reel of his moving picture."

"They came, Bwana, in a *moto* wagon with rubber wheels like Bwana's, but much lighter. Crooked Foot, having put the poison root in the drink, went back to the *moto* wagon and stood talking with that other one who was a fool. Then that other one took his gun and came back alone, as Bwana knows. But the crooked foot was too wise to come—for this other fool, the mechanic, has admitted that he told him this was the camp of the Bwana Kingi.

"So then the crooked foot, hearing the shot, came a little distance to learn what might be. But he feared to come close. At a little distance he stood in doubt for many minutes, resting his gun on the ground. Then fear overtook him and he went back to the *moto* wagon, running, and drove away; fast and far; for we followed a ways and came not up with him. That is all the story, Bwana."

"Hmh!" King grunted. "Just about as I figured him. Clever as a devil. But lacking just the guts to be an out and out gunman. We'll take after him in the morning with the car. If we have luck he may lead us to the gang's hangout; and then, with some good spearmen, bush fighters— But that brings us right back to your own crew. What sort of people have you available?"

"Outside of the office staff, who seem to be queer sort of babu blighters, I believe there are some six or seven native *walinzi* game-keeper johnnies whose real function is to watch out for petty native poaching and who bring in reports. But to tell you the truth, I—" Ponsonby reddened with an embarrassment that he had never known before—"I don't really know an awful lot about the thing."

"Fire them," said King. "I'll get you some fighters."

"But my dear fellow—" This much Ponsonby knew, as did every government employe from the moment of his arrival— "They are government servants, duly approved and appointed under the civil service regulations. They can't be dismissed without proper cause, charges drawn up and substantiated. They can put up a terrific howl; appeal right up to the governor of the colony, and what not."

"Fire 'em," King snapped. "The hell with regulations. Let 'em howl. Get your job done, and point to that while the clerks haggle over red tape."

Ponsonby was inspired to rebellion—he who would not conform to the straitly ruled conventions at home. King's impatience with governmental maneuverings was damningly logical.

"All right, dammit!" he said, "I will. I'll take on your men and let the rest howl at the governor's very gates."

King beamed upon him. An apt pupil. Distinctly a lad with the makin's. "Good for you. I'll have Barounggo pick up some of his own Elmorani, lion slayers." He called the big Masai to him.

"Listen well, Barounggo," he told him. "There is need to exercise thy little wit besides thy brawn. We must select quietly some eight or ten *askaris*, fighting men who are more than fools; for they must pretend to be *walinzi*, servants of the *serkali*, with no loud bragging and shaking of spears. Their pretence I shall judge when I see them. Their valor I leave to thy choosing."

The Masai swelled his great chest. "Bwana," he promised, "Myself I will put them to the test; and they that I shall bring—those who survive—will be warriors."

"Good. Tomorrow, as we travel, circulate amongst the villages."

King found time at last to fish out his pipe and blow luxurious smoke into the still evening air. He cupped his hands behind his head and grinned in review a good day's work well done.

"If we have any real luck tomorrow," he told Ponsonby, "the trail may lead us to the Big Shot who's organized the mob. He's low and smart enough to keep out of the shooting. If we can bring him in as clean as you got that bushwacking thug the rest'll be like running down jackals."

It seemed to Ponsonby that, for a man who consistently refused to embroil himself with this gang, King was taking an extraordinary amount of trouble. But he was learning to understand that this Kingi Bwana of the African bush country was a man quite extraordinarily different from the "set" that he knew. Somehow, he had never altogether admired that set; never whole-heartedly conformed to their narrow, caste-bound conventions. So they, outraged, had shipped him out to the colonies. Things were different in the colonies. Men were different— some of them. White men.

The morrow, however, brought one of the baffling disappointments of Africa. Pigeon Toe's car tracks wound through the tortuous scrub toward open plain country.

"Heading toward Magimagi," said King. "Likely they're operating around that water-hole."

The plain unrolled itself endlessly westward. In the shimmery distances low clouds of dust hung. King frowned at them.

"Herds of various beasts moving toward the water. Damnation!"

"But we may be lucky," hazarded Ponsonby.

"Not today," King growled, "That's wildebeeste ahead of us. He'll have been smart enough to get ahead of them."

The queer-looking creatures stretched across the whole front, thousands of them, straggled out in an endless panorama of slow motion, feeding as they went. Their grunting barks merged into a dull drumming of sound. King drove his truck among them. The nearest barked hoarsely and stampeded madly for a few hundred yards; then stood and stared in bovine stupidity.

"The luck is theirs that they're just lion fodder," said King. "Worth nothing. Else imagine what a machine-gun would do amongst 'em. And it's they, poor dumb brutes, that save him."

Then Ponsonby understood. The car tracks that they followed

came to the edge of the line of march; and there disappeared—trampled hopelessly into the dust by the myriad shuffling hoofs.

King spat in thoughtful disgust.

"Pah! As safe as covering his trail in water. He may be twenty miles ahead of 'em still; or he may have cut out any place and let yet other herds cover him. That man knows his bush. Thank Pete the rest are just killers."

AND THAT day's disappointment stretched out into the next, and the next. With the disappearing of that trail all trails disappeared. All the wild things of the open plain were closing on the remaining water-holes. Their tracks covered each other and other tracks covered those.

King made the long trek to the Magimagi slough-—circuitous on account of the deep, unbridged dongas that centered there. With the Hottentot he prowled the surrounding terrain, looking for signs of an encampment, listening for shooting. The Hottentot lifted his snub nose and sniffed the air for the faintest odor of lingering smoke. But only animal trails converged upon the pool.

They journeyed to other outlying water-holes. There they found the same peaceful conditions; virgin wilderness unsullied by sound or scent of man.

Ponsonby peered at scatterings of fresh bones.

"D'you think," a gruesome suspicion came to him, "they're using poison?"

King shook his head. "They'd be capable. But these are lion kills. Broken neck is a sure sign."

Three days to Unduli Pan, jungle country, spiny acacias, euphorbias, giant buttress-rooted figs; elephant country.

A wide belt around the pan, where sub-surface moisture lingered, was thick with scrub. Through the tangle, like dark tunnels, animal trails ran. A fringe of dense dead reed and a two hundred yard zone of cracked mud surrounded the slowly receding pool. A perfect open rifle range.

King hid the truck in a far-away bamboo grass and with Ponsonby cautiously sneaked up to the fringe to watch.

With the late afternoon drinking time the beasts came. Zebra first, as usual, impatient, kicking, biting, squealing; impala, leaping amazingly over each other, pretending they were not interested in the water; all the beeste and bok of Africa, cautious, on high-stepping feet, stampeding in wild flurries about nothing.

Later, with approaching dusk, came a general stampede in all directions: and then lithe, tawny forms, barely distinguishable against the baked brown clay.

Later again, with the beginning of darkness, there were vast shapes, incredibly silent, drifting like black shadows out of the shadow, the last of the light gleaming palely from their tusks.

The silence remained. Nothing disturbed them. No shattering fusilade. The African night closed sticky-warm and peaceful. Insects in solid masses drove the watchers from their hideout.

"Aren't we giddy lunatics," Ponsonby wanted to know, "to be going home through this jungle after dusk?"

"A leetle bit too early for lions to be hunting," King told him. "And they'll give plenty of warning, roaring the roof off of the landscape. That's part of their scheme—to scare the meat critters into blind stampede. You'll learn as we go."

And that was about the benefit that came out of their efforts. Ponsonby was learning Africa; learning how to travel, how to camp; to avoid the dangers of veldt and jungle. But to learn anything about the activities of the gang seemed to be impossible. And the anxious days were speeding alarmingly by.

"Durn funny," King growled. "They're hatching something particularly hellish. If we didn't know at first hand that a gun and poison squad was out for our hides, I'd swear this was all peaceful African back bush. The head that's running this is one smart and slimy *hombre.*"

Barounggo, the Masai began to bring in his recruits. Brawny, straight-looking spearmen. King explained to them that great honor was being shown them; they were selected by the *serkali*, the government, on account of their bravery. The young *bwana* was the duly appointed lord of all the game in all this wide district, and he had come many days' journey to look for just such men. He invented a solemn ceremony for Ponsonby to accept them into service.

Full of pride and zeal, they scoured a wide range of country, scouted every water-hole, hunting for news of evildoers who slaughtered the game. But they drew only a baffling blank.

"Could it be," Ponsonby hoped wildly, "that they've decided the business doesn't pay after all, and have given it up?"

"It pays all right," growled King. "You saw how much ivory came to just one pool in one night. Elephants often don't drink for three or four days at a stretch when they have far to go. There'll be other herds for that pool alone. Nossir, they're laying low for some reason."

"Perhaps they're afraid of us—you, I mean. And if they're as well informed as you think, they know you are booked up to go away to this Tadyeni place in a few days."

"And they figure then you'll fold up and quit?"

King put the theory in the form of a double question. He pretended to be scowling reflectively into the far heat haze; but from the thin corners of his eyes he was watching.

Ponsonby's face was set. Only the flush of his growing sunburn hid the whiteness that lay below. His jaw muscles swelled as he bit on his teeth and got up to stalk back and forth. Two weeks of the perplexing chase were nearly over; and the picture before him loomed dark and desperately alone. King noted the hard bulges in what was left of his breeches pockets and knew that the fists, thrust deep in, were convulsively balled.

"I—I—" Ponsonby swallowed. "Dash it all!" he cried in a choked voice, "I can't. I can't throw up the sponge and quit. Not now. You've shown me the beastly thing that's going on and—and—Damn it!" He flared petulantly against the merciless exigencies of Fate. "Your blasted gods of Africa do make it awf'ly hard for a man who'd like to think of himself as white!"

King got up and laid his hand on Ponsonby's shoulder. That was all the comfort he had to offer.

"Yes, they're hard gods," he rumbled ruminatively. "But somehow they sometimes stand by the white men who learn their book of rules. The rules are difficult to understand sometimes. But the first one of them is nerve. Stick to your nerve, feller— You've got it. And they may give us a break yet."

He thumped Ponsonby heavily on the back.

"Buck up, youngster. I believe in luck, and you can buy luck from the gods with your nerve. I've pulled out of worse holes. Hell, maybe the D.C. has squared Devanter already. We'll trek and go see."

But luck remained stubbornly aloof. From Lembu, Ponsonby wired to the D.C., a last forlorn hope, to inquire what progress might have been made about obtaining a release from Major Devanter. But after a delay—obviously for a further effort—the reply came.

With a set resignation in his face, Ponsonby handed the yellow paper to King.

"The man is obdurate. I can do no more. Officially I can exert no pressure."

King's hard fist crushed the paper into a tight ball and he flung it into a corner. The major fellow must be a stiff egoist as well as no sportsman. Enforced association with him over a protracted *safari* into a far and barren district would not be pleasant.

But worse than his own unpleasantness: this Ponsonby; he was a good lad. A ne'er-do-well at home? King snorted. Pah! A no-good, his hidebound old relatives at home might well think him to be; but he was the right material for the big, open, new country. All he required was showing. And he deserved showing—he had all the makin's.

King grunted his disgust:

"Hell, the D.C. might have forced his hand. The durn book of rules set up by your fussy colonial government is harder to understand than the African gods. But, damn, I don't give up yet. If nothing else breaks first, I'll rush this Devanter down to Tadyeni, get him his durned sable, and come back before you know it. You stall around for a while, worry the gang all you can, keep 'em moving; and maybe I'll be back in time to give you a hand with 'em."

Ponsonby was astoundedly overjoyed.

"Really, old man? Would you do that? Why, I thought you wanted nothing to do with this business that you didn't have to. By Jove, that'd be awf'ly decent."

"Aw!" King was embarrassed by the sudden surge of hope and confidence in Ponsonby's face. "As a hunter I do my share in shooting some of the dumb beasts; so I guess it's kinder up to me to do something to give the rest a fair break."

King's willingness to cooperate was sufficient to arouse Ponsonby to a flash of his studied nonchalance.

"Righto, old top. All I'll have to do is stay alive for a few weeks more."

Disgruntled and morose, King trekked back to Malende to present himself before this flamboyant Major whom he already despised for an unsportsmanlike boor.

Boor? Boer, he should rather say. By his accent he placed the man as a South-African and by his name as of old Dutch Africander stock.

MAJOR DEVANTER was a big, broad man, not unhandsome. A short, fair beard failed to completely hide a steely mouth and strong chin. Intelligent eyes looked keenly from under straight brows. A man who knew his mind and had the courage of his own opinions. He was all cordiality. Like many a colonial of uncertain social position, he tried to cover his accent with an affection of Oxford.

"Ha, Mr. King. Awf'ly glad you showed up. I was almost thinkin' I'd have to relinquish you to the commissioner. He was frightfully persistent. Appealed to my sportsmanship and so on. But dash it all, old man, I may be an arrant duffer in the field, but when a fellow's been makin' ready all summer, that's comin' it a bit thick, what?"

King eyed him sourly. "Did he tell you why?"

"Why he wanted you? Oh—er, yes. Yes, of course. He wanted you take young Ponsonby out to—er, sort of show him the ropes. Some trouble or other with poachers, he said."

"And you couldn't see it, I suppose?" said King crisply.

"Of course I couldn't quite see giving up my trip," the major harped upon his defense, "just because a young government man needed breaking in. So I did the next best thing. I popped over to invite him to come along with us. But it seems he was pottering around somewhere. So left him a note."

"Aa-ah!"

There it was at last. The luck that he had been expecting. His grin that had been absent for so long seamed King's face. He thought quickly. This wouldn't be so bad at all. Three white men together, and those quite excellent native spearmen that Barounggo had collected; they ought to be able to make a very successful little campaign against this slimy gang, machine-guns and all. And this Major Devanter. Not such a bad sort after all. He made out a very good case for himself.

"So I think we ought to have quite a decent trip, what?" The major voiced King's own thought. "That is to say if you won't find two of us—tenderfeet, you call us, isn't it?—Two such rank tyros too much of a strain on your patience for such a long trip as Tadyeni."

King's grin vanished. Tadyeni was ten days' journey away from the elephant country.

"Oh! You still want to go to the Tadyeni plain?"

"Positively, my dear fellow. There and nowhere else. I *must* have giant sable antelope; and you yourself told me that Tadyeni is the only place you know. You see—" the major was confidential—"it's this way. My fiancee's father is curator of mammals in the museum down at Capetown; and I've promised him a habitat group of giant sable. In fact—" the Major laughed a little sheepishly—"the old man's consent is in a way contingent upon my supplyin' him with the specimens. That's why I'm undertakin' a thing of this sort for which I have really no aptitude. Quite out of my line. I'm anything but a hunter. I'm strictly a business man."

"Aa-ah!" The exclamation rasped from King; and that was his only comment. This was not so good. The other, that flash of hope, had been too good to be true. Luck didn't come that easily, not for him. He had always been one of those Fate-bedogged men who had to go out and make his luck.

This time it looked as though Fate were deliberately conspiring against him. Everything was going too perfectly wrong—tied up months ago for just this season by a man who could make no other time; who was willing, it seemed, to go well over half-way to concede a favor to the D.C.; but was bound by very legitimate personal considerations to go to a far outlying place to get certain specimens that could be found nowhere closer.

That was more than just bad luck. That was a deliberate plot of malignant Fate. The sort of thing that stern gods of a hard land sent along to test a man down to the very fiber of him.

King swore savagely at having to take orders from Fate, even temporarily. Well, he would have to revert to the earlier plan. Hurry this major off, get him his specimens, and hurry back.

"Very well," he told him. "I'll be ready to start with tomorrow's dawn. I'll have all supplies and men. You'll need only your personal clothes and your rifle. See you at sun-up. I've got some final arrangements to attend to now."

There was a vast amount of detailed instruction and advice he would have to give Ponsonby before he left. That lad, with all the spirit in the world,—but with all his inexperience—was up against a deadly proposition. And he wouldn't shirk it either. That tradition of duty and service to empire and such was damned inconvenient stuff. But the boy had guts.

It was luck—a little luck—that most of the gang were inexperienced too; just gun men. Pigeon Toe was the danger. If he could but avoid that poison snake.

Those good spearmen. They knew their bush, of course. The most intelligent one of them, appointed as a leader, might—ha! He had it! The grin was fleetingly evident— He would leave Barounggo with Ponsonby as chief of the native force. If it came to fighting, there was a wise and cunning fighter. But the Masai— The grin faded—Dammit, the Masai would likely be reckless fool enough to charge his men against a machine-gun.

Truly was Ponsonby up against a deadly proposition. So that discussion with Ponsonby ran through the night and into the first light of dawn.

King got up without enthusiasm.

"So there you have it. All that I can give you. Take the Masai's advice in everything but barging into danger. I've got to go on my own chore. Good luck. I'll be seeing you before you know it."

Ponsonby was pale. He had absorbed all that he could of advice. But he had no illusions.

"I hope so," he said, not at all hopefully.

KING STALKED, scowling and swearing softly, back to his camp. Damn this duty and service stuff. Why couldn't the boy just lay low until he should get back from Tadyeni? He'd show him, by God, how to round up this murderous mob. But what use? If the youngster didn't have just those things he couldn't be worth bothering with—wouldn't have the right makin's.

King roused the Hottentot and told him to start up a fire for early coffee and a quick getaway. Then he went to see that the major would be up and ready. The sooner away, the sooner back.

But the getaway was not so soon. Fate—or maybe the dark gods of Africa that dealt out luck in recognition of courage— were indicating a small opening in their intricate game.

As King crossed the wide, wire-fenced Devanter compound
to the whitewashed house in the center he saw something in
the early light that stopped him as suddenly as though he had
met a bullet.

A track on the ground clear-cut and sharp in the dew-laden
dust. A track of a white man's boots—one of which turned
pigeon-toed.

He stared at it as Robinson Crusoe must have done at the
astounding track of a human foot. In the next second he recov-
ered his poise and made a show of fumbling for his pipe. He
filled it laboriously and lit it while his eyes from under the brim
of his double *terai* hat scouted the ground for more tracks and
squinted sideways at the windows.

They seemed to be dark and empty. But King's every nerve
was tense with caution. Caution and a dawning suspicion of he
did not know what yet. He made a gesture of impatience, as
though he had forgotten something, and he turned and went
back to the bustling camp.

"Kaffa," he called the Hottentot to him. "All thy cunning is
needed and all thy wit. Feet have been to that house in the

night. Come with me—it will be as though to carry the white man's bags—and whilst I am within, read me the story of those feet."

He strode back whistling, hammered loudly on the door, entered to the major's hearty, "Come on in, old man," and found him dressed and ready.

"Hullo, old fellow, *Jambo sana.* The best of good mornings." The major was full of enthusiasm. "Auspicious morning for my first *safari,* what? I'm all packed and locked up for a six weeks' holiday, and under your efficient supervision I hope I'll not find it too hard. But you won't find me weakening. I'll stick it out, by Jove, until the rainy season drives us in."

King contrived a smile and the conventional reassurance that was the requirement of all tenderfeet. But, "Until the rains!" His mind raced around the thought. Was it coincidence; or could there be some reason for that insistence?

The major busied himself with sundry final turnings of keys about the house. He made no objection to King's accompanying him through the various rooms. King had been half wondering whether there might be anybody else there. But everything was as it should be.

"There," said the major at last. "I fancy there's nothing left lying for even my native caretaker to steal. I sent my gear, rifles and everything, over to your camp last night; so we're all set. Just my duffel bag left! Did you bring a boy?"

King was glad for the chance to get away.

"I'll call him and take your stuff over and get it stowed."

"Right-o. I'll come over in five minutes."

The Hottentot shouldered the neatly packed duffel bag and stumped out, King at his heels.

"The feet," said Kaffa with positive assurance, "came to the house early in the night; for the dew is heavy on them. They went away again not two hours ago; for the dew is light upon their going. That is all the story of those feet. An innocent story. Yet, Bwana, it is in my belly that evil is here; for what dealing would such a man as Crooked Foot have for full six or seven hours with this white man who must go to Tadyeni which is the furthest of all places from here?"

The shrewd little man put his finger on the very thought that whirled through King's mind.

Tadyeni, ten days away. These exact six weeks; no other time would suit. Contracted months ahead. An unassailable reason for not acceding to the D.C.'s request for release.

Too perfectly wrong, King had cursed all these concurrent mischances when he had blamed them upon a malignant Fate. But to his now racing suspicions they all fell together just too perfectly right. King had little conceit; but he knew very well that he was the only man in the district of whom ivory poachers would be afraid. He was the only white hunter who ranged in the back country, and his sentiments about sportsmanship and game conservation were well known. These six weeks in Tadyeni would take him beautifully away.

And then minor confirmatory circumstances.

The quick readiness to oblige the D.C. and invite Ponsonby along—get him out of the way too—nice. And this insistence of the major's about being such a neophyte. Why should he be?— He was an old-timer in the land. If he were such a tyro as he pretended, how should he know to pick upon sable antelope that were found no nearer than ten days' hard journey distant? How did he pack a duffel bag so well? How know to send his gear over the night before? How be ready and have the house all locked against his absence? An amateur would be floundering and sunk with last-minute details.

Clever, devilishly clever, all of it. The whole plan and the working of it so far had been clever. This major man looked to be clever enough.

Vile suspicions to harbor against a man. But Pigeon Toe! What secret business could a decent man have with so vile a person as Pigeon Toe throughout seven hours of a last night?

That inescapable fact was reason enough for any sort of suspicions.

The major came striding from his house. Tall, self-possessed, dressed in exactly the appropriate clothes for *safari*—King noted that to add to his list—keen-eyed; a man who knew what he wanted and usually got it.

"All ready!" he cried heartily. "And, as you Yankees say, r'arin' to go."

King made a quick decision.

"Ponsonby just sent a boy down to say he'd be glad to accept your invitation and come along."

The major beamed. "Splendid! That's topping! Did he send a note? Where's the boy?"

King had to think fast. "I chased him back to tell Ponsonby to hurry up, and I'd be along to show him how to pack so he wouldn't keep us waiting all morning."

With that excuse he hurried away before the major should think of any other awkward questions.

PONSONBY WAS sitting exactly as King had left him. He had not moved. He sat gazing at the opposite wall as a man might in a death cell.

King burst in on him like a whirlwind.

"Quick, quick! Up! Get a move on! You're coming with us. Luck has busted wide open on us— At least, I think. What cars, trucks, anything, can you borrow or steal?"

"What—why—what on earth's happened?" Ponsonby was bewildered.

"You'll need transport for your crew—your spearmen. I have my light passenger flivver and the truck loaded to the limit with gear and two extra boys for the Devanter *safari*. We'll have to corral something for your army. I'll explain as we run."

Ponsonby's wits came to him quickly.

"There's a small government truck for the game department

in Newton's hide go-down. But I don't know about petrol and—"

"Get it! Get everything you have! We'll pile the men in and I'll rustle up an extra few sacks of mealie corn. Jump! Unless I'm a suspicious fool the gods have given us a sign."

Within the hour a startled native driver sat at the wheel of the truck and listened wonderingly to King's instructions to drive a wide circuit through the empty bush round Malende settlement.

King wedged himself with Ponsonby beside him and watched the ground as they went. Presently he found it. He jumped down to examine the trail. He whooped.

"I'd have betted on it. Look. Tire tracks. Fresh—the dust hasn't blown over 'em yet. Somebody left Malende not two hours ago, heading westward."

"Who would be going westward?" Ponsonby wondered. "There's nothing there."

"Not a durn thing—" King was exultant—"except the water-holes and elephant country. It adds up. By golly it adds up. My guess is that Pigeon Toe took his instructions and is off to join the gang in their hide-out. We'll be gone today—they think—and they'll have a clear field. Come on, let's get to the major; he'll be aching to start."

"I hope to heaven your suspicions are correct," said Ponsonby dubiously. "You—we've got nothing to go on but some tracks. We could prove nothing against him."

"Don't backslide." King warned him quickly. "Don't revert to your processes of lawful procedure. We're dealing with people who're smart enough to play rings around your clumsy law. The gods of Africa are giving us a lead. We'll go with this major man out into the open places of Africa and follow their play. I'll find out soon enough whether he's as innocent as he looks, whether he's such a rank tyro in the bush as he claims."

The Major blinked surprise at the throng that huddled in Ponsonby's truck. King, watching him like a hawk, thought that he noted a flash of uneasiness. But the major laughed bluff cordiality.

"Awf'ly glad you could come, old thing. But my word, you do travel with quite an escort, don't you?"

King lied glibly for Ponsonby.

"He's tenderfoot enough to feel that he needs three tent-boys. The rest are department men, going to be dropped off at Zimwe."

"Well, glad I don't have to feed 'em," said the Major. "If we're all ready, gentlemen, let's go."

The three white men rode in the passenger car. The two trucks lumbered and pounded behind. The major was affable, full of anticipation for a good holiday. He talked gayly about the shooting to come—King wondered whether with just the teeniest bit too much familiarity. He joked. He asked amateurish questions about the bush—perhaps the teeniest bit too amateurish for so clever looking a man.

They halted for a sandwich lunch and a stretch; and the major had not a care in the world.

They halted again for the ceremony of scalding tea in the prevailing ninety degrees of temperature; and the major only perspired and mopped tenderly at his face that was beginning to feel the sun.

It was toward evening camp time that he hazarded the remark:

"I say, aren't you heading a bit over to the westward, old man? Isn't Tadyeni more south?"

King's further eyebrow flickered. But he explained shortly:

"N'gwent River. Three days ahead. The old ford washed out last rainy season. We have to work round by Lokri's Shamba."

"Oh, did it? I hadn't heard that!" the major exclaimed. "I thought—" He stopped abruptly.

"You wouldn't know about it," said King, "being a business man in Malende. It's only us back-bush trekkers who'd be interested."

The major remained thoughtful.

The next day's travel bore even more to the West. Close to the equator, where the sun jumps up and seems to hang in mid-sky for most of the day, it is easy for a rank tyro to lose sense of direction. But the major ventured upon an expostulation again.

"Bad country to the south," King grunted.

At the lunch hour he, who never misjudged the way, ran the car into a dead end of thorn tangle. He got out and shouted to the Hottentot in the far following truck to come and scout a way out.

Out of view, he lay comfortably on his back and focused his field glasses on the empty sky. He frowned and handed the glasses to the Hottentot. He had long ago taught the little man how to use them as an adjunct to his own extraordinary sight.

"Read me the specks in the high heaven, apeling."

The Hottentot grimaced as if with all the throes of acute pain as he went through the still difficult process of adjusting the glasses to the close set of his eyes. At last he settled down to steady scrutiny.

"Vultures," he announced. "Very high and not circling; traveling in the direction of Unduli Pan."

"Ha! The swine haven't lost a moment's time," King growled. "How far, little wise one, do you judge Unduli Pan?"

The Hottentot stood on one leg and thought—not reasoned; he groped, rather, for the directional inspiration that some bush dwellers can evoke.

"This half-day, *bwana,* and another half-day, going fast in the small *moto* wagon. A half day and a whole day, going in the big *motos.*"

"Come with us in the small *moto,*" King told him. "Bring the grub box."

He headed the car openly for Unduli Pan.

Even Ponsonby from the back seat noted the major's restiveness. He kept looking at King nervously and at last burst out:

"You're sure you're not losing time, I hope. 'Pon my word, it seems we're coming a long way out of the way."

"I know very exactly what I'm doing—now," King told him.

The Major digested that for half an hour. As he turned over its possible meanings in his mind his face changed. The affability passed from it. A scowl had the curious effect of drawing his eyes together. He looked like an angry and a violent-tempered man—and dangerous.

"I want tea." He barked at last. "Damn it, I'm having enough of this."

KING STOPPED the car. An alcohol stove and a tea kit were a vital part of the outfit. They all got out. The major stamped back and forth, his hands in his coat pockets, scowling in furious thought. Like something trapped—an angry beast in a cage.

Suddenly he stopped and snatched his hand out of his pocket, a thick, stubby-barreled revolver in it; and in his handling of that he was certainly no tyro. His carefully studied accent passed from him as his rage grew.

"Now then, my bumptious Mister Kingi Bwana, you'll tell me exactly what you're driving at."

King looked at the gun, the gun hand, up the steady arm to the eyes. No foolish plays with this man. He would shoot. "Perhaps you know," King said evenly. "You're so clever."

The major's mustache curled away from his teeth and revealed startlingly the reason why he affected the softening effect of it with his beard. While his face twitched with uncontrolled fury, his eyes set in that menacing anomaly, the cold blankness of a killer.

"Pretty damn smart yourself, aren't you?" His words came like shots. "Even fooled me for a while." He crouched slightly and his shoulders stiffened. His pistol arm tensed. King began edging over toward the car.

The major's teeth glared out again. "That's not so clever. You won't fool me again. I know where your gun is. But it's the right direction. Closer to Ponsonby there where I can see the two of you."

King stepped quickly over and stood beside Ponsonby. The major pivoted slowly to cover them both.

"That's better. And you needn't grin. Ponsonby doesn't wear a gun either. I was clever enough as far back as last night to look through your clothes."

"Yeah?" King showed his annoyance. "That's one I didn't give you credit for."

But the major was deadly.

"You don't bluff me out of anything, my smart lad. All I'm wondering is how to dispose of you fellows." His eyes flickered to the surrounding bush. "Those damn trucks will be coming on our track and—"

He bit off the words in venomous thought.

"Perhaps you're clever enough to make 'em believe a lion got us," said King.

Expression flashed into the deadly blank eyes. Doubt. No man would be so cool unless—

"Yep," King laughed at him. "You're not so well heeled as you figured. Let him feel the point, Kaffa. Don't move, Big Shot."

But the major jerked spasmodically as a half inch of Somali knife jabbed in exactly over his spine and pushed with steady pressure. Then he stiffened.

"Not quite clever enough," King grinned at him wide. "Better drop the gun, because I'm going to have to pay him not to kill you."

Mustache and beard snarled apart again but the hand that had been tensing on the gun-butt relaxed.

King walked forward and picked it up. He laughed sardonically.

"Yeh, I don't wear one of these things in this law-abiding colony of yours. A mistake. I should. That was very nicely done, good apeling. There will be a reward of tobacco and a blanket striped as the lightning."

He looked over to Ponsonby, jauntily and with a vast satisfaction.

"Learning more about your colony every day, eh? Now here's where *you* decide. Me, I'd recommend for you to take this gun and shoot this snake for a venomous thing that's organized the filthiest racket in Africa and collected a gang that use guns or poison or what have you. But I reckon you've still got your traditions, and maybe you want to take him alive."

Ponsonby looked at King, wondering, hesitant. He had grown to rely on him for every move. King grinned at him.

"I'm not 'conducting' you any longer. My contract ran out yesterday. You're on your own feet."

"Oh!" Ponsonby assimilated that thought. Then his mouth tightened in decision. "Well, I—I shall arrest him."

"O.K. Go ahead. Take him," said King unconcernedly.

It was beginning to seep into Ponsonby's understanding that King expected him personally to go through the motions of making the arrest.

"Yeh. One of your laws," King accused him. "I've been up against it before. And what a yawp a defense lawyer sharp put up when I pulled in a sacred British subject—me having no 'authority.' The D.C. had to take it to the Governor to iron it out. Y'see I'm not even hired by you. I'm in mutiny and rebellion against this snake. You read up your fat book of regulations some day. It'll give you a gripe when you're out alone in these backwoods and things are happening fast. Though of course—" King's tone passed from the cynical to the insinuating—"You, as an officer of the law, can call upon me and my man to assist you in the performance—and et cetera and so on."

"Oh," said Ponsonby again, "I see. Well, damme if I'll call on you—yet."

King's grin was benediction. "Go to it, feller. And you, Major Big Shot, if you try to pull anything particularly vile, I'll give you to the Hottentot as a present. Kinder unfair to cramp your style that way; but it's the decent man who's got inhibitions that's always got the handicap."

The major snarled hate at King. "Ho, a fight promoter, yes?"

King shook his head. "Nope. A trainer. I've got some good material here and I'm showing him the ropes. This isn't going to be a fight. You're heavier 'n him; but you've been being a smart business man while he's been going through a couple weeks of the stiffest kind of training.

AND IT wasn't a fight. It was a scramble. Heave and punch. Knock down, roll over, squirm and punch again. Dust flew, clothes ripped, thorn bushes crackled, flattened and sprang up again. Neither man was a boxer. It was a test only of courage and stamina—plenty of both.

But finally Ponsonby sat on the major's back and held his arms twisted behind him. Torn, scratched up a good deal more. But on top.

King nodded. "Good. That is, not bad. Africa is a tough school, no?"

Then he explained. "You had to do this, youngster. Y'see, from the foolish kind of poke you gave Pigeon Toe in his face a while back, I guessed you'd never been in a fight before—back in your high-brow home. And you had to know you could lick a tough man. 'Cause we got some other tough people to go and lick. Now I'll show you how to tie him up."

He fished a piece of gun-cleaner drawstring from his pocket and tied the major's thumbs behind his back. Then with his hunting-knife he slit through the prisoner's shooting coat and shirt—two holes, wide apart, well up between the shoulders. He passed the twine through the holes.

"And that man," he hissed softly as he knotted it, "won't escape unless someone lets him. Y'see, a man has no strength to pull that way. He can sit and he can lie and he isn't tortured—damn him. I'm sorry at least once a week in this country I've got some inhibitions myself."

Far shouts back and forth and cursings of thorn twigs that

reached in and raked the drivers' faces indicated that the trucks were coming up.

"Since they've caught up with us; and since we know now exactly what's what," said King, "maybe we'd better keep the army with us. Looks like we'll be needing 'em. And by the same token they ought to be told just what they're going up against. A machine-gun 's an awful shock to men who don't expect it."

He told the men briefly what sort of a situation be expected to find. Desperate men were to be captured—or at all events their crime must be made to cease. There would be wounds; probably death. Therefore now was the time to say whether they would carry on, or would Barounggo have to search for other men.

"But, *bwana*, what talk is this?" The Masai was enormously indignant. "What need to offer shame to these men? These be Elmorani. See their garters? Each man of them has slain his lion with shield and spear."

"All right! All right!" King mollified him. "That they would run from battle I did not think. But they should know that a fight is before them."

"No man will go away," the Masai took it upon himself to guarantee. "Mine own honor is at stake. Did I not bring them, having first tested each one? As witness this scar on my shoulder not yet healed. That tall fellow it was, he who grins; for I bet him a cow that he could not touch me. A slip it was, *bwana*. A mischance. Else he would never—"

"I take over thy bet, braggart," King laughed at him. "I will pay it. If that tall warrior pricked thee it was well earned."

The tall man lifted his spear in salute.

"*Assanti sana, Bwana, m'kubwa, m'pagi.* Thank you indeed, *bwana*, great chief, generous one. For such a chief a small matter of some fighting is a good thing."

"You do not fight for me." King told them. "You are servants of the *serkali*. And as such, those who may receive wounds, the *serkali* will care for them; those who may die, the *serkali* will care for their women in their villages. My own men I have made provision to care for. Therefore there is no need of anxiety for this fight."

The men tapped their spears against their shield rims, a crescendo rattle of warriors' applause to a chief.

"Yes," said Ponsonby, "I've heard it said around the club and other places that Kingi Bwana knows how to handle Africans."

"Something else for you to remember," King shelved the compliment.

"And who," Ponsonby half-whispered the question to himself, "in all this merry-go-round cares for the welfare of Kingi Bwana? Seems like there's nobody left."

"That," said King quickly, "is the compensation I must pay for the privilege of being a free man. And brother—" he spread his shoulders and breathed deeply of the dust-laden air—"It's worth it."

But time was speeding and here they stood talking.

"Come along! Come along!" King bustled into action. "We've got ground to cover. Dammit, I doubt we'll make it in two stop-overs now. If only we'd gone direct we'd have been there by now. But you had to have 'proof' on this clever big shot."

He motioned to a couple of brawny spearmen to pick him up.

"We'll feel sorta cleaner, I guess, if your prisoner rides in the baggage truck. And I hope to God he tries to escape. These Elmorani lads aren't handicapped by any inhibitions. Come ahead. Let's get going. We've got two of 'em. Only a few more to get."

"Dashed if I don't believe," said Ponsonby, as the car bucked over the mimosa roots, "that you're jolly well pepped about bucking this gun gang."

"Who, me?" King flouted the idea. "I'm not bucking any gang. You're the game-warden. I'm just bringing my client, Major Devanter, along to let him see how you run your job. 'Cause your law is going to let him off easy on all the 'evidence' you've got on him; and I figure it'll be good for him to know, then, what happens around the water-holes."

The thorn scrub country began to open up into the familiar rolling plain.

King examined the sky with his glasses and checked the direction of the microscopic specks with a pocket compass.

Yes, Unduli Pan was the scene of operations. He urged the drivers to speed. Later the Hottentot lifted his snub nose and announced:

"There is dead meat in the air."

"Good Lord! Can he really smell it?" Ponsonby wondered.

"I wouldn't bet one way or the other. Some of those fellows can pretty near outsmell a dog." King wasn't interested just now in ethnological theories. What he wanted to do was to reach the tree country before night, hide up the car, and creep down to a favorable position somewhere near the pool before daylight should come again and betray them.

"If luck holds—if these cars stand up to the punishment we're putting 'em through—we'll make it," he insisted almost prayerfully.

And luck held. The gods, rewarding those who obeyed their book of rules, gave it to them.

They laid up the trucks, left the mechanics as guards over the prisoner, crept through jungle paths headed by the Hottentot's animal sense of direction and night vision; and presently their own noses told them that in the jungle about them were dead things.

Ponsonby could hear King swearing while he fiercely enjoined silence upon the others.

"What I can't make out about all this," he told King, "is whether we're afraid of bumping into them, or they're afraid we may find 'em."

"I don't know who else is," said King, "but I am."

The next thing they knew they could feel a moist vapor on

their faces from the surface of the little lake. In the tree fringe they bedded down to wait for morning.

"Elephants often drink at dawn," King whispered. "That'll maybe get the murderers to show their hand."

IT WAS a nerve-racking and gruesome wait. Warm eddying breezes brought whiffs of charnel odor from here and there. Out on the encircling mud belt and in sundry places in the jungle hyenas howled their raucous call and fought over foul food and gibbered the maniac wail that fools have called a laugh.

Dawn came. Everybody crouched expectantly. Soon something would happen. But what? Nobody knew. Attack or be attacked? Ponsonby found himself vaguely wishing that his own expression might be as fiercely expectant as those of the *askaris*. It came to him all of a sudden that here he was with these spearmen whom he had taken into service as native wardens, and he was not in any way expecting to arrest anybody.

"At any time now," King whispered to him, "a herd may come down to drink. Watch. Big as they are, you'll hardly hear 'em."

Ponsonby peered from amongst the leaves. The light grew stronger. Suddenly he stiffened. Across the mud slope some two hundred yards distant, he thought he saw a movement in the dry tops of the fringe of dead reed left by the receding water. He watched. It *was* a movement, an undulant waving. Something pushing cautiously through. Too small to be an elephant— that reed didn't grow high enough. The movement reached the edge of the reeds. The cause of it came out into view.

A man. He stood and surveyed the expanse of open mud bank up and down. Ponsonby's breath sucked sharply in.

"Pigeon Toe!"

He raised his rifle. He did not know why. Somewhere in the back of his mind was a realization that this was not self-defense, as it had been once before when he peered from cover and a man pointed a rifle at him. His hesitation almost lost him his life.

Pigeon Toe saw his motion. His rifle jerked up on the instant and fired.

It was only King's tremendous shove that sent him reeling and saved him.

"Durn fool!" King was abusing him. "I told you you couldn't get Pigeon Toe that easy. He's a hunter. Damn, I didn't spot him soon enough."

A startled squeal sounded in the jungle on the heels of the shot and behind the place where the man had stood. King gripped Ponsonby's arm.

"Baby elephant! They're coming!"

On the heels of that again two more shots rang muffled in the jungle and a short burst of machine-gun fire.

There followed a hell's pandemonium of hoarse giant screams, squeals, brazen trumpetings, and a crashing and thundering of vast bodies stampeding through everything in their path. A single furious trumpeting remained to split the air in short blasts, and short rushes crashed back and forth in the jungle.

King was swearing through clenched teeth.

"The swine! The filthy beasts! You heard 'em! Hell, I didn't like to believe it, in spite of the bones. But, damn 'em! They failed this time. Pigeon Toe's shot stopped the herd, and those dumb fools cut loose from poor position. But they hit one. The hellions! Not to drop him clean, blast 'em. Just to hurt him and make him sore."

Ponsonby was just as outraged as was King. His impulse was for immediate reprisal.

"Anyhow, that shows us where they are. Shall we up and go for 'em?"

King looked at the crouching men, fierce, eager.

"You're durn right, we'll—" But his habitual caution came back to him. "We'll have to be careful—can't rush a machine-gun. But we can cut across to that end before they get organized, and if they're dumb enough to stay in the jungle, we'll show 'em, by God, what jungle men can do."

"Well, I'm ready. Tell them."

"You tell 'em." King grinned maliciously at Ponsonby. "They're your men. I'm not going to get blamed for anything that your men may do in the heat of a fight. I'm just tagging along 'cause I'm scared to be caught by those devils alone."

"I can't tell 'em an awful lot in Swahili," said Ponsonby. "But damme, I can lead 'em."

"Good lad! The sooner, the better, then."

They pushed out from their cover and started to sprint, each man for himself, across an arc of the open mud slope, heading for the further fringe of jungle where the shooting had been.

The leading runner, a tall greyhound of a man, had barely gone fifty yards when a vicious crackle of another gun blasted out from the dark tunnel of an animal run to his left. His hands clawed out before him and his impetus carried him like a diver to land on his face and slide on the hard-baked mud.

The next runner came into the deadly zone, and eagerly racing a hand's breadth behind him, another.

The deadly crackle continued to spurt from the tunnel mouth. Both men pitched and slid on their faces. The spear of one of them stuck into the ground and slanted teetering. A bullet cut splinters from it; and the shaft bent over the hung.

The next leading man saved himself from the death zone by flinging himself sideway, from where he scrambled to his feet and followed the rest in a mad rush for the shelter of the jungle.

"Phe-ew! I'd never guessed that." Ponsonby was panting and furious. "How the devil could those rotters know we were hostile to them? They couldn't have understood that Pigeon Toe's shot was fired at humans at all."

"They didn't," King spat savagely. "This bunch was holed up to cut down anything that the other bunch missed. They took us as we came because I tell you they're letting nothing stop their business."

He addressed the remaining men, five of them, besides his own too.

"Warriors, this was a mischance that came upon us by reason of being over impetuous and rushing like foolish game beasts into the open. In the jungle path these men lie hidden. I know not how many. By stealth, then, they must—"

But the men, scowling and muttering, were already slipping through the tangle of bush and vine. There was nothing to do but follow them. King dropped on his belly and wormed into a low opening.

"You stay here," he hissed over his shoulder at Ponsonby. "This is jungle work."

But Ponsonby's face grinned close over his heel. "You're not 'conducting' me now. I'm on my own feet."

A short burst of fire crashed out a little to their right. King reached back and dragged Ponsonby up beside him.

"Damn-fool game-warden. So listen. That gives us their exact direction. Keep trees between as you go; or they'll likely cut you in half."

WITH ENORMOUS caution they crept forward. Nothing dared be brushed past. Twigs had to be carefully bent aside, dead leaves picked out of the way.

Another burst crashed out. The incredible clatter of bullets amongst leaves and twigs receded into the distance; then came back in crisp whispering echoes.

Again a spasmodic burst; and the shattering of twigs in another direction.

King's lips mouthed the barely whispered words:

"Nervous. Shooting blind at sounds."

Sounds apparently were everywhere; faint clicks and infinitesimal rustlings from every direction around the hidden gunmen, for frenzied bullets rattled away this way and that.

Chameleon-slow now. All the caution of that watchful creature stalking an insect—a poisonous, stinging insect. Even shooting blind, a machine-gun spray might cut a man in half.

Ponsonby's eye found itself before a camera-hole opening

between twigs; and in that strained position he froze. He did not dare move. The machine-gun seemed to be looking right at him.

There they were. Three men crouching in a dim funnel that bored through the jungle. Two of them held rifles, the other squatted behind the deadly gun; nervous, fear in their evil eyes.

Typical gunmen, callous enough to pain and death in their own haunts, but bewildered now in unfamiliar ground. Fear of their own death twitched their faces.

The gun whirled on its swivel and menaced another point, jerked round to another, then spun back to Ponsonby.

His breath froze in him. He was not aware of having made a sound. He dared risk none by moving.

Sounds were everywhere. The machine-gunner's eyes flashed about him. The gun muzzle wavered with them.

Then Ponsonby saw him suddenly clutch at his shirt front. Just as though a wasp had blundered in and stung him. The trigger hand jerked away to join the clutch. From between his fingers a spear blade protruded.

All in one convulsive, astounding second there was the blade and suddenly red fingers clawing at it.

Then the great form of the Masai rose up out of the bushes behind him.

"*Hau!*" he shouted, full-throated, like the coughing roar of a lion in its spring.

One of the rifle men turned to meet him. He left his spear and hurled his dark bulk at the man, arms and legs asprawl. Together they went down.

The third man was swinging his rifle up, when another dark form jumped high above the struggling pair and arrived upon him, spear first.

Then a rush of leaping naked forms and the hissing "*Ss-ghee*" of the Elmorani, gruesomely indicative of spears passing through flesh. Then the Masai, tugging to retrieve his spear.

Ponsonby stood beside King, big-eyed and a little sick.

The Masai lifted his red blade in the salute that courtesy to one's master demands and reported.

"Three of them, Bwana. Against three of ours. We are even."

"Yet it is not enough," came a voice.

"We are ahead," said King. "One slain before and one captured."

"How many more are there in the other group?" Ponsonby asked.

"Durned if I know. I'd always figured six or seven all told—and Pigeon Toe. They won't be so easy. Do you know how to use one of these things?"

Ponsonby shook his head. "No. I missed the war. Don't you?"

"Hell, no. I'm a hunter, not a soldier." King stood with his thumbs hooked in his belt and teetered on his toes, frowning. "So the handicap is still against us. Well, waiting won't help. *Andamani Wasikari*. Come ahead, men—I mean, tell your men to come along. But this time I lead. This bunch will know who's looking for them."

Keeping careful cover, they worked round the rim of the jungle pool. Ponsonby, exerting all his faculties to emulate the silence of the others, was surprised when King held up his hands to stop everything.

"Over there, a little to your left. About fifty yards, I'd judge it. Listen."

Then Ponsonby got it too. A slow rustling of leaves thrust aside. A successive crackling of leathery, half-moist twigs as a huge foot sunk deeper into the jungle debris. A long, windy snuffle and a woosh of expelled air.

"Something else looking for 'em," said King grimly. "And a lot madder'n us and ten times as patient. People'll tell you a wounded buffalo is the most dangerous beast in Africa. But I'll bet on an elephant every time 'cause he's that much cleverer. A good ally."

"But Good Lord." Ponsonby whispered it. "Won't he charge down on us?"

"Sure. Like an army tank—if he winds us. But what wind there is across. And their hearing isn't any too good, spite of their bat ears. A good man—like, say, a Kavinrondo hunter—can creep up to 'em and jab 'em with a spear. We'll just have to watch our wind."

The next thing, voices stopped them. An oath and a querulous complaint.

"Cawn't see a foot in this blawsted tangle. 'Ow the 'ell are we goin' ter shoot?"

And then: "You shut yer faice, Okey. If they tries ter do any stalkin' through this stuff we'll bloody well rip 'em wide open,"

They stood at the edge of a patch of elephant grass, stiff-stemmed canes that waved dusty plumes twenty feet in the air; dense, crowding out all other vegetation. No live thing could pass through that without betraying its course.

"Aa-ah!" King breathed. "Pigeon Toe's doing. Yeh, he knows his bush." He looked to left and right and he sucked in his lip.

"Yes, a crafty nest. A machine-gun spray would cut through that stuff like dead corn stalks.

To the right the cane patch bordered on the open circle of the lake. To the left the elephant snuffled and searched with vindictive patience.

The vagrant wind blew from the pool, quartering across the cane patch, passing on between them and the angry beast. To work around to the further side of the patch—even if that might prove to be of any use—would surely bring the man scent directly down wind to the brute. And then even an expert and cool-headed rifleman in that close jungle might not stop it; and any luckless spearmen in the way would be lost.

It seemed to be a checkmate; an endless game of wait for one side or the other to make a mis-move.

THE HOTTENTOT scuttled from behind his sheltering tree to where King and Ponsonby stood. His eyes glittered with excitement. He looked like a monkey contemplating a fearful and irresistible mischief.

"*Bwana,*" he whispered, "*Heitsi Eibib* himself has prepared this opportunity. If Bwana therefore permits—" He stopped to sniff the wind again, wetting his splay nostrils with his tongue and swinging his head to catch its exact direction.

"What's *Heights-I-bib?*" Ponsonby had to know.

"Hottentot nature god," King whispered shortly. "What is in thy head, Little Wise One?"

"See, *bwana.* Thus is the wind. There stalks the beast that they have wounded. It is in my head that I can draw him round to catch their scent."

King stared at him, and his own eyes began to shrink to thin slits as he contemplated the mad idea.

"By golly," he murmured, "I believe you could. Lord, what an ally! It will be a danger, Little One. Death will follow at thy very skin."

"A lesser danger, Bwana, than that devil-devil gun."

King's nod was reluctant. "Go then, bold apeling. And I myself will lay a stone for *Heitsi Eibib* with thee."

The Hottentot scuttled off. He whispered to the Masai and the other men. They edged down closer to King and Ponsonby. His agile form melted into the underbrush.

"By golly!" King felt for the wind. "If he does it, the brute will miss us by scant feet. If the wind shifts—" Mechanically he eased the breech of his rifle open to assure himself once over again that a cartridge was in the chamber.

A motionless minute passed. Another dragged itself on. Some small creature, encouraged by the silence, scuffled in the leaves. In the cane patch was a faint crackle of some man changing a cramped position. Ponsonby's mind groped with a Dantesque visualization of hurtling chaos and of the terrifying unsuspicion of the men within the cane patch—*If* the wind should not shift. Time crawled on.

The silence in the further jungle was startled by a loud whoosh, and a long steamy inhalation.

"Ha!" from King.

Followed a scrambling in the underbrush and a vast pushing aside of higher branches. A whoosh of expelled dust again— nearer.

A faster scrambling, and the crunch of huge feet. Right into the line of the wind over the cane patch! A quick succession of puffs from enormous bellows.

Then a blast of shattering brass—furious, vengefully triumphant. A bulk heaved itself to momentum with a vast crashing of twigs, branches, trees and the pounding of great feet.

Almost at spear's length an unseen tornado thundered past. It screamed brazen rage again. Then it was rushing through the cane.

Dry stems crackled like the gun. The gun crackled back. A short wild burst at blind destruction. Sharp shouts! Yells! A clank of trampled metal! An awful scream expelled with unhuman force! A further blind crashing through the cane and out to open silence beyond.

"*Ulu-lu-lu-lu!*" The Masai yelled. The rest of the spearmen took up their war cry and in a jostling pack dashed into the swath of destruction.

It came to King in a flash that they had arranged this concerted rush amongst themselves in order to forestall any restraint upon their vengeance for their fellows. He raced after them, into a pall of swirling dust that made fuzzy the outlines of twisted stems and broken reed. He stumbled to the central shambles in time only to hear the hissing accompaniment to spear thrusts and to see the heaving pile of dark limbs.

Outside somewhere the elephant trumpeted short angry blasts.

"Good Lord, he'll be back on us," Ponsonby warned.

King was tugging at struggling men.

"Kaffa!" He demanded. "Who has seen the Hottentot? Was he here?"

But it was from behind that the little man scrambled down

the lane of shattered stems, as pleased with himself as a monkey that has performed a difficult trick.

"Ha, apeling!" King's concern was allayed. "Splendidly done! I have feared for thy foolish life. We shall speak of this later."

Again the elephant trumpeted from outside; querulous; further than before.

Ponsonby was trying to drag the men away, to urge them by signs to run for the shelter of the jungle. King had time to explain their carefree laughter.

"He's lost the scent. Don't you see, in this tangle he couldn't see what was underfoot. He just charged ahead like a runaway truck, and now he's the other side of the wind."

The taut anxiety of furious events was passing from his own face. "Well, this looks like a clean-up. I'm afraid your men haven't taken any prisoners. But—" He shrugged. "I don't know that you can altogether blame 'em for that."

The Masai came to report with a huge satisfaction. "Four of them, Bwana. One—he who screamed—the elephant trampled like a slug in his path. The gun also is broken. But the Crooked Foot is not here."

"Ss-so?" King's own growing satisfaction clouded. "Yes, he was the only one smart enough to know what was coming, and he ducked just in time. There's still a danger then."

"But his gun, *bwana*, is here." The Hottentot rose from his close investigation of everything. "See, *bwana*, the iron plate at the butt. The screw is missing. Such a mark was left by the gun when Crooked Foot stood in thought upon the day of his poisoning of the drink."

"Ha! Then it must have been nip and tuck for him. He must have squeezed into the cane, and in the general uproar he wormed out—on the side away from us. He can't have gotten far. Out, you men! Out of here and fan out in the further jungle! That man of all of them, must be captured. What of that angry elephant? There too, remains a danger."

"The elephant, Bwana," a man came back from the further

lane of trampled cane, "has circled and has gone into the jungle again."

"The same side as we must hunt for Crooked Foot. The more need for care. Away! Away! Kaffa, see what trail may be found. The rest, fifty paces apart. Swift! Swift!"

KING PUSHED Ponsonby to the outer fringe that bordered the open belt of mud.

"Easier going for you."

Himself he took the next station, some fifty feet further into the jungle. Beyond him the men strung out; and the drive commenced.

Slow, of necessity; for Pigeon Toe would be clever enough to hide and double back. Zigzagging the men went. Every possible cover had to be probed.

Driven like game, the thought struck Ponsonby. Like the game he had so often driven to slaughter. Presently he was looking at great circular tracks in clay that led into a trampled lane through the brush. Even he could read those.

"Kingi, oh Kingi." He called softly. "Here's where it went in."

King's voice clucked impatience. "The same durn condition as before. It's somewhere in there, and the wind blowing across. If we cut its wind, we'll be charged. An elephant doesn't quit."

He passed the word on to the men. "Ears open for its presence, and pass immediate warning down."

"Aye, *bwana*," came a further voice. "But Crooked Foot, being before us, must cut the wind first."

"Ye-eh. That is so. That is so indeed. By golly, I believe we've got him between us and a deadline."

With inexorable thoroughness the drive continued. Everybody heard the explosive snort out of the jungle ahead. Everybody stopped; silent, alert.

Below the snort—between it and the pool—a stealthy scuffling sounded. Uncertain in its direction; a little forward, a little back. If that should be Pigeon Toe, he would know exactly what the snort indicated.

"And he's weaponless," muttered King.

From where the snort had come commenced a slow heaving of branches; questing snuffles and an advance down toward the scuffle.

Whatever it was that scuffled could not wait. Behind it were spears. Before it—well, a hope that if the vague wind should by good chance eddy for just a minute or so, it could pass through the zone of scent—and then the zone would stretch between it and the spears.

The scuffling pushed forward. The vast movement closed down upon it. The cautious jungle erupted furious sounds. A brass scream of rage; another scream of fear; rushing bodies; the rending of underbrush.

Ponsonby, out in the open, yelled with excitement.

"Halloo! For'ard away!"

Just as though he might have been out with the hounds and had seen the fox break cover. The next moment his joyous halloo changed to a strangled:

"Oh, my God!"

King pushed through to the outer fringe in time to see Pigeon Toe racing madly across the hard mud slope. Thundering enormously behind him, the elephant.

That was King's first view of it. Its shoulder, he saw in a flash, was gouted with blood that ran down and clotted over its flank. It limped on its nearer fore leg. But it gained horribly on the runner.

It was instinct for King to throw up his rifle. His sight moved to different points on the receding bulk. And then very deliberately he lowered his weapon.

"No," he said. "I can't stop it. A rear end shot like this. Only hurt it and make it madder."

Men broke from the bushes. They howled encouragement. It was easy to see where their sympathy lay.

King scowled, tight-eyed, at the grim race. With a grim sense of justice he said: "Let the gods of Africa decide. He's broken pretty near every rule in their book. Let 'em judge. If he can reach the water and swim under just a little ways the elephant will lose him. Then I'll shoot it for my damned inhibitions' sake and we'll make him a prisoner—if so happen there's no crocodiles. Let the gods decide."

And according to their dark wisdom they decided.

The man sprinted desperately, screeching terror as he ran. The vengeful beast rushed behind him like a pursuing engine. Twenty feet from the pool, when hope of safety for the man began to glimmer, the beast seemed to realize the fact too. It reached forward its trunk in a bunting sort of buffet. It seemed barely to touch the man; but it slung him the full twenty feet to the soft mud at the water's very edge.

For an instant he floundered desperately. Then a ponderous foot like a piston smashed down on him and drove him to its own knee depth into mud and spouting spray. Black bubbles gurgled up.

The beast screamed hoarse rage and disappointment at its sudden loss. Its trunk groped down into the thick ooze. It screamed rage again. Its feet kneaded the pulp beneath them ever deeper. Belly deep it stood in the black muck and trumpeted its blasts of unappeased fury.

"Come away," said King. "Under cover, all of us, before it sees us and comes. I don't want to have to shoot that good elephant."

In a long silence they walked to find their trucks. It was not till they had passed well away from the outlying odors of dead meat that King indulged in his characteristic stretch and deep inhalation of clean air and said very practically:

"Well, I guess that's that."

Ponsonby shook himself out of his thoughts. "Yes," he said. "I suppose so. I imagine that racket is quite thoroughly scotched. I have a great deal to thank you for, Kingi Bwana."

"Me?" King flouted the idea. "Hey, don't you try and blame any of your high-handed doings on me. You're the game-warden. They're your men. I've just been a spectator around here.

And if you want my opinion, I'll tell you I think the game department has done a pretty thorough job. There's only two things I'm sorry for."

"What?" said Ponsonby quickly. "Because I want—I mean, even as a useless spectator, I shall continue to need your opinion."

"First thing I'm sorry is for you," said King with genuine pain. "For the reports you'll have to write to headquarters about all this. Letters, explanations, acres of 'em. And ex-soldier clerks'll write acres back and want sketch maps 'cause they've been taught that's the only way to understand anything."

Ponsonby's face clouded. "Yes, dash it all, I suppose they'll want report. But dammit, I have a lot to do here. I must trek around and get to know the district and place these men where they're needed and organize my lines of information and—Well, I'll send 'em their bally reports when I have time to get around to 'em."

King beamed upon him. "Brother," he said, "I think you've learned. The clerks'll throw hemorrhage fits in their swivel chairs. But I'll tell you what I'll do—save you some trouble. I've got no job here now; so I may as well go in. I'll see the D. C. and tell him the story; so he'll understand the thinnest of your reports."

Ponsonby was immensely relieved. "That would be splendid. Save no end of bother. And what's the second thing you're not satisfied about? If you must go, I'll need all the advice you can leave behind."

"Yeh, but you won't take it," said King. "I'm sorry as hell that nothing happened to the Big Shot."

And so King told the story to the D.C. And the D.C. said: "Kingi Bwana, I believe you would demoralize an archangel. The needs of Colonial Administration subsist upon a diet of reports and office files, which I cannot change and you cannot understand."

"Yeh, but I've learned something," said King. "Putting it simple, the duties of Colonial Administration mean getting your job done. And Commish Bwana, that lad may be no good at home, but I'm telling you, you've got a game-warden back there now."

"**B**ETTER HOP over, Dickson," said the inspector, "and look into this. Something dashed queer up there. First Warren, not ten days ago, reported dragged right out of his house and eaten by something. And now this weird thing. Take the Moth. Flying time should not be more than four hours."

"Yessir." The corporal saluted. "Any special instructions, sir?"

"No, nothing special. Lord, I don't know what to say. This heliograph message is so incoherent. The new consul seems to be frightened silly. Babbles about black magic and what not— Er, you will be careful, of course, not to land across the border line. Those bally Abyssinians are so touchy."

"Yessir. If I can spot the break in the telephone line, I'll helio location, sir."

And so, owing to the modern magic of wings, the police corporal arrived at the consular station of Ewah before dusk; a distance that would have required three weeks of hard *safari*.

Consul Innis came forward with an eagerly outstretched hand that betokened his anxiety.

"I'm awf'ly glad you could come, old man. When they cut the telephone line—"

The police corporal raised one bushy eyebrow.

"Cut? How'd you know, cut?"

Innis looked up at him with intense eyes.

"I—er, I don't know. The things must have human hands."

Dickson stared down at the consul from his burly height.

"Probably just elephants, sir. White ant gets at the poles, or branches fall go that the wire sags; an' then along comes the blinkin' elephants an' barge right on through. Where is this new killing?"

Innis led the way to a gateman's lodge at the entrance to the consular compound; a wattle and adobe hut, but solid. From behind village huts naked forms peered with white, frightened eyes.

On the mud floor of the hut, sprawled as it had been left the previous night—nobody had wanted to touch it—lay the body of the gate orderly, a dark, mangled thing. Whatever it was that had killed it had the hardihood to eat of it right there without dragging away its kill.

Dickson had seen death in most of its horrible forms but the blood drained from his face at this nauseous thing. Not honestly eaten, but gnawed, slobbered over, nuzzled. It was an effort to stoop and examine it.

"Damn queer!" he straightened up. "That was never a leopard nor any of the cats. Nor no dog creature either. So then, what's left?" He drew away from the sickening thing, swallowing and grimacing. "Dashed singular. No one of the regular animals, an' so what else is there in Africa?"

A shiver shook the consul's slender frame.

"Just what—what I said in my S.O.S."

"Witchcraft? Bah! This is Christian Abyssinia, ain't it? This man was eaten by—by a—"The practical-minded corporal was at a loss to say by what strange creature.

Innis, wide-eyed, showed him the door of the hut. Its lock was the usual clumsy wooden affair, but strong and intact.

"Cat animals and dog animals," argued the consul inexorably, "can't open a lock like this. That needs—hands. And what thing with hands would—would gnaw at a dead man like that—except—" The consul whispered it in that dim hut heavy with

the odor of lacerated flesh. "Some half-human creation of black magic?"

The corporal stared at him. The idea was fantastic. Yet something with at least rudimentary hands had opened that door and something with teeth like no known African carnivore had eaten at the corpse. What new monstrosity of Africa was this?

THE QUICK tropic dusk was beginning to throw the grotesque shadows of an African village across the plain. Wide banana leaves spread wavering bands of blackness over the gray dust. Squat huts made ink pools that overlapped and merged with other blots of concealment. The first breeze of the night coolness made its ghost talk in the trees. The corporal shook himself out of the dusk spell to get down to practical business.

"Well, I'll get a couple o' these gapin' blacks an' get this—this mess—buried; then we can go into the layout of this place an' maybe get some reason into this mystery."

But at the corporal's first move every furtively peering figure dashed madly from him. "Uchawi!" was the terrified yelp; and the hurried scrape of heavy plank doors over mud sills and the clack of thick wooden locks indicated that the whole village was leaving the white men to whatever evil Uchawi might bring.

Uchawi. Witchcraft. The dread word that rules the lives of one full hundred per cent of black Africa!

Dickson had seen Uchawi scares before, but this one was a panic. He swore in perplexity. But he was a policeman, and certain jobs, however distasteful, had to be done. He set his teeth.

"Very well, gimme a couple your own men an' show me where; an' by hokey, I'll see that it's buried; an' buried right, too, so no filthy hyenas will dig it up."

"Yes yes," agreed the consul with a feverish anxiety. "So that no—hyenas—can dig it up."

The ex-soldier had buried men before, his own mates more than once. But never a thing like this.

There was something unmanly, insane in the terror of the wretched men whom he drove to the sickly task by lantern light.

To cover his own discomfort he demanded irritably of the men who toiled under his vigilance: "What is this witchcraft that so frightens this village?"

But at the first hint of Uchawi the African retreats behind a mask of stubborn dumbness. All that bullyragging and threats of the power of the police could get out of them was that this was the witchcraft of Those Who Devour the Dead. And further than that gruesomely suggestive title they would not—or could not—go.

"Pah!" The corporal came from that chore shivering. He swore angrily at himself. "It's this damned night chill," he growled. And to convince himself he repeated the white man's stock formula. "Dam silly nonsense! Hrrmph! Tommy-rot!"

But conviction did not come easily. And then into his perplexity broke the sudden hoarse howl of a hyena. Startlingly close.

"BLIMEY!" THE exclamation broke from him. "Rummy coincidence! Dashed rum!" Hyeneas were the filthy beasts that devoured dead things. This one must be snuffling around the gatekeeper's lodge, where death had been so shortly before. Dickson came warily through the gate, and suddenly he was almost upon it.

He flashed his pocket light upon it and shooed. An immense brute it was. Right at the door it had been nosing. Instead of scampering away, it stood its ground and snarled, not ten feet away. Its wicked eyes shone green; its tremendously powerful jaws, that could crack a buffalo's leg bone, were in the full spot of the light. In the outer circle of glow the stiff hairs bristled on its low-hung neck; its spotted hide was, as all its disgusting kind, mangy from carrion diet. Quite the biggest that Dickson remembered having seen. And there it stood and showed discolored teeth, while a grating rumble came from its throat.

Corporal Dickson was brave enough. And just now he was angry. Furiously angry with himself for the jangled condition of his nerves, that had been so startled by the nearness of the brute. His gun ready to fire at instant sight, he dashed after it.

And then his heart surged up into his mouth and he jerked to a standstill. There *was no hyena!* Instead, in the spot where he had expected to find it, a man! Or at all events a human sort of naked form that grovelled on hands and knees in the shadows. It lurched to its feet; an uncouth, heavy-shouldered creature with prognathous, brute features. Then the thing, bending low, galloped away into the darkness, whimpering. Whining—good Lord—like a hyena!

Dickson was too shocked to follow him. He stood staring at the spot for a moment. Then he raced into the house. His first action was to cross over to the rickety table and turn up the oil lamp, where he stood breathing hard. Then he shook himself. With a long reach he scooped up decanter and glass and poured himself a stiff drink. Then he shook himself again, like a man emerging from a knockout daze.

"Crikey!" he gasped. "This thing's givin' me the willies. If I wasn't cold sober I'd swear—s'help me Gawd, I'd swear I just seen a hyena turn into a man."

"Where? How?" Innis was on his feet, his eyes blazing. He clutched at Dickson's arm. "I told you there was witchcraft in this thing!"

Dickson shook him off. The man's crazy conviction was affecting his own judgment. He sat down heavily and with the back of his pistol hand wiped the moisture from his forehead.

"Crikey!" he muttered again. "Beasts that opens doors with hands an' eat dead men! S'help me Gawd, I'm half believin' you. This is gettin' to be beyond a police job." He stared at the lamp that flickered under the weight of his hand on the table. "There's one man in these parts I'd like to talk to," he murmured. "He's well up on African deviltries. If we could only get a hold of him—"

"I know," Innis broke in eagerly. "I've heard of him. Kingi Bwana. I heard he was somewhere in Northern Province and I sent out a drum talk to try and find him as soon as this—this last horror—happened."

"Ho, you did, eh?" That patent lack of confidence in police ability to handle the case nettled the corporal. It helped to bring him back to a practical realization of his job. Methodically he produced official notebook and pencil.

"Very well, sir. Let's get this thing down to common sense. There's been two o' these—er, mysterious attacks. Here, against the British consulate. Now, the first thing to find is motive. Who might have a reason? Who lives here besides these dopey lookin' blacks? What's the lay-out o' the place?"

But there was little enlightenment in that. Ewah was no more than a caravanserai village. There were the few huts of the villagers who catered to the caravans, and that was about all. The leading citizen and trader of the place was an Afro-Arab halfbreed from Zanzibar, Moussa bin Ullah, who was astute enough to claim British citizenship and protection therefore by the consul against confiscatory Abyssinian taxation.

"A blank enough lay-out," grumbled Dickson. "You say there's no witch doctor; no devil cult? Then, what have these people? What have these so-called Christian Abyssinians on the border to do with black magic?"

"*Whooo-oo-oo!*" The grating howl of a hyena rose into the night to answer him, and after it shrieked a quavering, maniac chuckle.

Innis clutched his chair seat.

"Gawd!" breathed Dickson. "Who the devil ever thought to call that thing a laughing hyena?"

And, "*Whroo-oo-oo-uh,*" it came again. Another one. And others. Howling, snarling, chuckling. Out by the graveyard.

The corporal listened tight-lipped.

"Tell me," he wanted to know, "was there any other death in the village today? I mean, anybody else planted out there?"

Innis shook his head.

"No. I'm positive. I would have known."

"Well," said Dickson with grim emphasis, "they're fightin' over meat an' nothin' else. And"—the words came through set teeth—"no hyena that lives could dig up the man I buried. We rolled heavy rocks over him."

The two men stared at each other as the uproar of a ghoul's sabbath continued in the outer dark.

DICKSON ROSE heavily. His rugged face twitched as he tightened his belt.

"S'help me Gawd, I got to go an' see. Else I'll get to believin' ghosts same as you. It ain't possible; an' I got to go prove it ain't."

Innis' whole frame shook as he gripped the table edge and heaved himself up out of his chair. "I'll have to come too. I must. If it's what I—what we both think—I must come and see."

Dickson shrugged. That sort of courage was beyond his understanding. It was the urge for exact knowledge driving the student beyond the limits of his nerve. But he would be glad enough to have a companion—any sort of companion in those eerie circumstances.

The cemetery ground was pitched in the nearest convenient spot, a scant stone's throw from the village huts. The night was ink blade, the air nauseous. Impossible as Dickson felt it to be for animals to have disturbed his recent work, snarls, howls, whimperings came from the site. Whatever they were, there were several of them. If brutes, and if as big and bold as the gaunt beast that Dickson had disturbed at the gatehouse door, caution was necessary.

At a distance of a hundred feet he pressed his flashlight button. A feeble and inadequate thing it was at that range; and Innis, clinging to his left arm, disturbed the steadiness of the beam. The two men could distinguish only dark shapes that milled and fought over something. Low shapes on four feet. Eyes reflected lambent green in the ray.

"Beasts' eyes," said Dickson with an immense relief. "No ruddy ghosts there."

"Beasts without hands couldn't move your rocks." Innis refused to be diverted from his fearful theory of sorcery. And then: "Look out! My God!—They're coming!"

The dark forms, with concerted agreement, had left off their fighting and were advancing slowly, growling in their throats.

A half dozen things of that size in their own night were as deadly a danger as lions by day. Dickson fired quickly into the mass. The pack roared fury and rushed in a bunch. The flash beam wavered drunkenly in the air under Innis' clutch. Dickson shook him loose furiously and fired again.

"Run!" screamed Innis' voice from behind him. "My God! You can't stop them!" And himself he raced in mad panic for the house.

Behind him he heard more shots. Something yelled in physical pain. Innis stopped. His impulse was to rush back. But he was alone amongst gravestones in the inky blackness, and he had no sort of a weapon.

"Come on!" he screamed again and stumbled frantically on for shelter.

At his door another wave of panic met him. It yawned blackly open—they must have left it so in the anxiety of their exit. The draught from outside had blown out the light. Innis lurched over the threshold, fell, lurched to his feet again, moaning incoherent cries to Dickson. Roars, howls, a flurry of shots, piercing yells came. But no Dickson.

In an insanity of panic Innis fumbled for matches, fumbled madly—for agonized hours, it seemed. When he found them they sputtered against the wick in his trembling fingers and went out. Cursing in a frenzy, he lit more, in bunches. When he finally got the lamp alight, only bestial roars, brute snarls came from the fearful dark—and maniacal laughter.

Innis screamed for his servants. He might as well have screamed for a guardian angel with a fiery sword. Servants cowered in their huts behind safely-barricaded doors. Innis had no sort of weapon in the house; he was a student, not a hunter or a fighting man.

Cursing helplessly, shamed by his own ineffectually, he shut his door and, like his servants, who knew the practicality of black magic, he barricaded it from within.

DAYLIGHT BROUGHT a measure of sanity; and— he thanked heaven—Kingi Bwana. Tall, sun-browned, coolly observant, his narrowed eyes squinting deceptively in the sun, but taking in every detail as he walked forward. With him his wizened Hottentot servant, who scurried about like a blanket-wrapped monkey and asked questions and took notice of everything; and his Masai, immensely naked, who leaned on a great spear and waited only to be shown something which he must fight.

There was an enormous comfort in those three hard men of

the African black lands, whose reputation had come even to a newcomer like Innis.

"Thank God!" he bubbled over. "Thank God you could come; all three of you. You'll all be needed in this frightful business."

"Yeah," said King. "I picked up a drum talk that sounded pretty frantic, and the drums said a police plane had flown over. So I made a night trek and came along. Plane still here; no policeman. More trouble, eh?"

"Worse than that. Oh, my God! I'm ashamed! But I couldn't do anything! In the night I just couldn't!"

"Hey, hey!" King laid a steadying hand on the consul's shoulder. "Take it easy, hombre. Come along into your house. Give me a drink and a wash and then get it off your chest."

In short, hysterical bursts, broken by shudders, the consul told his story. But his overwrought state gradually subsided, and he became more coherent as King listened, commenting neither one way or the other, shooting in only an abrupt question at intervals.

When it was all over King grunted.

"Has anybody been down to this cemetery place since Dickson disappeared?"

Innis shook his hanging head. "No native would dare; and I—I—"

"That's quite all right, too," said King. "I'd hate to walk into a pack of hyenas—or ghosts for that matter—at night without a gun, either. How about coming now and looking things over?"

Innis shuddered again but answered:

"Yes, very well— With you, yes."

King nodded. The man was not altogether a craven. He had been through some sort of a shocking experience. But he was getting hold of his nerve.

"Circulate about," King told his two blacks. "Talk with these people of foolish countenance and find out what you can— Come along, Innis."

In the graveyard they soon came upon the body of Corporal Dickson, or what was left of it. A sickening mess of shredded clothing and clotted blood and ragged flesh. Innis averted his head and trembled. King dropped a strong hand on his shoulder again. His own nostrils curled as he looked at the gnawed-over thing.

"All right, *amigo*. Steady. You couldn't have prevented it," he told the shivering consul. "Now come on. I want to see that grave."

The heavy stones that the corporal had placed as a protection were scattered, flung aside; the earth lay in heaps. That exhumed corpse had been almost wholly eaten. Its remains lay sprawled hideously.

King's eyes flashed to every little detail of the repulsive scene while he stood in silence and pondered.

"You see," quavered Innis. "That needed hands."

After a further silence King slowly nodded.

"Yes," he agreed. "That needed hands. Dickson knew well enough how to bury a man in Africa." He whistled tunelessly through his teeth. "Those Who Devour the Dead, eh? A singularly horrid conception, even for Africa; and it's beyond my guessing. Hyena teeth have been here; and yet, what are these other beastly marks? These slobbery gnawings?"

"Yes, yes; That's what I told you." Innis whispered in tremulous excitement. And then, after a moment of silence, "Mr. King, what if there are wounded men in the village today? Pistol wounds—Dickson shot something. And by daylight they must revert to human form."

King regarded him through narrow slits.

"You sound crazy to me," he said. "But come on in again and palaver this." Within the house he motioned Innis to a chair, while he himself stalked the floor, his thumbs hooked in his belt. "Now tell me, Mister Consul, what is this that you are ready to believe about black magic that kills and eats men and about which I know nothing?"

Innis shifted uneasily and refused to meet King's eyes.

"Go ahead," said King. "I've seen enough unbelievable things not to laugh."

Innis sensed an immense encouragement and sympathy.

"Well," he blurted at last, "I couldn't tell Corporal Dickson. But you—perhaps you'll understand. It's—I'm sure it's lycanthropy."

King stopped in his stride to stare at the man.

"That's the highbrow word for werewolves, isn't it? But good Lord, man, that's European. That's mediaeval superstition. And we're in Africa of today."

INNIS HITCHED his chair forward and leaned towards King to expound.

"Do you know that occult societies exist today—even in your own America—such as the brotherhood of Pow Doctors—who believe that not all mediaeval magic was just superstition; that some of them practice magic today? And listen again. Even you know that all Christian mediaeval Europe believed in the absolute practicality of a ritual which enabled certain adepts to transmute their bodies into the form of wolves. And you know"—he spoke with significant emphasis—"that Abyssinia was considerably under the influence of mediaeval Christianity."

In that primitive room, with its sparse, hand-made furniture and its mud floor strewn with reeds, the man's feverish sincerity sounded not nearly so wild as King might have expected. All that he could say, rather lamely, was:

"Well, but that's wolves. There aren't any wolves in Africa."

"Listen." Innis pointed a professorial finger at him. "In Europe the form of the transmutation was, very naturally, some local carnivorous animal. In Iceland, for instance, it was black bears. In Abyssinia—and these outlying borders have remained utterly mediaeval—it is—hyenas!"

A short laugh broke from King, though it was no loud snort

of derision. It was just that he did not know what to say; the thing sounded so damnably plausible. His only logical objection was: "All the same, a mediaeval Christian superstition is a far cry from three material killings in an Abyssinian border village of today."

"Listen some more," Innis insisted. "The writings of the mediaeval magicians, Hermes Trismegistus, give a detailed formula and ritual—gruesomely awful, as all such black rituals are—for effecting the transmutation of a human into a beast that must then raven after the flesh of other humans. I *know* that copies exist in this country. Africans—of mediaeval sensibilities, or less—can subject themselves to such revolting rituals—as witness voodoo and its inexplicable performances."

King prowled the room, scowling at the floor. Then he shook his head.

"I think you're altogether wrong," he said at length. "I'm the last man to say that things beyond all sane belief don't happen in Africa. But this—I can't swallow your theory—yet. Though I'll admit I've said such a thing before and had to swallow it. But even if you should be right—the Lord knows, anything may happen in Africa— Poor old Dickson was right, too. There's still not enough motive in sight. Come, show me your village— the people, houses, everything. Let's see whether we can't dig up something, just as your devil beasts do."

So tour the village King did; but from that he gained nothing. It was a quiet and very ordinary African village. There was no witch house; no skull-and-bone-festooned shrine of necromancy; no resident sorcerer; nothing. Just a village, hot and ill-smelling in the sun.

The villagers looked furtively at the two white men. They were by no means hostile; they looked as mediaeval Christians might have done upon a pair of excommunicates. The white men's house had been marked for Uchawi.

The utter absence of any sort of a background for the abnormal happenings of after dark baffled King. Although he growled:

"I agree with Dickson. They're a mangy looking lot. But hell, I don't connect any ideas out of that. Let's go talk to this British subjects of yours."

THE MAN Moussa showed the Arab half of his heritage by demanding more personal privacy for himself and family than the happy-go-lucky pure African. His house, more pretentious than the native huts, was surrounded by a bamboo fence. The Negro half of him was evinced by the slipshod condition of that fence. Through its gaps, as the visitor approached the house, a woman could be seen.

"Ha!" King stopped to stare. "Where's she from? Down coast? Yemen? She's no African."

But Innis did not know her. "I've never seen her close. Mohammedan fashion, he keeps her purda-nasheen."

Mohammedan fashion, too, Moussa bin Ullah was all hospitality. In feature he was more Negro than Arab, but his manners were the perfection of Arab hospitality. Personally he met his guests at the door.

"*Subakh Allah bilkheir,*" he called upon Allah to give them health. He conducted them in, placed cushions for them, clapped his hands and a Negro boy brought thick, sweet coffee.

King was too immersed in the mystery of all these happenings to have any manners. Instead of the customary long preamble about trivial nothings as demanded by etiquette, he came bluntly to the point. What did Moussa know of conditions, of people, of any man, witch doctors, devil priests, who might, would or could engineer witchcraft against the British consulate?

But Moussa spread his hands deprecatingly. Who would be interested in instigating any such thing against the consul effendi? Did not all men know that the consul interfered with no man, that he exercised jurisdiction and collected a just duty only upon caravan imports into British territory? And was he not particularly Moussa's friend and protector from aggressive Abyssinian taxation? As for witchcraft—he shrugged—these borderland Abyssinians were, after all, primitive Africans. Any untoward happening was immediately set down by them as witchcraft. Why should Innis Effendi let himself be troubled?

But, persisted King, hadn't the trader heard at least the hell's chorus of the last night's darkness and the shooting?

Moussa crossed his legs and exhaled smoke. Hyenas were everywhere—may Allah curse them. As for himself, his house was far from any such disturbance. Would a good Moslem build his house near a cemetery? And particularly near a Christian one?

Well, there was no information there. Or if there was, it was not forthcoming. Unless there might be any value in the trader's veiled suggestion that some Abyssinian caravaneer might resent the customs duty, and so—but more than that Moussa would not say.

King stalked from the house. With long strides he crossed the compound, head forward, frowning, his thumbs hooked in his belt. But suddenly he stooped.

A child was playing by the gateway; a lemon-brown little boy, richly dressed in absurdly grown-up pink satin coat, tight white pants, and embroidered cap and slippers.

Inquisitively King lifted the child's chin. It had the round, owlish little face with the soft eyes and extraordinarily beautiful eyelashes of halfbreed Arab descent. King lifted its hand and looked at its finger nails.

"Ha!" he grunted then and strode on. Outside the gate he remarked. "Just what I thought. That was a white woman. Wonder where he got hold of her? No bearing on this case; but what a hell of a life!"

Innis made no comment. He was staring at a man, a thick-bodied, blanket-draped native who, unlike the rest of the un-hostile villagers, scowled sullenly at them. Innis gripped King's arm.

"Look!" he stammered. "That's a new face in the village— And see his shoulder. He has a wound. Maybe a bullet?"

Quickly King looked the man over. A dull, brute-faced fellow he was; and he certainly scowled at the white men.

"Rubbish!" he said testily. "You've gone crazy with your mediaeval superstitions. Here, I'll show you in a minute that whatever his hurt is, it's no pistol wound."

But at King's approach the man sprang away and fled from him as a wild thing might, wailing and crying into the bush. King was too utterly astonished to follow until too late.

"And I've seen other new faces in the village," said Innis with dark meaning.

"Hell!" snorted King, "you'll have me crazy along with you." He frowned into the troubled distance. "The fellow's teeth!" he muttered. "Like a gorilla's. But even idiot apes don't eat dead men. Let's be sane— Now then, what is there in this hint about caravaneers having it is for the consulate as a customs collector? How would that be for a motive for sicking something onto you?"

"It might be. But caravans aren't due for two weeks. Still— some importer might have instigated a magic—might have sent a pack of beast-men on to clean out the consulate before his arrival with some prohibited goods or other. It could happen."

"Good Lord! A whole pack, you'd have it now." King growled in his throat. After a thoughtful silence:

"An instigator two weeks distant doesn't help. This thing is upon us here and now. Oh, I agree there's a physical danger aplenty. No one can laugh away three men killed and devoured by—by—" His voice trailed away in scowling perplexity. Like corporal Dickson, the night before, he was unable to say, killed and eaten by what.

He strode in silence till a thought came to him and the worry was removed from his face by a thin and very hard smile.

"Innis," he said. "Your ghost stories are getting me too. So before I go completely loco I'll tell you what I'll do. By golly, I'll lay for these ghost-beast things of yours. This very night.

And I'll catch one of them—alive! I've caught wild beasts before. And we'll clear up this madness."

"That," said Innis slowly, "sounds plausible—when you speak of it—by daylight."

KING ONLY laughed. His worry was gone; action lay before him. He went off to confer with his henchmen. Native gossip, and particularly in matters pertaining to witchcraft, came of course to them as to no white man.

Yes, new faces were in the village, they agreed. At least they did not live in the village; they had arrived recently and had taken possession of some huts that had been deserted on account of cholera a year ago; down by the dry water course that led to the sunset.

"Ha! So?" It was a weird coincidence. Callously these brute-faced strangers lived in a place of pestilence. And not only that, but in that same direction lay a heavy belt of thorn scrub in which hyenas, too, must lay up during the daylight hours. The donga, with its sandy bed, was the obvious path.

King blew sibilant discords through his teeth. Every new angle to this thing but bolstered up Innis' horrific contention of a man-beast sorcery. But—King grinned tightly—this night would show.

But a whole pack of creatures as ferocious as these—whatever they might be—could not be tackled alone. King must have the unflinching support of his black men. And that was a negotiation that called for diplomacy. He said to the two of them:

"Now the matter of this witchcraft that threatens us here. It must be fought."

He addressed himself particularly to the Masai, whose creed it was that life for a full-bodied man existed only for the purpose of combat. The big man shuffled on his feet. Not to stand by his master in a fight went sore against his manhood. But witchcraft!—

"Look!" said King. "I go into this fight to face whatever may come. Do I go alone?"

"Indeed, Bwana," the Masai's fierce face worked with emotion, "shame lies heavy upon my feet; yet it is known that white men in their wisdom are proof—or, at least, very nearly so—against magic that eats us black men up."

"Agreed," King quickly said. "Witchcraft made by a black wizard does not easily attack a white man—though we three together have seen it happen. But this, as all the village knows, is a magic out of the white men's religion. Therefore it is clear that not you, but I, must be vulnerable."

That indeed was an unanswerable logic. After a full minute of assimilation the Hottentot clucked his tongue against his palate.

"Association," said he, "with this great spear-wielder who exercises only his muscles has made me dull-witted, else would I have seen that myself."

A great grin began to spread itself over the Masai's face, though he still looked sheepish.

"My shame remains, Bwana," he said. "That I hesitated to go where Bwana went. Let me now but have opportunity to win back my manhood."

"Good!" said King. "We go then to set a trap, a pitfall in the donga path by which these witch creatures come. No man can set a trap like Kaffa. Man or devil, something will be caught this very night."

And the trap that little Kaffa then set *was* a trap. The simple old pitfall principle, but prepared with all the jungle lore that the Hottentot possessed. He chose a narrow spot in the donga. Stiff clay banks, scoured twenty feet deep by the torrents of a thousand rainy seasons hemmed it in. Lower down, sandy soil permitted a widening and a growth of straggly brush. At the edge of the brush the Hottentot dug his hole. The earth was carried back and scattered. A frame of thin bamboo strips was woven over the pit. Surface soil of the same surrounding kind was scattered over it. Even the little shrubs were reset in their original positions. Finally the faintly depressed animal run that meandered along the donga floor was cunningly continued as it had been.

The Hottentot stood back and surveyed his work as might an art critic. But he lifted his stub nose and sniffed the air with dissatisfaction.

"I yet smell man," said he. And with that he crept past the thin edge of his pit and went scouring down the lower brush. He returned with the body of a zoril, a skunklike creature with strong scent glands. He dissected the glands and with a stick smeared the unpleasant musk about the immediate bushes. At least he was satisfied.

"That," he pronounced, "is a trap."

"A good trap," said King. "Nothing less than human intelligence will avoid that; it's beyond any beast cunning."

"Perhaps," Innis interposed his obsession, "a combination of both—man-beast might—"

"Anything might be," said King. "But at all events tonight we'll know."

DUSK CRAWLED in on horridly laggard minutes. Even King felt a tension grow upon him and swore at himself for a fool. With the dying of the dusty red sun a thin slice of new moon showed in the sky.

"The wizard's moon of black magic," Innis croaked out of his occult lore.

King swore at him also for a fool.

"And I'll prove it to you before this night is up," he growled. "Or at any rate we'll settle something—one impossible way or the other. And so I'm going out with my boys and watch. Whatever falls into our trap mustn't be given a chance to get out."

"No—no indeed!—or be helped out by other hands." Innis harped on his fixation. He rose from his seat, closed his eyes tight and shivered. "I too, I must come with you."

King understood what the police corporal had been unable to do—the student's urge for exact knowledge. He did not argue.

"Better put on all the heavy clothing you have. Woolen shirts, sweaters— Not because you shivered. Look at me." He himself bulged under his khaki shooting coat. "Padding." He explained. "A tip I learned from a bear hunter. I'm alive now because of it. And what have you that would do for a weapon? A good knife, machete or something? A gun won't be so good if it should come to a mixup in the dark."

On the upper lip of the donga the little party found a place. Hidden in a brush patch they could look down—or rather, they could listen down to the place of the trap. The thin moon showed only shadows darker than the other shadows, and below them, a wide trench of solid black.

Waiting was as waiting always is—tense and full of tiny noises. Tight with the pulsing vibrations of a thin wire. King was alertly silent. The others he could not see, ensconced as they were in whatever little openings the brush afforded. But he could hear to one side of him a soft *whsh! whsh!* It was the Masai stroking the long blade of his spear with a little stone that he always carried in his knee garter of monkey hair. Then the grunted whisper of the Hottentot asking for the stone. There was comfort in those noises.

Then the abnormal ears of the Hottentot picked up something.

"Things move below, Bwana."

Their own voices would not carry down into the gully nearly as well as sounds would come up. King could hear them now. The quiet pad of feet, too faint to guess whether of men or beasts. Right up to the edge of the brash patch they sounded. Now was the imminent crisis of the whole venture. Another step and something would crash through the artificial floor.

But there at the brush edge was a pause. Faint shufflings, cautious whisperings—or was it the swishing of leaves?

Innis' hand groped out and found King. His whisper was an odd mixture of elation and awe.

"Nothing less than human intelligence, you said, would suspect."

King only gripped the arm that had found him till Innis' choked remonstrance gave him a realization of his nervous strain.

Then up from below came the whimpering, maniac giggle of a hyena!

King's pent breath drew in yet another gasp. Whatever was down there *could not be!* Something *must* fall into that perfect trap!

"Listen!" came Innis' whisper. "They are going back!"

Shufflings and scrabblings sounded. Retreating. But not far. Stones slipped. Earth fell in tiny cascades.

"They're climbing up!" said King grimly. "And on this side!"

D O W N T H E donga, where the bank was not so steep, scuffles and little landslides were plainly audible. The things— as though they understood fully that they had been expected— seemed now to be careless about concealment. The last earth clod rattled from the ravine lip. Then a long, black silence.

"If you can find a tree," King called to Innis. "Get up it, fast!" Himself, he rose from his prone position and drew his heavy hunting knife.

"They come, Bwana!" croaked the voice of the Hottentot. And the immediate crashing in the bushes told the rush of heavy bodies.

For the next demoniac five minutes King knew only that he fought with blurred shapes. The blackness was just pale enough to show that shadows detached themselves from the bush shadows and howled as they rushed in. He heard the shout of the Masai, a high pitched squeal from Innis, and then a low charging form hurtled against his legs and he went down. Something clamped viciously upon his arm and worried. Thank God it was well padded, but it was his knife arm.

King rolled desperately. His legs found and twined themselves half round a heavy body, half round a bush. He fought to change that entanglement; with a scissors grip he might have cracked ribs. The straining grunts from his own throat equalled the muffled brute growls of the thing that held his arm and heaved at it in great twisting tugs. His left hand found a fistful of skin and coarse hair. He twisted at it, rather ineffectually punched at it. In their joint plungings the body fell over his face. His nostrils were filled with a feral stench. Furiously he heaved his knife arm up and down against the grip that numbed it; this way and that, hoping somehow, anyhow, to stab into flesh.

Either he succeeded—he could not tell—or somebody else in the black mêlée connected with something. For the thing yelled and let go. King lurched to his feet.

"Innis!" he shouted. "Innis! Where are you?"

But he could not hear himself. He was in the indescribable uproar of an enormous dog fight with an undercurrent of the confused shouts of men. Then another shadow hurled itself at him; and down he went again, clawing and clutching at anything, everything, in the first desperate need to keep teeth from his throat. He had just succeeded—he thought—when the ground fell away from beneath him. He felt himself rolling, the beast with him. In a whirling scramble they went down together, gashed by stones, impeded momentarily by bushes that in the next instant tore loose, accompanied by rubble; till with a grunting thud they reached the pit blackness of the donga bottom.

Here King could not distinguish even shapes, only something that growled and fought with him. Grimly he had held on to his hunting knife. He stabbed out into the dark, and stabbed again. Heavy resistance gave him a spasm of triumph. But that was only sticky clay. Furiously he stabbed again, and yet again. Suddenly the thing yelled piercingly and rolled clear. King staggered to his feet, widespread, knife held forward for another attack. Then his heart surged as he heard feet go galloping away along the donga bottom.

Frantically he groped his way to the bank. In the pitch darkness that was a wild scramble, gaining a yard, slipping back two. But somehow, eventually, he made it—to find that there, too, the fight was finished. Howls of rage and pain streamed away in the direction of the village.

"Bwana! Bwana! Is that you?" came the Masai's voice. "Is the little light in a stick unbroken? I have slain me something."

"Where's Innis? Kaffa?" was King's first question.

"Here, Bwana. Bitten by many devils."

And Innis' voice, too, panting, half hysterical. "Here. But I think I have a broken arm."

King fished for his flashlight. By extraordinary luck it was unbroken.

"Here, Bwana! Just behind this bush! My spear still pins it to—Awah! What sorcery is this?"

From King, too, came a hissing breath. The thing that lay pinned to the ground by the great spear through his chest was a man!

"I fought—I swear I fought—" King's voice came hushed, as from far away. "Damn it, I fought with a hyena! I felt it; I smelled it; I got a mouthful of its filthy hide!"

Innis' face came into the circle of light, dead white, blood-smeared, but excitedly jubilant.

"It is the rule, the absolute rule. When they die they must revert to human form."

King's mind was reeling in an insane world beyond the power of coherent speech.

"Good Lord!" he breathed at last, "we're all crazy. Come away home—the house—where there's light and a stiff shot of hooch!"

WITH LIGHTS and four more or less stout walls came a certain return to rationalism—or, at least, a respite for thinking. Innis' arm proved not to be broken; but badly enough bruised and twisted, at that. His hurriedly-donned sweaters and shirts were shreds, ripped from him in streamers. King's, better protected by his tough shooting-coat and breeches, were in slightly better shape. But both men were a sorry mess of blood and grime and rags.

"Though at that," said King through his teeth as he winced under the smart of iodine, "it does seem that hyena teeth would have done more damage. Innis, my crazy friend, I'm half believing in your ghost creatures. This is Africa. And if not hyenas, with what infernal things did we fight? Listen to the brutes."

The devil's chorus of howling, and the even more awesome idiot laughing, sounded up-village. In the direction—King pointed it out darkly in between holding strips of bandage in his teeth—of the half-breed Arab's house.

"Curses go home to roost, they say. Does it seem to you, Mister Consul, that they're maybe looking for a lodging around the home of our smooth friend Moussa?"

"Moussa!" King prowled the room, frowning, connecting threads of circumstance.

"Moussa! An ill-omened name in East Africa. In the old slave days Ibn Moussa was one of the most unspeakable lieutenants of the infamous Tippoo Tib. He left a trail of half-breed sons like a poison toad's spawn. Now, what reason might our half-breed Moussa have for not liking a British consul?"

Innis was too exhausted to think.

"I don't know. He has always been so friendly. Still—as a trader—I don't know."

King's mind was racing away on a trail of possibilities, vague and tenuous, but any thread was as valuable as a rope in that mystery.

"These villagers. Why are they all so dopey? What—Wake up, man!—What d'you know about any trade in drugs? Do they have opium here?"

Innis shook his head wearily. "No opium. Nothing here. Up

in the Abyssinian highlands they grow *k'at*. It's a sort of hashish thing, only worse; sends people half-witted. And, by Jove!"—he sat suddenly upright—"Come to think of it, the French excise has trouble with it in Djibouti!"

"Aa-ah! A dope that sends people berserk. Your government wouldn't like that sort of thing, would it?"

For the first time since he had come into this so baffling affair King was able to laugh without care.

"Tomorrow, Mister Consul, I'll come and stand by while you have a long talk with British Subject Moussa. Let me put a finger on a motive and, believe me, I'll twist out of some one just what all this man-beast magic is—and tonight maybe we can sleep. Listen to those—things—up there."

But that proposal, like so many other plans in this uncanny affair, was suddenly diverted by another demonstration of sheer horror. With the morning came running feet, waking the weary white men from sleep, and the Hottentot's excited voice.

"Bwana! Bwana! The men-beasts have devoured the Arabi trader's child!"

King tumbled from his cot. "Home to roost!" were the words that framed themselves in his half sleep. "Come on, Innis! Wake up! Hustle!"

THE WHOLE village seemed to be in hiding. The mud road between the huts was empty. Doors remained close-locked. As King circled the trader's fence, sounds of struggle and feminine shrieks could be heard.

"Beating her up," King growled. "As though she could have prevented it. Come ahead."

He swung round the corner of the gate post—and there he stopped in his tracks. His nostrils crinkled with nausea. There the thing lay! Dragged barely as far as the gateway! Its bright-colored clothing in shreds! Half eaten, gnawed by inadequate teeth! Ghastly. Nobody had dared to touch it—Uchawi of the blackest!

King charged on up to the house. Confused voices shouted.

The door was locked. King thundered upon it. Voices babbled from within. King cursed furiously, took a run back and smashed the door clear of its hinges. In the room was Moussa. He cowered away as though King pointed a gun at him—as though the white men came with an expected accusation.

"Talk!" King barked at him. "What happened?"

The man only chattered, mumbling, his fingers at his lips. Gone was the Arab veneer of urbanity. Just now the man was pure Negro. Uchawi had reached out to him and he was mortally afraid.

From some far back place muffled moans came and a dull hammering upon a door. King's eyes went questioning in that direction. The man found his voice to drool an explanation.

"Grief, Bwana!"—He even reverted to African idiom. "And fear! They have rendered her hysterical, Bwana. She would have run forth and showed her face before strange men."

That sounded plausible enough. King let it go. The other thing was more important.

"Well, your women are your affair. But that—that thing that was your son. Pick it up and do with it whatever you do with your dead. You can't leave it lying there like a dog."

"Indeed, Bwana, I—Yes, Bwana."

"Now!" snapped King. "Or by golly I'll take you by the neck and shove you to it."

"Yes, Bwana. Immediately, Bwana."

From the doorway King watched the wretched man— alone—he could compel no servant to help him. Eyes averted, with a cloth he covered the body and hurried to some outbuilding.

"Come on home." King took Innis by the arm and led him from the compound. "I give in to you. The things that did that were man-beasts. Not clean, wholesome hyenas normally hunting their meat. There is black sorcery here."

Innis shuddered. "Thank merciful heaven they have left us. I am sure they've turned back on their instigator."

"Perhaps you're right. I'm ready to believe anything. Tomorrow we'll find out what it all means. We can hardly bullyrag Moussa in the face of his own tragedy. He will keep till tomorrow."

BUT THAT proposal, too, was diverted by Uchawi that was stronger than the disposition of men. Diverted as soon as came the darkness in which magic could operate.

With the night the devil chorus yelled and howled again around the trader's compound. At intervals came the shrieks and cries of human voices in mortal fear. Louder and more menacing than ever before was the uproar.

King looked at Innis. Innis stared back at him. Stiffly King reached for his weapon.

"Guess it's up to us. Not on Moussa's account. But that wretched white woman. We must get the boys and give a hand—and, personally, I'm almost anxious to take another shot at the men-beasts who do—what they do."

In a compact body the four men went warily up the deserted village road, this time carrying lanterns. But the chorus that made a witches' sabbath about the trader's house drew away around the fence at their approach, as though cognizant of their conquerors.

As the men came into the compound, the door burst open of its own accord and a frantic figure rushed towards them. It was the woman. She clutched at them indiscriminately. She was hysterical with fear, crazed with grief. Her broken voice shrieked high falsetto and hoarse baritone.

"My child! They devoured my child! They are devils!"

She spoke in English with a strong foreign accent. On the farther side of the fence a demoniac howl rose to drown her shrieks. But she screamed yet higher:

"They are *vrikulakas!* My child! They must be killed!"

"*Vrikulak!*" Innis seized avidly upon the word. "That's a Balkan country word for were-wolf! The country of Dracula!

Tell me, woman, where are you from? How did you get here? What do you mean?"

"Ah, what matter who I am—how I came to this brute? A beast he is! A beast, I tell you! It is he who sent for these wolf-men. He gave them the *k'at.* My child! They have devoured my child! And how they raven for him!"

Innis motioned to King. Together they took the shrieking woman into the house, assured her of protection, partially calmed her down.

"Tell us about these—*vrikulakas,*" said King. "If we are to fight them, tell us what you know."

Between bursts of hysteria and screaming the woman unfolded details of a grisly cult that was more revolting than anything that King had yet met in Africa.

Vrikulakas. In her country everybody knew about them. And here in Africa they were the same, only worse. They were men. They were not sane. They lived apart in packs and they had a secret beast cult of stupefying drugs and gruesome rites that made them quite mad. When they embarked upon their insane orgies they believed that they became—here in Abyssinia— hyenas. They ran on all fours like hyenas; they lived with tame hyenas; they acted like hyenas, howled like them. The maddest of them dressed in hyena skins, hunted with their foul pets, and even ate the loathsome things that hyenas ate. To all intents and purposes and their own belief they are hyenas—man-beasts. Those who dared to speak of them knew them as "Those Who Devour the Dead."

And now—the woman screamed hysterically—like hyenas they had devoured her son! And it was all the fault of that man, that brute, who called himself her husband— He knew about the man-beasts. He had sent for them because the next caravan was bringing down a big consignment of *k'at.*

Innis, for the time being, was more excited over this astounding revelation than about any illicit traffic in drugs. King felt that he could digest that fantastic phase of sorcery later; dig into it; find out all about it and add it to his knowledge of unbelievable things in Africa. For the present there was something else. Very quietly he asked:

"Where is Moussa now?"

"Hiding!" screamed the woman. "Hiding in the back rooms in terror; for the man-beasts now howl around the house for *him!*"

And howl they did. Fearsomely, in ravening chorus. Into the very compound they seemed to have come.

GRIMLY KING left the woman to Innis' ministrations and eager questions. He beckoned to the Masai and stepped with him into the dark labyrinth of a Moslem dwelling's back rooms.

Only dim Moorish lamps burned. They groped their way, poked into closets, peered under beds. The house seemed to be empty. Servants had long ago fled.

But the Masai, probing under a pile of rugs with his spear, suddenly flushed a disheveled figure, crazed with fear and yammering. With the agility of a rat it eluded them and scurried from the room. The Masai whooped a great shout and bounded after it. Screeching, it scuttled into another room and slammed the door.

King rushed up, to find the Masai bellowing laughter and kicking at its panels with naked feet. He pushed the man aside and hurled his weight against it. It held fast. Both men crashed their shoulders against it. It creaked and a panel split. From beyond came a despairing wail and the shutters of a window rattling madly.

"The crazy idiot!" panted King. "If he gets out there amongst those—Moussa! Moussa, don't be a damned fool!"

But Moussa was beyond all reasoning or listening. Mad he was with fears that beset him on all sides. The window shutters swung open with a crash against the outer wall. There came a final incoherent cry. A scramble. A thump. And silence.

"The fool!" shouted King. "The damned fool! He'd have been better off with us!"

He rushed from the door. In a dim passage he stumbled, the Masai over him. In other windowless passages they lost their way. Only a confused uproar from without came to them.

They burst into the main room to find Innis standing awe-struck; the woman with wild eyes, exultant. Here sounds could penetrate from outside. An infernal cacophony of bestial howls, satanic whimperings, triumphant yells. From farther out rose shrieks of insane terror that receded fast.

The sounds trailed away into the night. Shrieks and joyous howls and farther shrieks. At long last, silence. Only the African night outside. The insects of the night took up their trills and chirrupings that the greater clamor had disturbed.

That beast should hunt down and devour beast was the African rule.